Don't
Explain

**Novels in the Artie Deemer series
by Dallas Murphy**

Lover Man
Lush Life
Don't Explain

Other novels by Dallas Murphy

Apparent Wind

Published by POCKET BOOKS

Don't
Explain

•

DALLAS MURPHY

POCKET BOOKS

New York   London   Toronto   Sydney   Tokyo   Singapore

POCKET BOOKS, a division of Simon & Schuster Inc.
1230 Avenue of the Americas, New York, NY 10020

Library of Congress Cataloging-in-Publication Data

Murphy, Dallas.
    Don't explain / Dallas Murphy.
      p.   cm.
    ISBN: 0-671-86687-7
    I. Title.
  PS3563.U7283S76   1996
813'.54—dc20   95-8887
                                         CIP

First Pocket Books hardcover printing January 1996

10 9 8 7 6 5 4 3 2 1

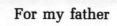

For my father

All my thanks to Jane Chelius, Jim Condon,
Peggy Crisco, Joe Gramm, Bill Grose,
Sarah Haviland, Bob Hogan, David Langhorne,
Marie Murphy, Sarah Shankman,
and as always Eugenia Leftwich.

Note

There is no Kempshall Island, no town of Micmac, no county called Cabot. I've changed names and salient features to protect the living and the dead, the guilty and the innocent, and me, somewhere in between, depending on how you look at it.

Artie Deemer
Poor Joe Cay,
Bahama Islands

Don't Explain

1

Without pressing engagements of my own, I watched Crystal dress for her tournament. She was sitting on the edge of the bed, drawing on a pair of black panty hose, smoothing them up her thighs, snapping the top against her belly. At that point, propped limpidly on an elbow, I wondered whether or not I could release the front toggle clasp of her bra with my teeth. It was a mere fantasy that arced across my consciousness unbidden. I never intended to try or even to mention it, and certainly not before a tournament when she needed to focus.

"What?" she asked.

"What?"

"You were looking at me funny."

Crystal Spivey, the woman I love and with whom I live on a full-time basis, is a professional pool player. She is ranked about eighth in the country, depending on whose ranking you read, but lately she's not been hitting them very well. She's not been staying down on the ball, she's been backing off some shots, particularly those requiring low cue ball. It's psychological. I hope it's not something I've caused, say by creating in her anxiety about oral assaults on her lingerie.

"Funny? What do you mean funny?" I asked innocently.

"Leeringly. You were leering," she insisted.

I try never to leer. Or to appear to leer.

"I can't hang around to be leered at. *I* have to go earn some money," she said.

By stressing the personal pronoun, she was alluding to the fact that I earn none, that I live entirely off my dog. Jellyroll is a star of stage, screen, and retail packaging. Now part of the pop-cultural fabric of this nation, Jellyroll got his start as the R-r-ruff Dog, spokesdog for R-r-ruff Dogfood, a position he still holds. His smiling full-color countenance can be seen on boxes by the dozens in the Pet Needs aisle of every supermarket in North America. His sweet, trusting temperament and keen intelligence are reflected openly in his face, and the motion picture camera loves it. That face has made me financially untroubled. Though Crystal lives with us, she supports herself, keeping her finances separate from Jellyroll's, because that's how she wants it. Something about self-image, but sometimes I suspect she wants to maintain the right to needle me about my absence of personal ambition.

I admit that I am intrinsically unemployable. Maybe once I was employable, once I had promise as something or other, but no longer. Without a famous dog, I don't know where I'd be. I nominally manage the charitable funds my lawyer and I established with Jellyroll's money, but I maintain a shadowy, anonymous stance as a philanthropist so people don't bug me, don't invite me places.

"So let's hear the details?"

"What details?"

"Of the naughty things you were thinking about me."

". . . It's embarrassing."

"Of course it is. Come on."

I told her.

"Go ahead."

"Go ahead?"

"Let's see if you can." She peeled off her shirt and put her hands behind her back—

I moved into what seemed an efficacious position. I didn't know how to go about this thing, but succeed or fail, the sides of Crystal's breasts would nestle against my cheeks, how bad could it be? But the phone rang.

Crystal said she had to answer because her start time hadn't been fixed yet. She was playing in a local tournament in a Brooklyn room that belonged to a friend of hers named Ronny. Ronny was delighted to have Crystal Spivey play in his tournament. She was warming up for the Southern Belle Nine Ball Festival in Memphis the following week. "It's Shelly," she said, offering me the receiver.

"Hello, Artie," he said, "just calling to see how—you know, if everyone's all right." Shelly was Jellyroll's agent, had been for years, but Shelly didn't make social calls.

"Fine, Shelly, why?"

"Oh, nothing, asking, that's all."

For a big deal maker, Shelly was pretty transparent. "Is something wrong?"

"Naw, not a thing."

I let him dangle.

"Well, a small matter. Probably nothing. Probably just one of those things. I got some mail. You know, kind of nutty mail. From a fan. Just a harmless eccentric, you know the type."

"What did it say?"

"Well, it implied certain threats to Jellyroll. Now take it easy. I knew you'd take it like that. That's why—"

"Shelly. Tell me."

"What?" said Crystal in the background.

I motioned for her to come listen. I hugged her head close to the phone.

"Well, a couple weeks ago I get this note. The note's written on the back of a bowling sheet. You know, a score sheet, lines and boxes, strikes and spares, from a bowling alley called Hi-Desert Bowl in Yucca Valley, California. That's way out in the desert near Palm Springs. I looked it up." Shelly was upset, but he tried to fake it. His voice quavered, and that scared me. "I'm sending it to you. I got a messenger on the way."

"What did it say?"

"Well, it didn't exactly *say* anything. I mean it didn't directly threaten Jellyroll. That's why I didn't do anything about it at the time."

"At what time, Shelly?"

"Hell, you know today. Today everybody's nuts. I got nuts for clients, present company excepted, of course. That doesn't mean they're dangerous . . . not all of them. Today I got another bowling sheet."

Crystal and I pronked straight up in the air when the

downstairs buzzer went off. Jellyroll began to bark wildly.

"Hang on, Shelly. I think the messenger's here."

"Artie—!"

"Yeah?"

"Make sure that's who it is," Shelly cautioned, sending chills up my back.

I peeked out the view hole. The messenger wore lime-green spandex pants, Doc Martins, a black leather vest with no shirt, black gloves with silver spikes on the knuckles, motocross shin guards, and a metal-flake purple motorcycle helmet with a black visor that covered his entire head. Nothing of his face was visible. Over his tit was a tattoo I couldn't decipher.

That's the trouble with having psychos on your tail—you just never knew. But since most bicycle messengers saw themselves as knights in some stupid post-apocalyptic road game, and since we were expecting a messenger anyway, I opened the door and took what this one offered. The bicycle messenger's tattoo said "Tough shit, Shirley."

"Thank you," I squeaked, signing his clipboard in return for the manila envelope with Shelly's logo.

"It's here, Shelly. We'll call you right back."

"No, I'll hang on."

Jellyroll knew something was up.

I mutilated the envelope trying to get the damn thing open. There were three score sheets inside. They were each folded in quarters. I spread them out on the bed side by side. Jellyroll jumped up and walked on them, trying to get our attention because he was insecure in the changed mood. I gently told him to get down, and he placed himself between our legs, joining us as we examined the score sheets:

"It's Cool Inside!" said a puffy snowman in icy letters along the top of the first sheet. This was the one Shelly spoke of—the Hi-Desert Bowl in Yucca Valley, California.

There had been two "players." They printed their names in Magic Marker, all caps: PERRY and DICK. Instead of a score, they had drawn graveyard crosses in every block on the fucking sheet. I could see through the cheap newsprint that something had been Magic Markered on the back, a cartoon of some sort, but I wanted to see the fronts of all three sheets together before we turned them over. I guess I thought I was looking for clues to their psychology, for something that said they were harmless cranks.

The second one was from Del's Bowl-More in Alasosa, Colorado. Del's logo consisted of an empty pair of two-stepping cowboy boots drawn against a bowling ball backdrop. There was some bullshit about their bar and grill being the Best in the West. The bowlers were the same, PERRY and DICK, and their names were printed in the same block letters with the same felt tip pen, by the same psycho.

"Are you looking?" prodded Shelly.

"Just a minute, Shelly."

The third and last score sheet was from Rock & Roll Bowl, Starkweather, Illinois. "Smoking permitted." The same pen, the same print, the same players.

Then we turned the sheets over. We knew we'd find the scary part on the back.

It was a big and crude cartoon of a TV screen with a talking head. The balloon from his mouth said, "All

Hollywood mourns tonight. One of its own is dead. . . ."

The same TV set appeared on the second score sheet. The talking head said, "The R-r-ruff Dog has been killed by an ax-wielding assassin."

The third said, "Live from our studios, we'll bring you an exclusive interview with the assassin, when we come back—"

Crystal swept them off the bed. They floated to the floor.

"When, Shelly? When did they come?"

Shelly said the first came a week ago. Three days later the second arrived, and this morning the third.

"Why didn't you tell me sooner, Shelly?"

"Look, I didn't want to upset you over nothing before I learned a few things. I took some steps, however—"

"Shelly, were they postmarked from these places? Alamosa, Starkweather, where the fuck else—?"

"No," said Shelly, "They were postmarked Los Angeles. All three of them."

I had to sit down. I sat on the bed. Crystal put her arm around me and continued to listen in. Jellyroll, ears down, looked from one of us to the other and back again. He knew.

"Artie, here's what I've already done. I've already done a couple of things. I've hired a guy, a private cop. I've hired him to trace these assholes." He lowered his voice conspiratorially. "You didn't hear it from me, but there are ways to handle this situation. The stalker situation. My man says you nip it in the bud early. Early is key. You don't let the stalker get stronger by feeding off your fear. You know what I'm saying? The earlier

the better. Don't let the stalker get into a routine. Whatever his routine is, you don't let him get into it.''

"What do you do?''

"Something so he goes away. Something strong,
Artie, something devastating. It's not my area. But it's
my man's area.''

Crystal asked, "Does most of his fan mail come to
you? Most of his fans wouldn't know who his agent is,
would they?''

"It's a curious thing you ask," said Shelly. "I asked
myself the same question. The answer is no. Most of it
goes to the R-r-ruff idiots or to the movie idiots, whatever idiots are appropriate, since Artie stopped answer-
ing it.''

Yes, I used to answer fan mail to my dog, but that
was a long time ago. I'd pretend that he was writing,
and I'd sign a cartoon paw print at the end. The apparent emptiness in the lives of his correspondents, those
over ten, at least, was the reason I started and the reason I stopped writing.

"But I don't keep Jellyroll's representation secret,"
Shelly continued. "Somebody could find out if they
wanted to.''

"But a person in the business would already know,"
I said, because that's what Crystal was getting at.
"Maybe somebody's playing a joke on you. Or me.''

"Who'd do such a thing as a joke? If they're in the
business, they know I'll find out who it was, and they'll
be exposed as flaming assholes. Jellyroll is the hottest
thing on four legs in America today. Nobody fucks
around with power like that unless they're totally nuts.
Or unless they're out to milk it for publicity. There's a
lot of ink to be had stalking the cutest dog in the world.

I don't think anybody's ever stalked a dog before, but the principle's the same, I guess. I got people looking into it, Artie."

"What about the police?"

"Well, it gets a little funny when you get in that area."

"What do you mean, funny?"

"I discussed that with my man. He points out that certain states have anti-stalker laws. This is one of them. Stalking itself is a crime in those states. But that doesn't do any good unless you know who the stalker is. An estranged husband, for instance. Also that law doesn't even so much as mention dogs. Some psycho could kill him—God forbid, I'm just saying—and not even go to jail. Which is why my man says you got to take private action, so to speak. I'm going to leave that up to my man entirely. But there's another problem about involving the police. The chance that publicity itself will create a killer out of some otherwise complacent psycho. Say your entertainment press got hold of this. 'The R r ruff Dog: Stalked.' That kind of heavy media onslaught can produce what my man calls the copycat factor. Picture all the crazy assholes sitting on their thumbs and rotating in front of their TV sets. You don't want to give them any ideas, Artie. You know what I mean?"

"Yes," I muttered weakly.

"You let my man take care of everything, Artie."

". . . Okay. Thanks."

I had intended to accompany Crystal to the tournament, leaving Jellyroll home, but I couldn't under the circumstances. And it wasn't only me. Crystal insisted I stay with him.

I ate some leftover Chinese that wasn't any good when it was new. I listened to Coltrane's *Ascension,* thinking it met my mood, but I couldn't handle its relentlessness. I wanted female vocalists. I took my place in my morris chair by the western window and looked out across the Hudson River, dead flat at slack tide, the yellow sodium lights of New Jersey undulating on its thick surface. Traffic had congealed on the parkway. A flashing ambulance was trying to get through, but nobody would move aside. Etta James sang "Let the Good Times Roll."

Jellyroll liked this—listening—or at least he was used to it. This is how we used to live, long solitary listening hours, the history of jazz, before Crystal came into our lives. Jellyroll circled in his Adirondack Spruce Bough Dog Bed and flopped on his side. He sighed, stretched, and flexed his paws with contentment. Everything was fine now. Whew.

But I couldn't let it go. I assembled the bowling sheets side by side. I wanted to study them for clues. I returned to the names. Three bowling alleys, the same names.

Perry and Dick. Who were Perry and Dick? The stalkers were actually named Perry and Dick? Or was it some kind of twisted hint, a psycho signature? I remembered Shelly's phrase: feeding off our fear, growing stronger on it. Was that what they were doing with this Perry and Dick bullshit? Or was there something to learn from it, thereby increasing our own strength. We had no strength. Who would you kill? Everybody who looked weird? I was gasping for air.

I called Wayne, a friend of mine who worked at the used books and video store on the corner. Wayne was the sort of guy who knew things. Hollywood was his specialty, but he knew some history, and he read serious fiction.

"How's it going, Wayne?"

"Oh, well, bad news. My uncle disappeared."

"I'm sorry to hear that."

"Well, it's not like we didn't expect it."

"You expected him to disappear?"

"The man's a genius, but he couldn't handle the structure."

"What structure was that?"

"So he tended to make things up, and this made them very edgy. Who could blame them for that? Lies are their business."

You can get in too deep with Wayne. "Hey, Wayne, do the names Perry and Dick mean anything to you?"

"Perry and Dick? In what capacity?"

"I'm not sure. Any capacity you can think of."

Crystal came home an hour later. That was too early for an amateur tournament. They can go on forever—unless you get eliminated, and Crystal had that eliminated look about her.

"I lost in the first round. No, no, I didn't lose. That's not accurate. I got stomped. By a beginner. I was supposed to be the centerpiece of the tournament, give it some weight, Ronny said. I got stomped in the first round by a beginner."

"You couldn't concentrate." I invited her to sit on my lap. Jellyroll came over to comfort her, too. She sat. Jellyroll put his snout on her hand.

"Ronny couldn't even look me in the eye. I told him I had the flu."

"Was she really a beginner?"

"Intermediate, tops."

I hugged her. Jellyroll and I cosseted her for a while, then the phone rang.

"Artie. Wayne here."

"Hello, Wayne."

"I thought of something. Perry and Dick. *In Cold Blood*. Truman Capote."

My heart sank—not *that* Perry and Dick—

"Killed those Clutters, those salt-of-the-earth Clutters. Tied up those Clutters and killed them one by one with a shotgun, for no reason. This was the pinnacle of the senseless-killing school of New Journalism. Largely a sensationalized and discredited genre today, this piece was a knockout. Perry and Dick were top-drawer psychos. They hung them in the end. Nobody minded. Fair movie, too, real grim black-and-white. Robert Blake and Scott Wilson. Why do you ask, Artie?"

2

First thing next morning, my friend Clayton Kempshall, as an evil high school principal, sprinted headlong off Pier Twelve into the East River. My snarling dog chased him all the way, but my dog stopped at the end of the pier. My friend did not. Clayton made quite a bit of it, slapstick sprinting in midair. Then he hit the water. Head cocked quizzically, Jelly-roll watched from the end of the high pier. People have made a lot of weird moves around him for years, he's used to it, but this—jumping into the East River— seemed particularly bemusing to him.

"Cut," called Kevin James, the director, a reasonably sane man who tried to make life easy for his collaborators.

The harbor is nature's great gift to the City of New York. We've turned our back on the waterfront, but without it there'd be no New York. When I first moved to town, I'd take the train down here, sit on a dock and watch it, absorb it somehow. I don't come down here much anymore because the South Street Seaport development turned it tame and lifeless and indistinguishable, but the water is still wild. Almost invisible out there, Clayton was being swept toward the Brooklyn Bridge by a raging flood tide.

I was feeling a little edgy about this whole business because I got him the gig. It would be an ironic drag to drown in that slate-gray water, boat-hooked ashore seriously bloated somewhere in Queens, for the sake of a gig as an evil high school principal in a Jellyroll movie. Precautions had been taken. He wore an inflatable life jacket under his charcoal-gray suit, and chase boats were waiting to pick him up. Besides which, he didn't *need* to jump in the river. They had stunt persons who got paid to do that kind of thing—

"No, Artie, I think it's important that I do my own stunts. It'll come in handy in case I ever get a real role. Not to say I don't appreciate that of an evil high school principal in a Jellyroll movie, no indeed not."

There seemed to be some kind of problem with the chase boats. Why hadn't they picked him up yet? Both, low-slung plastic boats with enormous twin outboards, had gathered around his little head bobbing in racing water. But his head zipped out between them. They'd missed him cold. A police boat was standing by, as required by law, and it, too, raced after Clay, now waving his arms, trying to beat back the panic, heading out into the big middle of the river.

Jellyroll looked over his shoulder at me to see whether or not to be upset about it. I shrugged at him. He looked back at the river.

I saw a guy in the chase boat leaning overboard. He came up with Clayton in a bear hug, while his colleague maneuvered the boat in the current. Clayton seemed unable to help himself over the side, so the boat driver left the wheel to help. Up he came stiff as a plank. It's a cruel business.

Back on the pier, he sat on a low stool and, despite a thick down sleeping bag around his shoulders, shivered. Jellyroll licked his arm. Jellyroll liked Clayton.

"Hey, Joey," I called to a guy at the coffee-and-doughnut table.

"Yeah, Artie?"

"Can you get this guy something hot?"

"Sure. Like hot chocolate?"

"You like hot chocolate, Clay?"

"Yeah. Great." His shoulders were hunched. "It looked good, didn't it, Artie? I mean the running gag? I don't think it's out of character, do you?"

"No, it's good." I hadn't actually read the whole script on this one. I'd skimmed it. The plot had something to do with stolen Nazi treasure, an evil school board, a sympathetic little boy, and, of course, his dog. The latter two set the world right at the end. At least I assumed so; that's what usually happens, but it doesn't matter. People don't go to Jellyroll movies for the narrative. They go to watch Jellyroll be sweet and smart, maybe do a trick or two. It's not an artistically rewarding gig for the humans.

"Jellyroll, what do you think? Was it top-drawer physical comedy or not?" Clayton asked.

Jellyroll cocked his head from side to side inquisitively as he does when you ask him a question, and all the while he smiled up at Clayton. Jellyroll smiles. His sweet nature reflected in that smile has made him the most famous dog in the country. He barked sharply at Clayton.

"What?"

"He wants to chase you off the pier again."

"Fun idea."

Kevin James, our director, approached pursued by a half-dozen folks who wanted his undivided attention. He'd directed a few other Jellyroll movies, *Nick Danger's Dog, Dog of Poker Flats,* and another one I forget, but the projects he cared about were not getting any green lights, as he put it. I could understand his fear he'd be pegged as a dog director for the rest of his life. Consequently he was a little cold to me, but he never fucked me up. What more can one ask?

"Great leap, Clay. Love the running in midair. Classic gag, no kidding."

"Hey, thanks a lot, Kevin." Poor Clayton leapt to his feet.

"And Jellyroll—brilliant as always."

"You don't think it was out of character?" Clayton nudged.

"What was?"

"The running. Too slapstick?"

He patted Clayton and Jellyroll on the shoulder and moved along, but he didn't get far before another group of attention seekers headed him off.

"He liked it," said Clayton to me. "Then why doesn't he use me as something *other* than an evil principal? Kevin's doing some interesting stuff. Did you hear about the Bosnia Project?" He hugged his legs to his chest and shivered like a little boy at the end of a day at the beach. Clayton had a face full of angles, like a broken pencil, with a stiff shock of hair that stood

16

straight up in an electrocuted way. His brows furrowed vertically and twitched. The poor sod. He was getting a little too old. "Plus, Kevin's adapting *Three Sisters*. Don't you think I'd make a great Judge Brack?"

". . . Judge Brack?"

"I don't think I'm right for Masha. You free? You want lunch? Maybe we can find a little fish *boîte* that takes dogs? You want fish?" he asked Jellyroll, who cocked his head side to side.

"We've got to go uptown for a R-r-ruff Dogfood shoot."

"How is that? Is that a good gig?

"It's lucrative but not rewarding."

"Yeah, I know that kind of gig."

"Jellyroll's just walking through it now."

"What about those tricks? The tricks are new. Do you teach him that?"

I said I did. I teach him a trick or two to keep him interested.

"Hey, Artie—" He lowered his voice. "I heard a disturbing thing the other day. I heard that there's a stalker after Jellyroll?"

"What? Who did you hear it from?"

"Woman I've been seeing from the soap."

"When was this?"

"Yesterday. But she said she'd heard it from her personal trainer out on the Coast last week."

"Last week?"

"I guess it's true, huh? There is a stalker, from the look on your face."

"I've been getting threatening bowling sheets."

"What are you doing about it?"

"Well, I'm trying to keep it quiet, but that hasn't been successful, has it?"

"Apparently not."

"I wonder if the stalker himself's putting out the word," I said.

"Publicity, huh?"

"Yeah."

"I played a stalker in a reenactment on *Serial Killers Update*. Severely twisted fucker. I got to talking to the writer. He told me he couldn't say on reality TV what he *really* learned from his stalker research."

"What was that?"

"That the best way to handle a stalking situation is to kill the stalker before he even gets started."

"Come on, Clay—"

"I'm sorry, I'm just telling you what he said."

How did all those people know? Why was I the last one to know they knew?

"Hey, Artie, you all right?"

"Yeah."

"Look, maybe you don't need to take it so seriously. It's probably nothing."

"Yeah. Probably."

". . . Did you say you've been getting threatening bowling sheets?"

"With cartoons on the back about ax murderers."

". . . Artie, I have an offer for you. Why don't you disappear to my island?"

"Did you say *your* island?"

"Absolutely. I'm a very rich young gentleman. You don't think I'm jumping in the river for the bread, do you? Absolutely not. I jump for the artistic satisfaction. Look, I'm not kidding you here. It's remote and un-spoiled, way up north on the ocean. You'll stay in the boathouse at the head of a pristine cove. Well, it's not

18

really a boathouse, but that's what we always called it. Why don't you and Jellyroll and your lovely new squeeze—what's her name?"

"Crystal."

"Crystal. Why don't you and Crystal take the boathouse with my compliments? Have a private little interlude, no show biz, no commercials, no psychos."

"It's really your island?"

"Kempshall Island, absolutely. Kevin's been up there, as a matter of fact. He came in his own boat and spent a week. He loved it."

Kevin passed us again with a determined stride. He didn't slow down or make eye contact, but he said, "Take him up on it, Artie. His island is one of the world's beautiful places."

"It's true," said Clayton. "I never go."

"Why?"

"Well, because of my old man. The islanders despised the bastard. He was a millionaire over and over by the time he got up there, but he was still an acquisitive little Dickensian prick. He was real wrinkled, and he always had bad breath. He took over their island. It was pretty easy since the locals don't have two nickels in cash money. He built his dream castle and ran them off. In fact that's what he called it: the Castle. That's where I spent summers until one night my father burned it down with me in it—I was ten—and he disappeared one step ahead of the feds." His expression no longer matched his glib tone. "I was lucky to get out with my life."

"Jesus, Clayton, I had no idea."

"Oh, yeah. It's movie-of-the-week-material, my youth."

19

"What became of him?"

"He was never seen again."

"Never?"

"About two years ago, I hired a detective agency to find him. I got the best. Your best detectives, by the way, are still based in L.A. I spent a lot of the old man's money to pick up the trail. But there was no trail, not a trace, nothing to go on. The agency eventually fired me as a client."

"Could he have died in the fire?"

"No, the local law had top experts in to poke through the ashes. There were no remains. He was running all kinds of financial scams, robbing people who trusted him. He was scum, but he was very good at whatever he put his mind to. He put his mind to disappearing."

"What about your mother?"

"Dead. She died while I was still an infant. . . . Some of the local people are great. I'll fix it up with Dwight. Dwight's a prince. He'll pick you up at the little one-horse airport and take you to Kempshall Island. What do you say? You got me this gig, let me give you a vacation in the boathouse. It looks like you need it."

"Does it really look like I need it?"

"Oh, bad."

3

Jellyroll was supposed to play dead when his person tries to feed him some "ordinary" dog-food instead of his usual R-r-ruff Dogfood. His person prods him, picks him up, jostles him, cajoles him, but nothing works, he remains "dead," hanging limply in his person's arms—until offered some you-know-what. He's great at it. Playing dead is a Lassie bit we copied one melancholy Saturday afternoon.

But under the present circumstances, the playing dead part made me edgy. I decided, however, to let it go because the young writing team of Marsha and Brad was so delighted with the "concept," I didn't have the heart to make them change it. After all, he was just *playing* dead. Besides, the cool, dark studio felt safe, and the people inside greeted us warmly, asked if we'd like anything, coffee or a snack.

Mr. Fleckton and his two always-terrified assistants greeted me, but they were as stiff as potato chips today, and I could tell by the way Mr. Fleckton's brow throbbed that something was uniquely wrong. He made small talk with me for a little while, then he said, "Uh, ahem, Mr. Frank would like to, ah, see you on thirty-five."

The corporate headquarters, the brains, of H. & R. Casswell Comestibles, the corporate parent of R-r-ruff Dogfood, was known to its minions as "thirty-five." It was always spoken of in hushed, reverential tones, even when ridiculed, as in "those dickheads on thirty-five." It had its own elevator, a carpeted, paneled, and mirrored one that stopped only there. On thirty-five.

"Uh, Artie," said Fleckton in a quivering voice, "no animals allowed on . . . thirty-five."

I paused. "He's been up there before," I told Fleckton.

"Yes, but that was special." Mr. Fleckton's eyes pleaded.

Did I want to leave Jellyroll alone under the circumstances? Or did I want to tell them all to fuck themselves?

"We'll take great care of him right here," said Marsha and Brad. Jellyroll loved Marsha and Brad.

So I agreed. The elevator shot upward at orbital velocity putting undue strain on the ligaments in my knees. Nobody needs to go that fast unless he's an astronaut.

A jovial, round-faced fellow in an expensive suit met me when the door opened onto the decorated (the concept was mauve) reception area. On thirty-five. He pumped my hand and led me into his corner office. The floor-to-ceiling glass walls overlooked the southern reaches of Central Park and most of Manhattan to the north.

"Artie, nice to see you again. Barry Frank, you re-member me?"

"Sure. How do you do?" I'd never laid eyes on this guy before. Why was he so nervous? His smile was about to fall off his face and disappear in the mauve carpet. Was this about the stalker? Had they, too, heard about the stalker?

"Come on in, have a seat. Coffee?"

"No, thanks."

He pressed a button on his desk somewhat smaller than a snooker table. "Wanda, coffee. Wanda, ASAP." He smiled at me. He sat on the corner of his desk, swung his leg back and forth. "So how've you been?" he asked as if we were old buddies at the frat house smoker. "Have a seat."

I heard water plashing somewhere. Did he have a fountain in here? I looked for it, didn't see one.

"Oh, that?" he said. "That's a little idiosyncrasy of mine. Nature tapes. That's the *Babbling Brook*. For re-laxation purposes. Does it bother you? I can turn it off. Dam it up, as it were, ha-ha."

"It doesn't bother me." I sat in a leather chair facing him. His smile never faltered, but beads of sweat sprang from his forehead.

The coffee arrived, delivered by a beautiful young woman in a tight little black skirt and ruffled white silk blouse. She bent from the waist and placed the tray on a glass coffee table. Then she turned and walked out.

"Artie, I'm afraid the fact is we're going to have to get a new R-r-ruff Dog."

"What?"

"Well, Artie, first I want you to know this is not my

23

idea. I was against it from the gitgo, and I made my opinion known. Very loudly. But the corporate board-room is not a level playing field. Frankly, Artie, there is a faction on the board that, well, to put it charitably, is concerned with values."

"Values?"

"Appearances, ah, in the family-values arena."

"What are you talking about? Jellyroll's neutered."

"Ha-ha, good one, Artie. No, Artie, actually, from their point of view, it's not Jellyroll that's the concern, it's you."

"Me?"

"You see, Artie, they learned that you live with a professional pool player. And, well, this faction on the board, the one concerned with family values, can't in good faith be seen to support the homosexual house-hold. Now, I have no problem with gay people. Some of my best friends are gay."

I sputtered inarticulately at first, but then I said nothing.

"I know how you feel, Artie. I tried to tell them, but they were adamant—"

"She's a woman."

"What? Who is?"

"The pool player."

"A woman pool player? I didn't know there was such a—"

And at that moment I felt suddenly sorry for Barry, just a minion who probably made three hundred thou-sand bucks a year, but still a minion without a wealthy dog to rescue him from the workaday humiliations.

"You're not ga-ga—?"

"Barry, I want to talk to you about this coffee. This

coffee is cesspool overflow." I handed him the cup. "This coffee doesn't even deserve the name coffee. I'm going to sue you and the board for attempted murder by antifreeze poisoning."

The poor guy was trembling in fear and confusion. Coffee was sloshing over his index finger.

"Artie, we can discuss this."

I headed for the door.

Barry pursued me out into the reception area. "Artie, who knew she was a woman? I mean, Chris Spivey. Who knew it was Christine, not Christopher?"

I kept going.

And suddenly Barry stopped pursuing me. "Yeah," he sneered, "go ahead, be righteous. You can *afford* it."

He knew he had a point. This R-r-ruff gig paid big bucks, but the fact was Jellyroll and I didn't need it. We used to, but his career has taken off since then. I *could* afford it, and freedom to walk is one of the sweets of wealth. I hustled through the heavy glass door toward the elevator. I free-fell thirty-four floors back to the studio. A hush descended as I stepped from the elevator. Heads turned. A dozen people on the floor, five more up in the booth, they all stopped work to watch us. They all loved Jellyroll, and now he was going from their lives. Jellyroll sensed the difference. His head pivoted.

I strode straight to him, took his leash from one of Fleckton's assistants, who flinched as if I were going to belt him. Long faces prevailed. Marsha was sobbing in the corner, while her associate Brad, also in tears, patted her shoulder blade. I felt this impulse to go over and try to make *them* feel better, but I ignored it. I walked out wordlessly.

New Yorkers develop keen alertness to anomalous movement in the street. Anything jerky or sharp, anything faster or slower than the daily pace leaps right out of the background. Heads turn, shoulders hunch, and like prey animals, no one relaxes until the anomaly can be identified, evasive action taken. Jellyroll and I hadn't even made it the half block from the side exit of the studio to the corner of Sixty-eighth Street and Broadway before I spotted the stalker sprinting at us with a baseball bat in his hands.

From somewhere a woman screamed.

He was about fifty, bald on top, wearing an undershirt, snapping sandals, one of those misfit types at whom, from the time he was a tiny child, bullies threw lighted matches. I didn't think it would happen like this.

But the stalker skidded to a stop ten feet away and began to beat the shit out of a parked car. Big overhand swings. The windshield exploded. Cords in his neck straining, the guy screamed, "You'll never get away with it, never, never, never!" as he pounded deep dents in the hood. "I'll always be there! Watching!"

I stood gasping for breath. My knees wouldn't lock properly, but the muscles in my thighs couldn't keep my legs straight. The adrenaline, subsiding now, had burned out all my muscles. Raggedy Andy. I leaned against a mailbox. Did Jellyroll think the bat was meant for him, or was it just me? He got behind the mailbox and peeked out to watch the guy beat the car.

Others watched, skittish, keeping their distance. That

kind of wild, primitive rage has a terrible attraction. The rubberneckers didn't notice me hugging the dome of the mailbox like a wino. They crouched to see who was in the car. But there was nobody in the car. Nobody at all.

The guy was tiring visibly. The frequency and severity of his blows diminished to slow motion, until finally he couldn't lift his slugger off his shoulder anymore. Apparently spent but satisfied, he walked off.

After a while I let go of the mailbox. I'd left my handprints in its soot. My knees were suspect, but I directed us west across the avenues. We picked our way around Lincoln Center, avoided the congestion at Seventy-second Street by cutting west on Seventy-first, a block north on West End Avenue and we were in the park. I had a plan to stroll north in Riverside Park to my place at 104th. Jellyroll would love that.

Riverside Park can soothe the ravaged nerves on its good days. This could have been a good one; the sun was still high, yet a cooling breeze ambled down the Hudson. The air seemed clean. Children and dogs frolicked and gamboled. People shot baskets. I passed a couple of refrigerator-crate shantytowns in the field north of the Henry Hudson on-ramp, but I could still dig the fantasy of urban civilization and the human impulse to preserve the greenery within it.

We passed the children's playground and took a little side trip down to the promenade along the bank of the river toward the tennis courts. The temperature dropped five or ten degrees down here. A red Moran tug pushed a cement barge upriver against the current. White water boiled up from its struggling propeller, and I was reminded of the children's story about Scuffy the Tugboat. That was kind of a melancholy, bittersweet recollection, but it felt a lot better than scared shitless.

I sat on a bench while Jellyroll rolled on his back in the cool grass. As I sat there watching Scuffy, the muscles in my neck began to soften their grip; but you can't sit long on these benches, because as the wood slats rot in the damp air, they become homes for ants. The slats are infested. Probably prime real estate if you're an ant. Ants crawl up your thighs. If you ignore them, they'll marshal their forces to carry you back to their queen.

Jellyroll was circling and sniffing a young husky named Roger. But I didn't recognize the walker. He was a big man in a small singlet and Yankees cap. Roger's owner was named Phil. I didn't need to be told. Phil had had AIDS.

"Yesterday," said the man in the Yankees hat. He didn't wait around to see my sadness at the news. He'd probably had enough of that. He leashed Roger and bolted. I didn't blame him.

"Artie—"

"Haw!"

"Little tense these days? As you know, I can relate to that."

"Hello, Seth."

Seth was a depressive playwright. Seth's dog, a black Lab cross named Buchner, was also depressed—by association, most of us dog walkers figured. Buchner hadn't always been like that. He and Jellyroll used to wrestle and chase as puppies. Jellyroll still tries to get up a game, but Buchner is distracted, morose.

"You want to hear some ironic shit?" asked Seth, sitting with us on the bench.

"Not really."

"I got this showcase production in the East Village, right? New piece. Well, an old piece, but I fixed the ending. This is mean, biting drama, this has undercurrent and edge, the kind of shit nobody wants. But guess who shows up out of the blue on opening night. Margaret Seagraves! I can't believe my eyes, it's her. At a showcase! So I'm shitting hot bricks through the whole thing. Margaret Fucking Seagraves! It went well. I'm lurking out front trying to overhear something, but she comes right up to me on the sidewalk. She shakes my hand and says, 'It's a rare thing these days to see mean, biting drama.' "

"That's great," I said without energy.

He began to scratch at his crotch. Ants. "She walks away, I feel like shouting with delight, right? Margaret Seagraves, loves my play. Her review is going to put my young ass on easy street. I'm thinking stardom, right? Ten seconds later a shot rings out."

"A shot—?"

"Pow! The slug hits the Greek deli six feet above her head. Blew a hole you could stick your fist in!"

"So she didn't write the review?"

"I call over there today and pretend like I'm concerned about her, but she's not even in. So I ask her lackey, is she going to write my rave, or what? 'Oh, I doubt it. Ms. Seagraves is very upset by the experience.' Upset? What kind of thing is that? That's totally unprofessional behavior! I mean, take Bosnia. The theater critics in Sarajevo, they never stopped reviewing despite constant bombardment. What is this *up*set bullshit? It killed a deli!"

I sighed.

"Goddamn ants! You want to walk?"

"Sure."

When we got to the grassy spot just north of the tennis courts, somebody shouted, "Hey, you want to call your dog before I break his legs?"

What?

It was a solitary picnicker/sunbather in a little black nylon bathing suit reading the paper. He was about thirty, with long flaxen hair, a Gap model's face, and tight abdominals. He'd established his place with a blanket and laid out his lunch from Zabar's. He had half a roasted chicken, several bottles of designer water, a container of macaroni salad, a couple of kaiser rolls, and some unopened condiments. Languidly slathering lotion on his shoulders, he wrinkled his ruggedly handsome face in revulsion apparently at the very existence of my dog—Jellyroll was passing fifteen feet away, not even slowing down.

"What did you say?"

"You want to get him away from my lunch or do you want to lose him?"

I remember distinctly hearing that. I didn't make it up. Okay, he made no threatening gestures, but there was the quality of threat inherent in his words—

Without further ado, I strode into his foodstuffs like a field-goal kicker. The macaroni salad was my first intended target, but not my last. It exploded under the impact. The handsome young man, up on all fours, tried to shield his face behind his hands, but it was too late. Macaroni and mayonnaise hit him like shrapnel from incoming artillery fire. I made snarling noises as I kicked the shit out of his lunch.

I leapt up and down on his waters until the containers belched out their contents. That done, I backed up to get into chicken-kicking position. Splat. The carcass pirouetted over the guy's head, shedding limbs. I knew this was insane behavior, but I simply didn't want to stop. The guy's terror at my insane rage filled my heart with delight. I was a dangerous man at that moment north of the tennis courts on the banks of the Hudson River.

Wait, one translucent bucket of something remained intact. I booted it. Pickles. The juice soaked me. Having pretty much completed my work, I walked off panting.

Jellyroll followed, but he kept his distance.

On the balls of their feet, a skittish group of witnesses watched us go. A few were dog-walking acquaintances of mine. I avoided eye contact. Tennis couples clutched their rackets to their chests as if to deflect psycho rage. The Latino eel fishermen discussed the event. I heard the word *loco* more than once. The picnicker was screaming at me high in his clenched throat. He was hysterical. I didn't look back.

"I agree with you," said Seth, coming along. "Fucking picnickers, a bad element, they need to be driven from our public places, same with tourists."

By the time I got to Riverside Drive, Seth and I had parted company. I was spent. The walk home was grueling.

"What's *that?*" said Crystal when I got there.

"What?"

"That—" She pointed to my throat.

I scooped it away, examined it. "A noodle."

She looked me up and down. "Why?"

I told her. Her brow furrowed with concern for my sanity. And then I told her about how they had summoned me up to thirty-five and fired Jellyroll.

She was flabbergasted. Tears came to her eyes. "Why?"

"They heard you were a pool player, so they figured you must be a man. Christopher."

"You mean—?"

"Yep."

"They can't do that! That's not even legal!" She was outraged, but only momentarily. She looked down at Jellyroll, who watched her with his mouth clamped shut, a sign of worry. He worries when his people seem to be upset. She giggled. "Well, at least you don't need the money. I'll kind of miss his face on all those boxes, though."

Then I told her about Clayton Kempshall's offer of his island.

"His own island? It sounds wonderful. Why don't you accept?"

"I don't want to leave you."

"Well, I could go with you."

"You could? But what about that tournament, the Southern Belle?"

She sniffed me. "Pickles?"

"Could be."

"You need to get away."

The phone rang. It was Shelly.

"I just heard they fired him. I knew they were stupid,

but who would have imagined? What do you want to do about it?"

"Do whatever you want, Shelly."

"I was thinking about enveloping them in litigation. I haven't enveloped anyone in a long time."

"Have fun. I'll be in touch."

Can you tell us how it feels to own the R-r-ruff Dog and know that at any time a stalker may strike?" the handsome, sandy-haired media person shouted after us. He and his crew of two were catching up. I could feel their hot lights on the back of my neck as Jellyroll and I accelerated down the concourse ramp at La Guardia.

Travelers' heads turned all around us. Suddenly I was looking down a dozen different gaping mouths. Jellyroll attracts attention anyway, but here he was in a major transportation center pursued by about twelve million candlepower of stark white TV light and three straining assholes.

There was no refuge for us, nowhere they wouldn't follow. Running would only encourage them. The breathless reporter in hot pursuit of the truth. If he'd been eating lunch, I'd have kicked it in his face. But of course you can't do that on TV. TV demands deadpan; you can't ever be real on TV or it will eat you alive. I would have to deal with him. I stopped. We turned to face the light.

He had this thirty-million-dollar smile. His teeth fairly sparkled. He was an all-American boy. I hate that kind of fucker. I'd seen him somewhere before, but I couldn't place where. His camera operator was a woman, but the camera covered her identity. All I could see beside the fish-eye she jammed in my face were enormous tits erupting under a black sweater. The sound man, tall and gangly, in tight jeans and lizard cowboy boots, proud of himself, smirked at me.

"I'm Rand Dewy from *Celebrity Tonight.* We hear that there's a stalker situation with respect to the R-r-Ruff Dog. Would you care to comment?"

"Weren't you a figure skater?"

"Why, yes, I was, Olympic bronze, actually."

Jellyroll sniffed his shoes.

Rand knelt down to pet him—

"Don't!" I said.

"What?"

"He'll take your hand off."

Jellyroll thumped the floor with his tail, peered sweetly up into Rand's face.

"The R-r-ruff Dog?" Rand looked devastated.

"Vicious. He's always been vicious. He was born vicious. Two weeks old, he killed his littermates."

"No—"

"Rand, could we step over here and talk in private? It's very important." I didn't wait for an answer; I took the microphone from his hand and handed it to the sound man, who seemed to have something stuck down the front of his jeans, a rope or something. I led Rand to a seat in the back of a vacant departure gate area. As I seated us in the plastic chairs, I made a big thing out of positioning myself between Jellyroll and Rand. "Now, Rand," I said, jaw clenched, "where did you get the idea that Jellyroll is being stalked?"

"Well, Mr. Deemer—your name is Arthur Deemer, isn't it?—I'm not at liberty to—"

"Rand, look at all the people watching us. People traveling to all parts of the world are watching us." I itched to disfigure the bastard even as I looked into his baby blues, but I tried to maintain an air of calm, never mind the beads of sweat running down my flanks. "Nobody's stalking my dog at this time, but any one of these people watching us could stalk him at some future time. Maybe the only reason they aren't stalking him now is because they never thought of it. You understand? I don't want you to suggest it to them."

"You don't need to patronize me," said Rand. "I'm not a moron."

"I'm not patronizing you," I lied. "I'm asking you, don't do this story."

"My producer sent me to get it. I got to get something."

"Say you missed us."

"Serge and Tammy would never support me on that."

"Who?"

He nodded at his crew. Serge and Tammy. Did I see the traces of tears welling in his blue eyes? "You think I'm a sellout."

"No—"

"You think I'm a cheap little tabloid-TV clack has-been, don't you, some submissive, bought-off talking head, don't you?"

"No, I—"

"What would you do in my place? Join the Ice Capades? Coach? Live vicariously through a fifteen-year-old skating bunny? Until she misses a double toe loop and accuses you of sexual abuse? Huh?"

"I don't know, Rand, I've seen your TV work," I lied again. "It's not bad. It's good. You have presence. Not everybody has presence. I'll make you a deal. I'll give you an exclusive if you'll drop this stalker story."

"Exclusive? About him?" He didn't dare point his hand toward Jellyroll, so he extended a finger close to the vest.

"Absolutely. But you have to stay away from this stalker story. Deal?"

"Well, I'd have to hear the news first." Rand Dewy wasn't born yesterday.

"Okay. The R-r-ruff Dog and R-r-ruff Dogfood are about to terminate their association over irreconcilable artistic differences."

"No kidding? Wow. You're ready to go on record with this?"

"Not me, I'm just his trainer, representing the syndicate that owns him. But you can attribute it to an unnamed source without fear of contradiction."

"The end of an era," he said thoughtfully. He raised himself in his chair like an Olympic skater alone on the ice as the first notes of his music swell. "All right, it's a deal. I'll just tell them I'm not going to do the stalker story because I have this scoop. Right? It is a scoop and it is true, right?"

"Absolutely."

He shook my hand.

"Let me ask you this, Rand. What gave your producer the idea that the R-r-ruff Dog was being stalked?"

"Well, probably the spot on *Celebrity Sleuth*. My producer didn't like getting scooped on that one."

"Are you saying it was on TV already?" Calm, rational, clear—

"On *Celebrity Sleuth*. On their 'We've Heard' segment. 'We've Heard' comes on right after 'Celebrity Birthdays.'"

"What did it *say*? I mean, what did it say?"

"It said they'd heard that a psycho was stalking the R-r-ruff Dog."

"What else?"

"Nothing. It's real short. That's the point. . . . You've never seen *Celebrity Sleuth*?"

"Oh sure. Hasn't everybody?"

"How can I get in touch with you?"

"We'll be out of town for a while."

"Where?"

I looked left, then right, as if for eavesdroppers. "Pensacola."

"Florida?"

"Florida, right." Suddenly I felt sad and tired. This was bad. The stalker was common knowledge.

"Where in Pensacola?"

"I don't have a number yet."

Rand fumbled in his inch-thick wallet for about two days and finally came up with a card.

I snatched it. "So I gotta go. But we have a deal. You'll hear from me." And then I bolted down the concourse with Jellyroll on my heels.

The concourse came to an end. Our gate was near the top of the ramp, but I didn't want to lead them right to it. I glanced back; so did Jellyroll. Rand, Tammy, and what's-his-name were still standing together talking in a clot. I sat down. My flight would wait because Jellyroll and I were its only passengers. I picked up a discarded *USA Today* and pretended to read it.

Rand and his crew turned and walked off, Rand leading, the crew elbowing each other as they blatantly ridiculed him behind his back. As soon as they were out of sight, I ducked into the rest room in case they doubled back.

Except for one guy, we were alone. He was middle-aged, wearing a blue blazer, chinos, a London Fog draped over his arm. It took me a moment to notice precisely what was wrong with the picture. The guy was standing between two urinals peeing on the wall. I double-checked to see if it were some kind of optical illusion, but no, he was peeing on the wall. A trail ran between his shoes. Jellyroll and I turned on our heels and exited. There's no telling what a wall pisser will do.

We headed for the nearest telephone. It was in a bank with about twenty other telephones. I finally found one that worked—

"Shelly, goddamnit, they all *know!*"

"What! What do you mean? Who?" Shelly shouted.

I told him about Rand Dewy, about *Celebrity Tonight* and *Celebrity Sleuth.*

"Okay, Artie, you got to relax. That's the thing to do, relax. Deep breaths." I could hear him wheezing.

"Maybe the stalker's telling them. Maybe he's making his own press."

"Artie, did they know where you were going?"

"No, I tried to throw him off by giving him the scoop on the R-r-ruff business."

"I could threaten to sue their firstborn. They fear your lawyer. They know Myron'll have their hair on his belt, but what good would that do? It would just call attention to us, give the loonies all kinds of sick ideas they didn't have before. Look, I'll ask my brother-in-law how he thinks we should proceed."

"Who?"

"The man I was telling you about before—Sid Detweiler's his name. What, didn't I mention he was my brother-in-law?"

"Sid Detweiler? Shelly, I don't need a CPA."

"CPA, your ass. This guy recently retired from the NYPD, homicide branch. You ought to hear his stories. Sid has seen the heart of darkness. Besides, he's family. Family's always best. Speaking of R-r-ruff, those idiots have been calling about every fifteen minutes. I'll let 'em stew in their own juices for a while, unless you have strong feelings one way or the other."

"I don't."

"Call me as soon as you get there. I'll make some inquiries about how they all know. In the meantime, take lots of deep breaths. Oxygen does wonders."

Then I put in a call to Poor Joe Cay in the far remotest Bahamas, a low, flat, peaceful place more of the sea than the land, to talk to my friend and bodyguard Calabash. His Uncle Warren answered. Trying to sound reasonably calm, I chatted for a while with Uncle Warren before I asked for Calabash.

"He at sea."

"At sea? When will he be ashore?"

"A hard t'ing to say about Calabash when he go to

sea. He do so periodically. Get off by hisself somewhat."

Then that crass white TV light struck us from behind, jerked our necks like a big comber at the beach.

"Gotta go, Uncle Warren. I'll call again. Good talking with you."

5

*T*he adrenaline surged again, the same blast as in Riverside Park, the sort that takes years off your life. It would be tough to maintain the deadpan. Jellyroll was peering up into my eyes. I scared him. He knew every nuance of my mood, and he didn't like it. I turned to face the wattage—

It wasn't for him! The cameras weren't even pointed at us. They were aiming at someone else, apparently a notable or a group of notables deplaning in an entourage, and we were being hit by the light spill. The camera crews bustled about the edges of the entourage, poking into gaps to get a look at the object of all this fuss. I was curious. Who needed fifty people to carry his luggage? This entourage, made up of some very tough customers with stern faces and darting eyes, moved like a phalanx that parted the ways for the honcho inside. I liked the concept.

"That's His Excellency," said a thin man with a pencil moustache and a black suit standing nearby. He was obviously an admirer of His Excellency. He was bobbing his head with obeisance even as he mentioned Him. "This is His Excellency's first trip to the Apple. He is very pleased. He has tickets to *Les Miz.*"

"Well, I hope he has a grand time," I said. I was panting with relief. It was clearly time to get out of town, get way out of town.

All my major joints had turned runny by the time we took our seats on the airplane. But now we could relax. We didn't even have fellow passengers to engage, because I had chartered the whole airplane. The world is not a fair place that I should have the wherewithal to hire a twin-engine aircraft while others must crawl, but there it is. We were aboard an Airstream by British Aerospace, I think, the one with the big wing strut running across the aisle. It was meant for about fifteen passengers. I hadn't asked for such a big airplane.

The pilots turned in their seats, head to head, to wave at us. They wore starched white shirts with crisp epaulets. The pilot was dark, the copilot fair, but both had rugged outdoors faces. They were probably based in Crested Butte, Colorado, and Big Sky, Montana, respectively, where they liked to ski with their well-adjusted, tight-bodied wives. I'd like to have been a pilot of some kind, even though I don't look the part. I look more like the navigator.

"Welcome aboard, Mr. Deemer. I'm Ron," said the captain. "And this is Dave."

"Call me Artie."

"Well, it's good to know you, Artie. We'll be getting airborne right away, but before we fire 'em up, the FAA wants us to tell you a few things you probably already know." Ron had fine pearly teeth.

Meanwhile, Jellyroll investigated the passenger compartment, sniffed everything as if he were considering acquiring the airline.

Ron recited from a plastic card, and I felt safe for the first time in days. I like airplanes. My father got killed in one before I was born. I used to read books about angles of attack, lift, drag, inertia, and thrust, but I don't anymore. Nor do I read about air combat anymore. Maybe I've buried my father; though literally, there probably wasn't much to bury, a smoking boot, perhaps. Had he lived, he might have looked something like Ron and Dave, tall, slim, stalwart, cool, sunglasses rakishly worn up on the forehead. At least that's how he looked in the old photographs.

They started the engine on the left side, and the plane began to vibrate, then the right, but the noise was surprisingly light. I motioned Jellyroll to jump up on my lap for takeoff. I hugged him tightly against my chest. I've never been able to think of a better way. Seat belts just don't work for dogs. He licked my ear as our wheels left the New York metropolitan area.

After we leveled off at about ten thousand feet, Captain Ron asked what my ultimate destination was—after we landed in Oglevie.

I felt a stab of suspicion. "Why, Ron?"

"Up north where you're going, there aren't many rules. We got some flexibility with regard to flight plan. Sometimes people like to overfly their cabin or whatever."

"Oh, I see. I'd like that. It's tiny, I hear. A place called Kempshall Island. Near a town called Micmac."

"Let me see if I got the charts."

"Okay."

A door latch opened behind me. There wasn't supposed to be anyone else aboard, yet someone was coming out of the lavatory—Christ, it was Barry from the thirty-fifth floor!

"Barry, what are—" Then I saw that Barry had an ax in his hands, a big two-blade Paul Bunyan ax.

"Look, Artie, I don't want to do this, but the board insisted. I tried to talk them out of it. I got two daughters in the Ivy League. Do you know how much that *costs?*" Barry was advancing on us down the short aisle. "I'm going to have to kill him for family values."

"Don't kill him, Barry. You said yourself it wasn't him, it was me they object to. Kill me."

"I'm sorry, Artie, but I have no choice in this thing—"

"Haw!"

The copilot—what was his name?—was tapping my forearm. "I'm sorry, Artie, I guess you were dreaming."

"Yeah, I guess I was."

"Ron found Kempshall Island. Wondered if you'd like to see it from forward."

"Oh, great. Thanks a lot."

"I'll sit back here and pet the star dog, if that's okay with you."

"You stay, pal." He hated those words, and he gave me the stink eye, but sometimes he has to stay.

I slid over the throttles and into the right-hand seat without kicking anything vital to level flight.

The azure ocean was spattered with green islands. The largest were about the size of a New York City block, and the smallest nothing more than barren rock piles and exposed ledges around which waves broiled. Humans played no part here, only the long slog of geologic time. Even the verdant, forested islands looked forbidding. Few had protected coves, none had anything like a natural harbor. The ocean clawed constantly at them. Maybe the ledges and rock piles had once been islands, but the elements had reduced them to their essence—rock.

"There it is," said Ron.

At this speed, geography took form quickly and flitted away under our wings even faster. "Where?"

"The nose is on it . . . now."

Two domes formed Kempshall Island. Both were wooded on their flanks, bald on the very top. The naked rock had a pinkish hue that glinted in the sun. The domes were soft and, compared to the other craggy and truncated islands we'd flown over, sensual, almost gentle. And then it was gone.

"No roads. You notice that?" said Captain Ron.

I hadn't, no. How does the islander move about a roadless island? By boat, I guessed. Or he just stayed put. I liked that prospect. "Could we go around again, Captain?"

"Sure." He called back to Dave, "Hang on, we're going around again."

"Okay," called Dave. Then Dave told Jellyroll that we were going around again.

From the new angle, I saw that one of the domes had

twin peaks with a low saddle joining them. In fact, the island was made up of three, not two, domes, the sides of which plunged almost vertically into the surf.

"Look at that!" said Ron as we completed the turn.

It was a huge crack. Something had cracked Kempshall nearly in half. One dome lay to the south, the twin peaks to the north. What can crack a solid rock island? Volcanos? Time? The rift cut deeply enough into the island to form a long, narrow harbor. There were a few boats and docks inside. I could see stairways zigzagging down the rock face to the docks. And then Kempshall Island ducked under the nose. There were no more islands ahead.

We were over open water for about ten minutes before the mainland came into sight. I mused on isolation and solitude. Life out there on the island would be very different from that on the island Manhattan. There would be nothing on the islands to distract one from the inner life. You would need a well of inner resources to tolerate yourself in such solitude. You'd need something other than controlled substances to fall back on. Part of me wanted to retire Jellyroll, chuck in the whole career and make do with things as they are, tinker, plant, observe nature's ways. Jellyroll would dig it, but would I turn sullen, distant, angry in the solitude, given to weird eccentricities and sudden psychotic outbursts? I didn't know.

The mainland was equally unpopulated, evergreen forests right down to the black rocks and the white surf. Somewhere around here was a town called Micmac from which I was to catch a boat to Kempshall

Island, but I didn't see a single roof or road as we crossed the coast.

Captain Ron was talking about a summer camp he'd attended as a boy in this area. Apparently there were a lot of mosquitoes and bullies, but I couldn't really hear. I nodded and grinned and longed for Crystal. The sun was going down, and I would be dependent on my own inner resources in the dark.

6

Now, in the falling light, I would try out the Jellyroll disguise. It wasn't originally a disguise; it was a costume. A friend of his made it for Halloween out of fake fur left over from her production of *Cymbeline*. I think it was *Cymbeline*. Anyway, we went to the party as a couple of pagan village-sackers from the *Sagas*. It's a tufted cape that fits over his back and shoulders and fastens around his chest and belly with elastic hasps. He didn't like it then, and he wouldn't like it now, but he'd comply. I asked him to stand up for a fitting. He did, but he was going to make me feel like shit about it. I held it for him to examine. There was a two-year, closed-closet whiff to it, but not bad enough to clear a room. At least not to the human nose. He looked up at me. "After years of loyalty, this is what I get from you, a stinking Shakespearean remnant?"

Nonetheless, I was committed to the disguise. He watched it go on, feeling sorry for himself. He blew out his cheeks in protest. I stepped back. Not terrible. I told him how pretty he looked, but he didn't buy it. Sometimes I think he doesn't respect me.

The copilot called back for us to take our seats and buckle up. We were landing. But where? I couldn't see a single sign of civilization, not even a headlight. We were flying over wilderness. Suddenly a dim macadam strip popped from under the wing, and the pilots put us down with barely a jolt.

We turned at the end of the runway near the forest wall, taxied back past parked single-engine puddle jumpers and a lovingly restored DC-3 to a new, square, cinderblock terminal building, where we stopped. OGLEVIE it said in spiffy aluminum letters, "Gateway to the North." I couldn't see anybody inside the terminal, and there was no activity out here, no fuel-truck drivers, baggage handlers, or small aircraft aficionados hanging around. To urbanites, absence of activity always seems menacing. But that's exactly what Clayton told me to expect in Cabot County, exactly what I wanted.

The pilots opened the door. I thanked them very much. They said it was their pleasure, and they leaned down to pet Jellyroll—until, simultaneously, they noticed the ratty fake pelt on his back and they froze.

"He gets cold," I said.

They nodded and went about petting him places the pelt didn't cover. He licked their hands.

"Do you have children?" I asked.

Naturally, they both did. Daughters.

"Maybe they'd like a photograph." I have glossies taken by a late girlfriend of mine. Jellyroll's head is cocked to the side inquisitively, eyes alert and glistening at her behind the camera. It makes me sad to look at the picture, so I don't. I gave them each one, shook their hands and deplaned.

The linoleum-and-fluorescent waiting room was abandoned, except for a guy manning the rent-a-car booth. Flesh spilled over the top of his starched collar, and the brown company blazer caught him way up the arm. Nonetheless, I'd try the Jellyroll disguise out on him. We were pretty conspicuous. How could you miss us?

But the rent-a-car guy did not bat an eye. Maybe he never batted an eye. He stood behind the counter staring forlornly at the opposite wall. His eyes were fish flat. Life hadn't rewarded his hopes and dreams. He wasn't alone in that, of course, but he seemed to be taking it particularly hard. Maybe nobody ever rented a car around here. I thought about renting one just to lend his evening some meaning, but there were no roads where I was going. Directly outside the glass door, twenty feet away, the Airstream's engines revved hard. The windows trembled, but he still didn't bat an eye. He was not a good test of Jellyroll's disguise.

I left our gear and took Jellyroll out front for a pee. It was chilly.

"Mr. Deemer?"

I spun—

"I'm Dwight."

Clayton had arranged for Dwight to pick us up. He might have been seventy, but he could have been much younger. His face looked like a piece of old unraveled hemp. His massive shoulders strained the buttons of his flannel shirt, leaving vents. The hand he shook mine in was the size of a dinner plate.

"Call me Artie."

Here was a man of the sea. You could almost smell the salt breeze and the fish gurry. I wish I were a man of the sea. I would like to look like Dwight when I grow old, weather-beaten, tough, yet somehow gentle, humble for having witnessed nature in the raw, but of course you can't look like that unless you live the life. "This is the dog himself, huh?" Dwight leaned down to show Jellyroll his enormous hand. Jellyroll licked it.

"He likes you."

"He does?"

"Oh yes, I can tell."

"I wish the wife could see. She tapes his R-r-ruff Dog commercials, plays them back with no sound. I think he's even cuter in real." Dwight straightened, towered over me, and said, "Clayton told me I wasn't to tell anybody this dog was coming to town, and I haven't."

"Thank you, Dwight." I had the impulse to tell him about the stalker right then and there, he being so solid and dependable, but I resisted the temptation. A conical sign on the roof of his old station wagon said TAXI? CALL CAPTAIN DWIGHT.

We drove through utter darkness on either flank. The moon was up and the sky starry, but they seemed to bring no light down to the road. I kept expecting to pass a gas station, a convenience store, a private dwelling, a trailer, a hovel, but there was nothing human in sight except bullet-pocked road signs. Even though there were no abused, amoral, Glock-toting thirteen-year-olds out in that forest, no commuter-crazed pedestrian-killers from New Jersey, no psychosis at all, the darkness was still disorienting me. I decided to engage Dwight in conversation.

"What are you captain of, Dwight?" I asked.

"Not much now. Lobstered offshore all my life, but last winter I couldn't face the cold no more. Man kids himself he's tough enough to take it, but no, he ain't. I stayed inshore this year. I'm gonna quit it altogether next year."

I had been thinking about doing a little boating myself. Lately, I'd been reading nautical literature, but I hadn't done much actual boating. I asked him some questions about lobster boats and lobstering, and he asked me about life in New York City, which he kept calling the Big Apple. Dwight had always wanted to go to the Big Apple. In fact, when he was a kid he wanted to be a tugboat captain in New York Harbor, but he'd never been there. Later, he said, "We got a little problem with tonight's lodging."

"What?"

"Well, it's too late to go out to the island, and there ain't suitable lodging here on the mainland. This ain't a big tourist area. I could take you up to the Double-O Truck Stop on the highway, but it's two hours away, and you wouldn't like it none, anyway. Drunk and lonesome, listenin' to sad songs, them truckers start stabbin' one another dead about this time of night."

"I think Clayton mentioned a bed and breakfast—"

"That'd be the Indian Pipes Lodge. But it burned down."

"It did?"

"Just last week. It'll turn out to be somebody with the volunteer fire department. That's usually a wintertime thing, but economy's been slow—"

"What is?"

"Your arson by volunteer firemen. They get family troubles, financial difficulties, they sometimes set fires in order to put 'em out. Feel good about themselves as fire fighters. Most of those fellas is salt of the earth, but every so often one goes a tad funny. The wife'd be thrilled if I was to bring home the R-r-ruff Dog and his person, but you wouldn't like that either. The Selfs is havin' a big reunion. A Self reunion ain't as dangerous as the Double-O, but it's just as loud, and they'd never give your dog any peace."

"Are you a Self?"

"No, I'm a Reed. There ain't any more Reeds, but there's still Selfs. Even out on Teal Island."

"Teal Island?"

"Well, Kempshall Island. Used to be Teal Island. Until old Kempshall bought up the whole thing and put the families off who'd been out there two hundred years. Renamed it after himself. Now, nobody's got anything against his son. Clayton was an innocent little boy at the time. I ain't alone in sayin' we'd like to have Clayton come up for a visit sometime."

"What was his name?"

"Who?"

"Clayton's father."

"Compton. Compton Kempshall."

"He's dead now?"

"Can't say. Nobody ever saw him again after his mansion burned down."

All this time, we had passed nothing at all.

"If anybody defied him, he'd ruin that person."

"How?"

"The bank'd call in the loan on his lobster boat, for

example. Or he'd start havin' IRS problems. Like that. Grown men feared Compton Kempshall. He put up a sign in town sayin' that men must tip their hats and ladies must curtsy when they pass him."

"Did people do that?"

"No, they closed the town. Everything closed. People from away need local resources, even if it's just a roll of toilet paper. . . . People's spirits was being damaged treated like that. It was like occupation by the Nazis."

"Who lives on Teal Island now, anybody?"

"No, there's a few. See, when Clayton went twenty-one, he returned all the deeds to the original holders from when his old man bought them up. A branch of my wife's family lives out there. You'll be sharin' a cove with Hawley Self. Plus there's some summer people who bought in over the years, but it's not a crowded island. I know you people from away like your solitude when you can get it." Dwight didn't say "from away" disparagingly, and I felt relieved at that. I wanted welcome. Welcome, especially at night, always bolsters the inner resources.

The road grew curvy. I began to worry about Jellyroll's stomach, but he seemed okay, sniffing the window crack. It was too cool to keep the window down.

"Do you have any children?" I asked.

"Yes, I do. My daughter's tryin' to make it as a country singer in Nashville, Tennessee, and my son is growing salmon smolts up near Burntcoat Head in the Minas Basin. Gettin' back to the question of tonight's lodging, I'm doing a little yacht sitting right now. This Belgian fellow owns it, but he's off in Belgium for the economic conference. There's nobody aboard."

"Stay on a boat?"

"Well, just for tonight."

"Terrific."

"Oh, you like that idea? Okay, good."

The town of Micmac was a mystery in the dark. It was tiny, that much was clear. Captain Dwight drove right out onto the dock. The ancient wooden beams and pilings clattered and groaned. It was a big, tarry industrial dock with full-fledged trucks parked on it. Salty workboats were tied to it, and at the end a small, brightly lighted ship was loading pallets of things. Jellyroll peed on a piling.

I didn't see my yacht until Captain Dwight walked us to the edge of the dock directly above it. The Belgian's boat was huge. It was a ketch or a yawl. I couldn't exactly remember which was which, but anyway it had two masts. Everything—deck, masts, cabin, booms, rails—was made of wood and richly varnished. The elegant curves made the Belgian's boat look more like sculpture than a utilitarian object.

"Hardest part of sittin' this vessel," said Dwight, "is keepin' the bird shit off the varnish."

I giggled. I liked this place. I felt safe, bright, and wide awake. I felt that I was breathing off tension, filter-feeding on the air, expelling toxic waste.

"Got a spring tide tonight," remarked Dwight. "There's a ramp over here—" The ramp led down to a floating dock against which the Belgian's boat was actually tied.

"Go," I said to Jellyroll, who was taking in the sights with his nose. Delighted and surprised, he hopped aboard the boat. His toenails skittered on the wooden deck.

I couldn't see many details, but in places the varnish sparkled as if it had its own independent light source. Dwight led us back along the deck to the cockpit. In the dark I kicked a protrusion of some sort—there are many protrusions on boats—and I tried hard not to moan with the pain.

The tongue-and-groove carpentry in and around the circular cockpit was dizzyingly complex. We went below, Dwight turning on the lights, into a mahogany sitting room with a buttoned banquette around a table decorated with a compass rose that was made of different-colored wood inlays.

"This is some boat," I remarked.

"Yep, nothing wrong with this boat a chain saw wouldn't fix." He led us down another set of varnished steps to a bedroom with wood walls and round portholes. The smells were heady and complex.

"You don't like this kind of boat, Captain?"

I think his nose wrinkled, but it was hard to tell with a face that rugged. "Sure I like it. Who wouldn't like it? The only guy who wouldn't's the guy taking care of it. The marine environment eats stuff like this, not so bad as in the tropics, but it still eats wood boats. If you listen close as you go to sleep, you'll hear the molecules chomping on the hull." He laid a set of towels and bed sheets out on the built-in chest of drawers. "There won't be any provisions in the boathouse. I could pick up a few things on my way in to get you tomorrow. Eggs, milk, like that. I'm sure the Selfs'll fix you up with enough food for everybody you ever met."

I passed Captain Dwight two hundred dollars cash.
"What's this? Clayton's already sent me a check."
"Yeah, but this is for me."
"I'll bet we can work something out, Mr. Deemer."
"Artie."
"I'll be back first thing in the morning, Artie."

7

*T*he Belgian's boat had rocked us gently, creaking every now and then, wavelets lapping our bilge. We slept in peace and awoke new men. I could dig this whole littoral, nautical ethos with no strain at all. It was only six when we awoke. 0600. I never awoke at 0600. We bounded up the ladder into the cockpit. Well, technically, Jellyroll didn't bound. He tried, but dogs are not equipped to bound up varnished ladders, so I gave him a boost from behind. Once up, we stood in the cockpit, our heads pivoting, absorbing our new environment, I with my eyes, he with his nose.

Thanks, Clayton.

The harbor was postcard material, yet there were no condo time-shares, no ye olde frozen yogurt and macramé shoppes, nothing whatsoever of popular culture. Except Jellyroll and me. There were some incongruous folks up the hill on the other side of the pier, but I didn't pay them much notice.

I sat down in the back of the boat behind the steering wheel and breathed deeply. So did Jellyroll. I took the wheel in hand, stood behind it, fantasizing, like a little boy, that I was driving the big boat in heavy weather, sailing hard, water coming over the bow. . . . I leaned out over the stern to see what her name was. Her name was *Names.* Hmm. Evocative, in a moody sort of European existential way. Everywhere I looked, buttery light sparkled on varnish and water.

We were tucked into a deep, round harbor, rocky and wooded with an equally round granite island lying just beyond the mouth as if it had been cookie-cuttered out of the mainland to make the harbor, then placed seaward a diameter to protect it. Shorebirds went about their business. Fractious herring gulls, beaks wide, screamed in each other's faces. Cormorants dried their wings on various vertical perches. Waders I couldn't identify, plovers or sanderlings, ruddy turnstones maybe, flitted in and out with the little wavelets on the gravel shore. I wondered if I could buy a bird book around here.

The shoreline seemed to consist of truncated and cracked rock shelves that slipped away beneath the surface at a shallow angle. Pink and black and white veins flowed through the granite. Why had this sublime little harbor not been nullified by hucksters, theme park moguls, image meisters, marketeers, and mass media shitheads? Maybe it was too far north to be vulnerable.

None of the stocky, seamanly fellows in high rubber boots unloading boats around us, throwing boxes of ice up onto the dock, seemed even to recognize Jellyroll. A forklift driver glanced our way but didn't show a glimmer of recognition, even as he nodded at us. I wondered if that was because of Jellyroll's disguise or because they'd never seen him before.

The smells were rich, almost psychoactive. Jellyroll's nostrils were going a mile a minute. Fish, salt water, wood, creosote, low tide. Jellyroll with all that canine olfactory gear must have feasted on the newness of it. He looked up at me with a big smile on his face.

A man with powerful round shoulders and a weathered-granite face pushed a loaded wheelbarrow past the *Names.* It contained coils of greasy cable and massive metal fittings of some sort. "Mornin', Cap'n," he said cheerfully, passing.

"Morning," I said.

That was a friendly little exchange. The "cap'n" irony didn't escape me, but what the hell, smartass irony is much better than psychotic malice and senseless hostility. Delicate morning light, sweet salt breeze from the ocean, professional fisherfolk who'd never seen a R-r-ruff Dog commercial, this would do fine for a decade or two. The man wheeled the cable to the little ship at the end of the dock. From aboard, crewmen swung out a wooden boom to block-and-tackle the coils over the rail. I breathed deeply and wished Crystal were here. I always like to hear her responses to things.

Micmac consisted of four wooden stores, one with a new red paint job, standing side by side along the road that ran perpendicular to the dock. Micmac huddled around the harbor, and the dock was the focus of the harbor. The stores all had back entrances onto a wooden walkway connected to the dock. The half-dozen houses I could see all faced the water. In the old days, I imagined, life came from the sea. The continental forest to the west meant darkness and death. No wonder people imagined witches and hassled Hester Prynne.

The people up on the hill on the far side of the harbor were not moving. At first, I took them for members of a bus tour: Perillo's Picturesque Harbors and Ports. But they weren't just passing through after grabbing a few snapshots; they were acting like this was their destination. Besides, they weren't looking at the harbor.

On their side of the dock, the circular shoreline continued its jagged bend, but the land rose abruptly from the water to form a stubby bluff with a craggy top and grassy slopes. There was a small, level, meadowy plateau on the slope. Something was happening on that meadow, something out of step with life down here.

They were clearly not locals—they were from farther away than me. They were all looking up at the same thing, like tourists at a rocket launching. All I saw was backs and craned necks. Whatever they were looking at was located up among the rocks and small crags on the top of the bluff. Some of the lookers had climbed beyond the plateau to the place where the grade grew too steep to walk upright. They shielded their eyes from the new sun with their hands or their hats. People pointed. A handful looked through binoculars.

Was it a jumper?

Nobody down here on the dock was paying the crowd any attention at all. Anyway, the bluff was too short for suicide. This would be the place to jump if you meant to tear some ligaments in your knee. The scene jangled me. There was something weird about it. I didn't need to come this far for the weird. I could get weird any time I wanted it just by walking up to

Broadway. . . . Maybe they were bird-watchers here to spot some obscure species resting en route to spawning grounds in the High Arctic. . . .

Others were arriving singly and in family units. Some carried aluminum folding chairs and Igloo coolers. What were they all looking at? They had turned their backs on the harbor, which must have been picturesque from above, to peer up at naked rocks. Geologists?

There were children, too. Some children watched as intently as the adults, but a few rolled in the grass. A couple of dogs wrestled. Here and there, people poured liquid from thermos bottles or ate pieces of fruit as if picnicking, yet nobody was relaxed. They were tense, expectant. They pointed up there for the newcomers. And again for each other.

"The Jesus people," said the wheelbarrow man heading back empty.

"The Jesus people?"

He stopped, set down his barrow, wiped his forehead on his sleeve, stood for a while watching the people on the hill, his back toward me. From the cockpit I looked down on his bald spot. "Yeah, that's what folks have taken to calling them. The Jesus people. But then I guess they got the right."

"What right?"

"At least until they create an unsanitary condition."

"What are they doing up there?" I asked.

"Waiting."

"For what?"

"Salvation." He picked up his wheelbarrow, but I didn't want to leave it at that.

"Why here?"

"They got a sign. They got a sign in the fungus."

"Fungus?"

"Lichens. That's all a lichen is, fungus."

"What was the sign?"

"The face of Jesus. Up on them rocks. Sort of in pro-file. There's goin' to be an unsanitary condition de-pendin' how long it takes to get saved."

"How did they know that there was a face in the lichens? I mean, in the first place."

"Goin' to be a parking problem pretty soon." He walked away.

I watched the Jesus people assemble. I hoped at least a few of them would be saved. I took Jellyroll for a pee.

I didn't get any coffee because the tiny restaurant was jammed with customers. I peeked in. It had a planked wooden floor and lovely glass and mahogany counters, little round tables with ice-cream parlor chairs, all occupied by people who would probably recognize Jellyroll.

He peed in the grassy strip beside the road. Traffic was beginning to congeal on this the only road into Micmac. I saw license plates from ten different states. Had they all come to be saved? A few people in the crawling traffic showed glimmers of recognition, so I hustled Jellyroll back toward the dock, toward the peo-ple who'd never heard of him. He didn't care, it was all new and exciting to him. But I'd have to forget the coffee, and that made me a little edgy. I wasn't certain I could be responsible for my attitude without coffee.

There was a marine supply store at the head of the dock. We went in. There were no displays inside or any other attempt at marketing. Heavy-duty chain was displayed by size in piles on the undulating wood floor. The old salts who shopped here knew what they wanted, and they didn't want a load of advertising bullshit. Some very esoteric stuff was stacked here and there, suspended from wall hooks and left in packing boxes. I couldn't even guess at the purpose of most of the objects hung on pegboards or stacked on olive-drab metal shelves. Oars, boathooks, fishing rods, antennae, and other long things lay across the rafters.

"Mornin', Cap'n," said the wheelbarrow man with the big shoulders from behind a dusty counter.

"Good morning," I said. I liked that. Captain Deemer. "I'd like to buy a navigation chart of the local area."

He spun on his stool to a wooden chest with thin drawers, whipped one open, and in a single motion swept a big paper chart back up onto the counter. The air settled from beneath it. It was beautiful. The land was tan and the water blue. He rolled it up, banded and handed it to me.

"Could I see those?" I pointed to a serious pair of binoculars in the case below the cash register. I supposed there were discount emporiums where the prudent seaman shopped. I'd pay top dollar here, but then people with wealthy dogs can engage in whimsy, while others must budget wisely, and still others live in pain and degradation. The world is not fair in that respect. I bought a top-o'-the-line nautical/military pair with a stout rubber covering, no metal exposed to the elements, but they were very big and heavy. These were the kind of binoculars you see around the necks of corvette captains on Discovery Channel documentaries about convoy escort duty on the Murmansk Run, not dudes with dogs from the Upper West Side, but I didn't care.

"A pleasure doing business with you, Cap'n."

"The pleasure's all mine. Let me ask you something. Have you seen the face in the lichens?"

"Me? No." He seemed surprised at the question.

"Do you know anybody who has?"

"Well, let me think now. No, can't say I do."

"It might not even exist?"

"Might. Might not. I don't see it makes much difference."

After we left the store, I showed my new binoculars to Jellyroll. He sniffed them skeptically.

Lobster boats with wire traps stacked in the stern were tied side by side three deep along the opposite side of the dock from the Belgian's boat. Salty-looking lobstermen stood in a clot smoking, talking in accents so thick it sounded like they were speaking Norwegian. They giggled now and then at a joke. They nodded at us in a hospitable manner but didn't say anything as we strolled by. Jellyroll sniffed their gear on the dock, nets and things, and one of the captains called him Bowser. Hell, maybe his disguise was working.

We walked out to the end of the dock where the little ship was moored. It was called *Slocum*. It had a low center deck with the wheelhouse in the back and a high upswung bow in front—but it was tiny. Aboard the low center deck, sailors were lowering a refrigerator by rope from the stout wooden boom overhead. Jelly-roll and I stopped to watch. Two burly guys waited with their arms up to receive it, while a third stood somewhat aside, at the base of the boom, and lowered away.

The third deckhand, the one lowering away, was a woman. She wore shorts with wool socks and heavy

hiking boots. Her muscular legs were bent, her body
centered. Her thighs twitched as she paid out the rope.
It creaked around the cleat under the load. She wore
nothing under her olive halter, and her arms squeezed
her breasts together into a deep valley. I would love to
see Crystal lower something heavy. Perhaps at the right
moment, after a nice dinner, I could ask her to lower
a major appliance.

But the fact is, just then, I was overcome with lust.
I stood there staring at the deckhand's straining body
like a testosterone-crazed juvenile peeking through a
knothole in the women's shower room. Beads of sweat
ran down her flanks as she lowered, and the curve
formed by her neck and chin as she looked up, eyes
fixed on the refrigerator, turned my knees to rubber. I
couldn't tear myself away from the sweaty physicality
of her lowering. This was raw, inarticulate, pounding,
boyhood lust. I forced myself to waddle off, disoriented, back toward the Belgian's boat, where I meant to
go below and consider the matter, but I didn't get far—

A scream of raw female terror froze us all in our
spots. Sometimes I hear screams like that in my neighborhood in the middle of the night. But here where
human relations seemed simple and stable, the sound
of terror in full voice chilled my blood. Jellyroll's, too.
The salts and I hunched our shoulders as if something
were about to explode in our midst. When it didn't,
we uncoiled, only to be blown back by another peal.
Everybody looked for the source.

The coffee shop had a back porch, with picnic tables,
built out over the harbor. It must have been a nice spot
for breakfast under normal conditions. Even now all
the picnic tables were crowded with diners. That's

where the screams had come from. The commotion grew.

The woman began to scream again, now in short staccato blasts. She wasn't very far away, a half block maybe, but I looked at her through my binoculars: She had bobbed black hair. She wore jeans and a Hard Rock Cafe sweatshirt. She was obviously from away. She covered her face with her hand as she continued to scream. She had bangs that she kept flipping away from her eyes. Her eyes were wide and round and darting.

She pointed at a wooden shed built into the corner of the porch. It seemed to have a door, but the door was closed. She was pointing at the door as she screamed, all the time backing away in mincing steps until she came up against the railing. There she began to sob breathlessly—

"Looks like they got some trouble up at the Cod End," one old salt commented.

"Ayah," another agreed.

"From away," another said.

Some diners on the porch went to assist the screaming woman, while others started hesitantly toward that door and its terrible secret. Other diners remained frozen at their picnic tables, forkfuls of food halfway to their mouths. It's troubling how human tragedy can often look so comic to the observer—

"Brains!" the young woman began to scream. I didn't understand at first, but she said it again and again. "Brains!"

"What's she say?" asked a salt.

"Didn't get it," said another.

"Brains," I said.

"Brains?"

A man in a matching shorts and shirt ensemble boldly grabbed the door to the shed and flung it open—outward toward the dock, so I couldn't see inside. The sign on the door said GULLS. The guy in the lime-green shorts recoiled from the sight inside. Somebody else looked in, then still somebody else. They recoiled. Everybody who looked in recoiled. They knocked cups and plates and maple syrup off the picnic tables as they recoiled.

A uniformed cop with a pear-shaped torso showed up on the porch from inside the restaurant. He held his holster down as he ran around the corner. Everybody pointed at the shed, and the cop looked in. I could only see his shoes from under the door, but he didn't recoil. After a while, he closed the door, pointed to an ununiformed, lanky guy in the doorway, and motioned for him to stand in front of the door. The uniformed cop herded everybody off the porch. Most of the Jesus people had turned from the face in the lichens to look down at the porch.

"You know who he reminds me of?" queried a salt.

"Sheriff Kelso?"

"Ayah. He reminds me of that TV cop, the confused one with the wrinkled raincoat."

"Colombo."

"Colombo, right. What's his real name?"

"Walter Matthau."

"Ayah."

I told Jellyroll to heel. We hurried back to the Belgian's boat. We went below and just sat stiffly.

An hour later, Dwight showed up in his boat. It was that distinctive type of lobster boat almost identical to the salts' boats across the dock. Dwight passed me a line, but I didn't immediately see anything to tie it to, so I held onto it until he came aboard and took it from me.

"Do you know what happened at the Cod End?" he said. "One of the Jesus people just got murdered. Somebody chopped her skull in half, for Chrissake! She was taking a piss on the porch right over there at the Cod End, somebody split her skull in half. Literally in *half*. Whack." He made a deadly chopping motion with his open hand. "Jesus. Somebody must have been in there waiting, but how the hell can that be? It's a one-holer." He kept shaking his head as I passed our gear to him over the rail. He had bags of food from the Selfs in his boat, and he had an old-fashioned plaid-painted thermos. "Want some coffee?"

"Deeply."

Dwight's boat smelled like a living thing of the sea, like a starfish in a tide pool. I inhaled as if air were a drug concocted to drive out cruelty, despair, murder, all the generally savage shit people do to one another. I hung my new binoculars around my neck and unrolled my chart on the engine box. I weighted its curling corners with bags of dogfood. The chart was full of information and symbols I couldn't exactly interpret, but I could immediately find Micmac Harbor because it was incongruously round. The island just outside was called Round Island.

A pair of ospreys stood side by side on their nest atop a dead cedar tree, necks pivoting as we passed below. I took a close look at one of them through my new binoculars. His black pupil was ringed with bright yellow, peering back at me across that great gulf between species.

I wondered what Dwight thought of my binoculars. Dudeish probably. You really have to be Supreme Allied Commander of the European Theater of Operations to pull off binoculars this big. All Dwight's stuff was worn and slightly shabby. It had that look only time and use can give a utilitarian thing. Dwight himself was like that.

I scanned the horizon. It was empty. We headed out into the emptiness, our wake straight and confident. I wanted to maintain my sense of adventure, but Dwight was tense. He manipulated his boat in a relaxed, casual way, but he kept clenching his jaw and pursing his lips. Occasionally he shook his head. He was talking at times, but not loud enough to be heard over the engine noise. I asked what once, but he didn't increase the volume, so I decided he was talking to himself. This woman had gotten her brains chopped out in his hometown, not my own.

In fact, Micmac wasn't even my destination, merely the departure point for the last leg of my trip. I was just passing through. One can't take on all atrocities as one's own, especially when passing through. I hadn't even bought a cup of coffee in Dwight's hometown. Wrongful death and senseless injury come wholesale in mine. But in Micmac, they still asked, *why?*

The air was cool and crystalline, free of known carcinogens. Beautiful. The edges of objects—buoys, rocks, birds, waves, the bow of Dwight's boat—seemed to my eyes unnaturally sharp.

"Even Teddy Kelso was shook," said Dwight audibly. "Teddy's seen some horror. He's the local law, but before he come up here, he was twenty years a homicide cop in New York City. Comes in the fish co-op sometimes, tell us stories'd curl your hair. But he didn't have no color in his face when he told me what he saw at the Cod End." He decreased our speed as the ride got lumpy. "Teddy married a Self just like me. We have that in common."

Out in open water, the shape of the waves changed from ripples to shallow rolling hills, I suppose because the water got deeper. Dwight didn't slow down, and the boat began to move more excitedly. A rolling motion joined the lengthwise rocking. Jellyroll's nails skittered for traction on the painted plank deck when a big one ran beneath us. I began to worry about his stomach. Jellyroll has a weak stomach.

"Did she have friends or family?"

"No, she was from away."

"I mean among the Jesus people."

"No, but Teddy said she had ID on her. She was from Hartford, Connecticut. There was pictures of two little daughters in her wallet."

We went on in silence for a while. I scanned the horizon all around. It was bereft.

"Christ, looks like somebody killed her for the hell of it. I mean, she weren't robbed. There was money in her wallet, Teddy said, a watch on her arm. You'd almost feel better if there was a crazy husband, or she was killed by the mafia 'cause she was a stool pigeon, or . . . some foreign death squad killed her 'cause she pissed off a mucky-muck in Peru. Something sensible."

"Have you seen the face in the lichens?" I asked.

"The Virgin?"

"The Virgin? I heard it was Jesus."

"Oh. I heard it was one of the Virgins. Who'd you hear it was Jesus from?"

"The guy who owns the marine supply store."

"People around here tend to let others do pretty

much what they want, 'specially when it comes to religion, unless of course they go to sacrificing house pets or declaring themselves the Deity. But now, with this killing, I don't know what's gonna happen. Whoever did it could still be up on that hill. Could do it again. To anybody. That changes things. It ain't from away no more. It's here."

A flock of herring gulls followed above our wake screaming invective at each other. I scanned the water again with my binoculars. That kind of magnification took some getting used to on a moving platform. It made me a little bilious.

Dwight said something I couldn't hear.

"What?"

He pointed straight ahead with his thick, scarred hand—"Kempshall Island."

What? It was fully formed, close enough to identify individual features. I looked at Dwight. Had he played some kind of tenderfoot joke on me? But how could he have? You can't make an island appear when a moment ago there was no island in sight, not even the hazy hint of one. That's what happened, however. I had *looked.* . . . Maybe it was some kind of atmospheric anomaly caused by refraction or something, like those fiery sunsets over New Jersey, caused, you soon learn from the cynics, by particles in the polluted air reflecting the sun. Maybe one grows so used to seeing the world through tailpipe smoke that its sudden absence dazzles the eye and brain. Maybe it was my new binoculars, maybe I needed some practice, or maybe they were defective in this rare, weird way that causes island myopia. I wished Crystal were here to tell me what she saw. I looked over at Dwight. He didn't bat an eye.

Dwight was saying something about the island. He pointed over the bow, then left the wheel to show me on my chart, but at that very moment, Jellyroll drew himself inboard and began to retch. His whole body convulsed and jerked. It's a disgusting thing to watch, and it seems to go on forever, as if his gut were thirty feet long. Dwight watched openmouthed, never making it to the chart. Finally Jellyroll curled back his lip and expelled the usual yellow bile. I wordlessly swiped it up with a paper towel I'd brought for the purpose and tossed it over the side. Jellyroll watched me do that, licking his lips.

9

We turned sharply around a rocky point and I saw the boathouse for the first time. Until my eye caught the straight-line roof, I didn't realize it was a man-made thing because it nestled so gently into the forested hillside at the top of the cove. It was roofed and sided with spruce shingles painted forest green, and the foundation was made of shoreline stones cemented together. The window and door frames and the railings of the porch were painted the russet of autumn leaves. A wooden porch cantilevered out over the water.

Dwight slowed the boat, once inside the cove. He said something, but I didn't catch it.

"What?"

"Sunkers."

"Sunkers?"

"See, over there." He pointed just off to the left where dromedary humps of black rock roiled the surface. Leathery kelp and black weed sloshed back and forth. A sunker.

" 'Nother off there to starboard."

This sunker didn't even break the surface, but I could see its menacing presence. I had stopped looking at my chart to take in direct reality.

"This is Dog Cove," commented Dwight.

"It is?"

"Yeah. See the two islands out there?" He pointed astern.

Both were just beyond the mouth of the cove. About the size of toppled-over Upper West Side brownstones, they guarded the cove from the sea, calming the water inside.

"Near one's called Dog Island, other one's called Outer Dog Island."

Jellyroll knows that word, of course. He clapped his jaws shut and looked around for one of his fellow men. "Why so many dogs?" I asked Dwight.

"You ever heard of John Cabot?"

"The explorer?"

"Yeah, him."

About 1497, Cabot, a Venetian exploring for English merchants, made a successful voyage to Newfoundland. Some people think he came down this far.

"Cabot's supposed to've heard barkin' when he passed by here in a fog. Must've been terrifyin' approachin' this coast in them ships." Dwight paused, probably to consider with a seaman's knowledge the terror of doing that back then, then said, "Modern people killed off all the seals, so you don't hear no barkin' these days, but seals is probably what he heard." Then Dwight seemed to muse on millions of murdered seals.

We slid past a big orange float, and I asked what it marked.

"That's a moorin'. Belongs to Hawley Self. He's an urchin man. He mostly lives aboard his boat on that moorin'."

"Urchins?"

"Yeah, this Japanese guy in Micmac buys all he can get. They love their sea urchins, Japs. Urchin divers make decent money. If they live. Lot of 'em don't. Drowned bodies never come up in these waters."

"Why?"

"Because of the gasses."

"What gasses?"

"The gasses in your gut. By-product of bacteria and so forth. That's what causes a dead body to float up after a couple days. Water's too cold for the bacteria to grow. Cold like that day after day makes addled old men outta thirty-year-old urchin divers."

There was another mooring float nearby. He said it belonged to Clayton. Dwight passed the mooring and headed for shore. He stopped his boat beneath the boathouse porch against a flat rock six inches out of water, put there by nature as if for a dock. Dwight stepped ashore and attached lines to rings imbedded in the boathouse foundation.

"Is this natural?" I asked.

"Nope. We cut it out." Dwight started to unload. I passed things over the side to him. I was delighted with our new environment. So was Jellyroll, who leapt ashore and ran into the bushes. In two loads, we had our gear stacked at the foot of the steps beside the house leading up to the porch. This was the front entrance. There was another door at ground level in the back, but it opened onto the side of a steep hill.

Jellyroll struck up a relationship with a chipmunk

inhabiting the woodpile near the back door. Shucking and jiving in and out, the chipmunk ran Jellyroll ragged.

Dwight and I picked up shopping bags full of food from the Selfs, and I followed him up onto the porch. This porch is where we'd spend our time, Crystal and I, sitting at the weathered picnic table peering peacefully out across the cove toward the Dogs and the empty ocean beyond. Sights and smells this sweet and gentle could change a melancholic back into a romantic. Upper Broadway raises calluses on the old worldview. I'd lose them here, but I supposed I'd raise others. I couldn't imagine just then what kind they'd be. Jellyroll sniffed a circuit of the porch, glanced at the view, and decided he'd rather crash around with the chipmunk.

Dwight opened the little French doors. The interior space was proportioned like a large house trailer, because only a long and thin building could have fit on this site. The walls were unpaneled, joists visible, and like the floors and ceiling, they were painted gloss white, giving the place an open, bright air, like a house in the Bahamas.

"Still a little musty," said Dwight. "I opened it up yesterday."

I didn't smell any must. It smelled like a seaside pine forest. I caught myself grinning with delight.

The bedroom was off the living room to the left, kitchen to the right. The kitchen was not separated from the living room except by throw rugs. I lugged over the foodstuffs. There was a genuine cast-iron stove with lion's-paw legs. It had burned wood before somebody, maybe Dwight himself, had converted it to gas.

There was an old-fashioned refrigerator, the kind with the rounded tombstone top and deco flourish of chrome. Windows looked out on Dog Cove and the wooded hills beside the house.

The Selfs had made me a lasagna, a meatloaf, a stuffed chicken, twelve fish cakes, a lobster casserole, a corn chowder, and a deep-dish apple cobbler. I sort of wanted to go to the Self reunion. We would see each other as exotic, maybe share with each other the best of our foreign worlds.

"Now you got no electricity out here on the island," Dwight was saying, emerging from the bedroom, opening windows, finally inspecting underneath the refrigerator. "But the propane tanks is all full, and everything works. I checked myself yesterday."

"Please thank your wife and the rest of the Selfs. Anytime she wants to meet Jellyroll, please tell her she's welcome—"

"I will."

The furnishings were summer-house simple. A wicker couch stood in the center of the living room on an ancient, threadbare Chinese carpet. There was an embracing, high-backed armchair, and an oak table with four distinctly mismatching chairs.

"Dwight, is there a boat I could rent?"

"Like for transportation? Or are you a high-speed recreationist?"

"No, transportation. I want to pick my girlfriend up in Micmac. She'll be coming in a day or two."

"You know how to operate a boat?"

"Absolutely."

"Well, don't worry, you already got the binoculars for it." His face didn't move, but his eyes twinkled in a boyish way. "Just don't take nothing for granted. That's when people get in trouble around here, when they take things for granted." And Dwight went off to see what he could do about my boat.

I watched him go. I listened to the water sluice over the round, cue-ball-sized rocks beneath the porch. What did he mean? Take what for granted? Birds flitted in the trees and floated on the water. I spotted a great blue heron slow-marching in the shallows and put the glasses on him—

I have a fantasy. There is this family of which I'm a member; it is big and close, tolerant, even nurturing of its members' eccentricities, interests, phases. You can be yourself in this family without fear of losing its support. Its extended members gather annually for summer holidays when the evenings are endless, bathed in limpid light, fireflies blinking at dusk, a place just like this, bigger maybe to support the various branches that come from far and wide with smiles on their faces. I've never known such a place, such a family. Jellyroll and I could have bought a summerhouse that matched the fantasy as nearly as anything concrete could, but it wouldn't be the same. After all, the fantasy is about the family that inhabits the place, and Jellyroll couldn't buy that. I sat at the picnic table and grew pensive. The island promoted pensiveness. I stared out across Dog Cove, where life probably hadn't changed since the Pleistocene. . . .

And then I began to feel that flood of eroticism again. I could almost *hear* the hormones roar, as if I were paddling toward a waterfall in the wilderness. My feet itched, my torso tingled. Just like back at the dock when the muscular woman lowered the refrigerator, the same mindless adolescent eroticism, and just like then, it was interrupted, not by someone screaming bloody murder but by strange howling.

Jellyroll heard it first. His ears pricked. He snapped to his feet, cocked his head. Then I heard it, too, or I thought I did. Was it a howling? It was more like keening. We were both unacclimated to the absence of sirens, horns, alarms, explosions, salsa. Maybe in the silence, like in one of those sensory-deprivation tanks, we were hallucinating. My dog and I are very close, but not so close we share hallucinations. No, the sound was real, it existed. The hairs on the back of Jellyroll's neck stood stiffly erect. The sound was moving fast, changing in pitch and quality. . . .

Dogs! Christ, that's all—dogs. A pack of barking dogs, in Dog Cove, which was sheltered by the Dog Islands. Jellyroll began to bark his high-pitched, excited yap-yap bark.

I saw the underbrush rustle and then, here and there, a flash of dog flesh. Ten dogs seemed to materialize from the undergrowth and gather in the clearing at the foot of the steps, where they swirled in excited circles. Jellyroll hesitated, watching the signals, then bolted down the steps to meet them.

Dogs are not mere will-less servers of a master. Dogs are egotists. Everything they do around people and their fellows is rich with self-awareness and expression. The pack, a mix of mutts and purebreds, froze as Jellyroll neared the ground. He stopped on the bottom step. Tails down, they all waited for the ritual to resolve itself. A well-bred chocolate Lab, the biggest dog in the pack, dropped into the play posture, forelegs on the ground, rump in the air, and barked once, the cue for everybody to chill, we're here for fun, aren't we? Then they all moved at once.

A springy Jack Russell bounced up on the steps to welcome Jellyroll, and he bounded into the play posture to accept. They swirled and sniffed and panted and leapt over each other's backs. They had the look of a pack of hooligans feeding off each other's energy. The Lab kissed Jellyroll, so did one of the two coyote types, then they all started running headlong back into the underbrush and up the hill the way they came. Jellyroll started with them—

I gave that some quick consideration—a city dog running with the local pack—and I whistled for him to stop. He did. He always does, but this time he didn't turn around to look at me. A couple members of the pack stopped, looked over their shoulder at him. Then they ran off and left him standing there. Their wild barks faded to that keening sound, then to silence.

I felt like a cruel bastard. Jellyroll still wouldn't look at me. He didn't return to the porch. He flopped on his side. No relationship can run smooth all the time. Even in a fantasy family.

Then from along the shore in the opposite direction, we heard something else. Of course, Jellyroll heard it first. Someone coming on foot, walking along a shoreside path I hadn't noticed yet. Jellyroll forgot his despair. He began to bark. This particular bark sounds like a dangerous dog's bark, and sometimes I like that.

Hands in his pockets, a gangly guy in his forties shuffled out of the woods into an open area at the side of the house, the only spare flat ground. He wore blue jean cutoffs, hiking boots, and heavy woolen socks. He had pale bird legs. His head bobbed forward and back with each step, like a great blue heron's.

"Christ," he exclaimed, "I thought you were Clayton Kempshall for a minute there. I thought I'd seen a ghost."

"A ghost? Clayton's not dead."

"He's not?"

"No."

". . . Are you sure?"

"I just saw him a week ago. He didn't die since then, did he?"

"Oh no, years ago."

"You must be thinking of someone else."

"Clayton Kempshall?"

"Yes."

"Not dead?"

"No."

"Oh, man, I feel relieved. . . . Look, I'm Dickie."

"Artie," I said.

Jellyroll watched him suspiciously.

"Wow, that's really great about Clayton."

"Uh-huh."

"There hasn't been anyone in the boathouse for years, of course."

"Why?"

"Well, because of Clayton's ghost, but now, of course, we know that's bullshit, what with Clayton being alive. Yeah. I wonder whose ghost it was. You haven't seen any . . . paranormal shit go down hereabout?"

"No, but I haven't been here long."

"Yeah. . . . Maybe it was *Compton* Kempshall's ghost."

"People have seen a ghost around here?" People other than him?

"Locals, mostly. Don't trust a local. Fuckers will hurt you. Have you seen a dog come by here?"

"A pack of them went up the hill a little while ago."

"A pack? Christ! Fucking locals see some dogs playing in a group, and it gets them nuts. They get into some kind of crazed caveman head, competing predators, or some bullshit. They'll shoot the dogs."

"They will?"

"Fuck yes, they think the dogs are running deer. I say, 'You inbred lout, there *are* no deer on Kempshall Island.' And you know what they say to that? They say, 'See, that proves it.' Island wit. Have you met the cop?"

"No."

"Nazi." This guy was ardent, waving his hands before his face as if troubled by swarming insects. "That cop subscribes to *Skinhead Nation*. I've seen it folded in his back pocket. Kind of fucker who'll beat you senseless, then ask for ID. I've seen it happen, but only to people from away. He'll never beat a local. You know why? Because he married a Self. The Selfs are dangerous people, I'm telling you."

"Where are you from?"

"Central Islip, Long Island. Not that that's any paradise. You?"

"New York City."

"Yeah. I like New York, weird kind of postapocalypse head to New York I dig."

"What do you do here?"

"Here? I'm on the run. I'm underground. I'm hiding out from the FBI. They want me for sedition. Back in seventy. I'm Dickie the Red. Maybe you heard of me? No? Well, I got to get my dog before some inbred Natty Bumppo smokes her. Speaking of dogs, that one looks a lot like the R-r-ruff Dog. Maybe I'll see you at the launching. Are you going to the launching?"

"What launching?"

"This guy built a submarine. I mean, a *real* submarine. Up scope, like that."

"When is the launching?"

"I don't know. You'll hear. There ain't all that many conflicting activities out here. When did you come?"

"Just now."

"Then you were in town when it happened? The murders."

"Murders?"

"Weren't you there? A whole family got hacked to bits. These Christians are a dangerous element. They'll hurt you."

Dwight rounded the point going fast with a big white wave at his bow.

"Dwight Reed. Don't trust him. He ain't a Self, but he's pussywhipped by one. One of the *head* Selfs. The tribal leaders are always women, savage Brunhilda twats."

Dwight docked against the flat rock.

"Hey, Dwight," called Dickie, big smile. "What say? Long time."

Dwight completely ignored Dickie. "I think I found

you a pretty good boat. I used to own it when I first got married. It's over in the Crack right now."

Jellyroll and I climbed aboard. So did Dickie. Dwight asked him where he was going.

"Over the Crack."

"What about your dog?" I asked, but Dickie didn't answer.

10

"Everybody around here calls it the Crack for obvious reasons," said Dwight at the helm as we neared the entrance. "Nobody ever calls it Kempshall Harbor." He wrinkled his lip as if the words tasted metallic in his mouth.

The Crack. I'd already seen it from the air, but airplane dimensions had softened its effect at water level. Sheer pink-granite faces rose three stories straight up out of the water. The walls rose so steeply and the rock was so smooth that a swimmer could not have climbed out and would have drowned like a turtle pawing against the glass in a flooded terrarium. At the mouth, the walls spanned fifty feet of water, but inside they narrowed steadily to an acute angle, then to nothing. Brown, leathery kelp clung to the rock and undulated in the swell as if beckoning us to watery death. This was a primal place.

Some unimaginable force had cracked this island nearly in two. Did it crack gradually, eon by eon, or did it explode apart volcanically? Even Dickie shut up as we entered. The place seemed to demand solemnity from the people who entered, even those who did so often. I stepped from under the wheelhouse in order to look up. The cliffs loomed. Only lichens could live on them.

The Crack could be explained, it had a knowable geologic origin. Uplift, volcanism, crustal plate tectonics, glaciation, one of those world shakers, but the feeling of the place didn't encourage that kind of curiosity. Entering the Crack called up primitive anxieties, the kind that probably brought shivers up the spines of our ancient progenitors huddled around the paltry light of a campfire in an utterly dark world. I imagined otherwise extinct predators, saber-toothed tigers, dire wolves, giant marsupials peering down at us from the rim, licking their lips. Fresh meat. It felt like we were entering the blunt mandibles of a monster sprawled on its side. Inside, daylight dimmed. The cliff walls fell away to a shallower angle, still too steep to climb up, but shallow enough to build stairs down to the water—

The apex of the Crack, the hinge of the creature's jaw, formed a natural amphitheater, and there the submarine perched on a stand of interlocking railroad ties, a log cabin without a roof, twenty feet up on a ledge. The submarine was painted industrial orange, like the primer coat on highway bridges. The thing was as long as a pickup truck, but cylindrical, like a thick conduit. It was festooned with tanks, pipes, valves, hoses, connectors, adapters, nuts and bolts. It couldn't be real. I looked through my new binoculars. It sure looked real. In front was a big Plexiglas bubble, like on those

M*A*S*H helicopters. The captain would squat in there to con his ship. Its bulbous eye glinted in the sun.

Dwight had slowed his boat to a crawl. The span narrowed. Several motorboats were tied nose and tail in a line down the middle, making the quarters very close near the apex, in the shadow of the sub.

"Why did he bring it all the way over here to launch?" I asked.

"This is where he built it," said Dwight.

"What? I thought there wasn't any electricity on the island."

"There ain't."

"He's a genius," said Dickie.

Dwight docked his boat against a narrow wooden float near the apex of the Crack. Strings of wooden stairs ran up the rock in switchback flights. Some stairs came only halfway down, as if the rest had dropped into the water. Some step units were old, the wood black and grainy, others were fresh, and the rest fell somewhere in between, all heading in the same direction like a visible demonstration of decay.

"There's your boat," said Dwight, tying his own to a corroded cleat on the float. "If you like it. I mean, you don't have to take it. Don't feel no pressure." It was tied to the adjacent float.

I stepped up onto the floating dock, which needed a little more flotation. Water leapt up through the cracks in the boards. I leaned against cool pink granite and looked at my new boat. It was open, wooden, about twenty-five feet long with a faded red hull and white insides. There was a steering wheel with spokes mounted on a short pedestal in the center of the boat on the left side. Her ribs were visible, thick and closely spaced. Here and there rust streaked her red paint. This was a salty boat. This boat had been used, it had been out there. Things were worn in the way old craftsmen's tools are worn, the way Dwight's gear was worn. I was glad. I didn't want a tourist boat painted metal-flake magenta like a motorcycle helmet. I didn't want a boat that had molded indentations to hold your rum swizzle. I wanted a salty craft, and this was it.

"It's a Hampton boat," said Dwight. "Well, I guess you'd have to say it's a modified Hampton boat. I pulled up her sheer a little 'cause I liked a jaunty look in those days, and raised the stern some just for balance."

"What? You mean you built this boat?"

"Yeah, but it was a long time ago. She's gettin' old now, on her way out, but she don't leak too bad yet."

Dickie said something about Hampton boats, but it was clear even to me he didn't know shit. Dwight ignored him.

"She's gettin' a little hogged, as you can see."

I couldn't. I didn't even know what hogged meant. She looked perfect to me. I wanted her. I had a feckless impulse to buy her right then and there, but I repressed it.

"Everything ends," said Dwight.

Even so, building a complex thing probably develops one's inner resources. Or did one have to have inner resources to begin building?

"Immediate problem," said Dwight dryly, "is gettin' to it." The modified Hampton boat was tied to a float identical to the one we stood on, long and narrow, but fifteen feet of water separated us from it. There wasn't enough room for Dwight to raft his boat outside the

Hampton boat because another boat, a decaying red clunker, was moored lengthwise near the apex of the Crack.

Two-by-six planks braced somehow into the cliff formed a catwalk that technically spanned the rock between here and there, but it looked suspicious. Dwight was testing it with his foot.

"Say, Alistair," he said to a guy on the red clunker.

I hadn't noticed Alistair, my attention occupied with my own new boat. Nor had I noticed the carelessly hand-painted sign tacked to the roof of his boat, RED LOBSTERS. There was a crazy cant to the roofline. Green weed grew like long hair along the waterline. "Say, Dwight?" said Alistair, an old man with a face as granitic as the Crack itself.

"Would you trust that catwalk, Alistair, you was me?"

Alistair wiped his enormous hands on a mechanic's cloth and scrutinized the catwalk in question. "Can't say, Dwight. However, the last cat on that walk ended up in the drink."

"What happened? Did the catwalk crack?"

"Weren't no fault of the catwalk. Fault of the cat."

"So did you rescue him?"

"Fuck no, Dwight. I'm busy sellin' lobsters. I can't be rescuin' every damn fool falls off the catwalk. What do you hear about the killin', Dwight?"

"Killing?" said Dickie, shifting his weight from one foot to the other, rocking the float. "You mean kill*ings.* Like a string of them. Like mass murder in Micmac."

They ignored him.

"We better go up and around," said Dwight.

So we did. For some reason stairs delight Jellyroll.

He bounds up them and looks back at me with a big smile on his face. But I didn't feel quite so confident of the stairs. They moved far too much. Dwight climbed casually, but I stayed a few steps behind so as not to strain the stairs.

The rock was not uniform here. At the mouth, it had looked uniformly brown, but back here veins of starkly different colors ran through it. Some were pure white and crystalline, others smooth and black, with complex branches reaching out horizontally, sometimes intertwining with veins of a different color, a petrified bloodstream.

As we went, Dwight said, "This all gets cleared out come November."

"All what?"

"All you see. Stairs, floats, boats, everything. The whole harbor. All the boats get out by autumn. We take everything apart and store it up in the woods over the winter." He paused on a crooked landing near the top and pointed toward the opening. "See, out there— that's dead northeast. In a nor'easter the Crack is hell on earth. Water comes through that opening like a fire hose. We'd get swept away standin' here in a *weak* nor'easter. In a strong one, waves'd be breakin' up there in the woods." Dwight's face was largely immobile, but just then a look of respect, even awe, flicked across his weathered features at the image of the sea in the narrow confines of the Crack; then he said, "Of course, you don't get nor'easters in the summer."

I lagged for a moment trying to picture the scene. That kind of power was hard for a landsman urbanite and his dog to imagine. I followed Dwight up out of the Crack onto flat land.

Dickie tagged along, walking stiff-legged as if his scrotum itched.

There were two small barns or sheds with no windows near the apex. They were built on foundations of stacked logs. I realized that they, too, must get moved back from the reach of the sea. Within a block-long radius of the Crack there were no trees. Dwight told me that flying seawater had killed them generations ago.

"When I was a kid, we'd dare each other to stand close in a nor'easter. Like the city kids I read about that ride on top of elevators."

"I've been goddamned near carried away when I was standing way over there," Dickie pointed. "I remember one year—"

"Aw, bullshit, Dickie, you ain't even been here in November."

"Well, I stayed that one bad year. I gotta run anyway. Gotta get my dog. Hey, thanks for the lift. Boy, that sure *looks* like the R-r-ruff Dog," he said, but made no move to leave.

Twenty yards away at the far end of the clearing, there was an abandoned red building that looked like a rural train station circa 1940. I looked at it through my binoculars. It *was* a train depot, in ruins now. Weeds and shrubs grew out of the windows and up through chinks in the walls. I could see the tracks in front.

"Kempshall built himself a railroad to take his guests and his gear over to the Castle. That's what he called his mansion."

We started down the adjacent set of stairs, even shakier than its neighbor. Jellyroll didn't care, bounding ahead, having a grand time. I could tell by the way the stairs bounced that Dickie was still with us.

Descending, Dwight told me that the Hampton boat now belonged to a man named Roy. Roy and Dwight had gone to school together, played on the same line of scrimmage. "Roy had his esophagus removed back about two years ago, talks through one of them electric vibration devices. As a result he don't like to talk to strangers. Thinks his voice sounds weird. Does." So Dwight had already made a deal for me, but I didn't have to take it, he assured me. Roy wanted eighty-five dollars a week. How they arrived at that, I had no idea, but it sounded great to me—

"Say, Alistair."

"Say, Dwight."

Dwight introduced me to Alistair across the water. He said he was proud to meet me. I said I was, too.

"Now would that be the R-r-ruff Dog?"

"Yes." I had removed the disguise, not that it ever worked.

"Goddamn. The R-r-ruff Dog. Dwight, did you ever imagine the R-r-ruff Dog'd make it to Teal Island? That's my favorite dog in all Hollywood."

"Of course that's the R-r-ruff Dog," said Dickie confidently.

Dwight went aboard my new boat. Jellyroll leapt aboard, and I followed.

Dwight started the tour at the bow. "She sits low, so she's gonna take water in any kind of chop. You can fold this canvas cover back a little ways to protect your valuables." He moved to the control console built of plywood and showed me neutral-forward-reverse on the transmission lever beside the steering wheel. The chrome-plated lever with its red plastic knob was the only modern thing on my new boat.

"Okay, this is the most important thing—" Dwight kicked the engine box located near the stern. "This's a gasoline engine. It ain't a diesel engine. A gas engine can blow you to bits. You don't ever want to start this engine without giving it the sniff test—"

A sudden whirring interrupted him. We looked toward its source—the top of the cliff above the submarine—but there was nothing to see. The whirring grew louder. The thing, the whirrer, was approaching the cliff edge. Then a white mechanical arm with a cable and hook hanging from it appeared. The arm extended out over the water, telescoped back into itself, extended again. It withdrew again, and when it next extended, a nearly naked man with an ascetic, wrinkled body stood in the hook hugging the cable with one arm and gesturing to the crane operator with the other—

"Take it down, Edith. Down goddamnit!"

He was a circumcised man in a tiny Speedo with stars and stripes. His only other clothes were work boots with woolen socks. He was old to be riding crane hooks in skimpy Speedos on cool days. The guy was easily seventy-five. His body was hard, tanned, and wrinkled like your father's ancient old catcher's mitt in the back of the closet. He twisted in midair on the hook. "Take it *down!* What language am I speaking, goddamnit, Edith? Down!"

The crane whirred, and he spiraled down.

"That's Commander Hickle," said Dwight.

"Stop!" shouted Commander Hickle.

The hook and Hickle stopped a foot from the roof of

his submarine. Hickle stepped off onto the sub. But then the hook started again. It clanked on the sub.

"Stop, goddamnit, Edith! *Stop!*"

"Goddamnit, Edith," Alistair mocked, sitting on his transom. "Sparky's been doin' that all day. It's cuttin' into my lobster trade, Commander Sparky goin' up and down. Gets the customers edgy."

"The commander's a genius," said Dickie. "I worked with him on that sub." Dickie stuck out his chin. "We consulted on certain hydrodynamical matters."

"Yeah, right," said Alistair, "then he ran you off for stealin' his tools."

"Slander."

"Hey, Dickie, did Sheriff Kelso find you?" asked Alistair.

"What—?" said Dickie, deflating.

"Yeah, he looked pissed, if you ask me." Alistair didn't bat an eye, and I could see Dickie strain to figure out if he was being kidded or not, poor bastard.

Bored with the routine, Dwight continued with my orientation—"A cupful of gasoline in an enclosed space overnight can make enough fumes to blow your ass to bits when you go to start it next mornin'. I've seen it happen. There's a blower—" He flipped a switch mounted in the steering console, and I heard a fan go on. "But don't trust it alone. Lift up the engine box and sniff. If you smell gas, leave the box up for a while before you start the engine."

Alistair said, "Yeah, you remember Russell Cass? Got blowed to kingdom come out in Cabot Strait. It rained Russell for two days."

"Yeah," said Dwight. "Used to upset my daughter to see gulls gulpin' little floatin' bits of Russell."

97

"Around here lotta folks with gas engines don't bother with the sniff test. They use Dickie to start their engines for them. How much you get per engine, Dickie?"

Dickie looked hurt, but he didn't leave. He put his hands in his pockets and bobbed his head slightly as if trying to pump up a retort.

"There was one other thing, what was it?" Dwight asked himself, rubbing his chin. "Oh. The dinghy. Right there." He pointed to a battered little fiberglass boat tied to the same float. "That's yours. See, you can't use that flat rock as a dock. Tide'll come up and set your boat down on it. You got to leave your boat on the moorin' and dinghy in."

Alistair waved at somebody coming down the steps. He greeted Edith by name. Like the Commander, Edith was over seventy, but she was coming fast. I could see she had zeroed in on Jellyroll. You can always tell. He can tell, too. Edith wore a print shift and high-tech sneakers with ankle socks, the kind with little pom-poms at the heels. She held up the hem of her skirt so as not to impede her pumping knees.

"Hello, Edith," said Dwight.

"Hello, Dwight."

"Hi, Edith," said Dickie.

"Edith," said Dwight, "I'd like you to meet Artie Deemer. He'll be staying at the boathouse for a while. Artie, this is Edith Hickle."

She shook my hand warmly, even though she wanted to meet Jellyroll, not me. Many people aren't nearly so gracious. I used to get trampled by cute-crazed fans until I learned to lean forward and put a shoulder into them. They don't even notice when you put a shoulder into them. It's a powerful urge they feel.

"And this is the R-r-ruff Dog," said Dwight with a little ta-da move.

Edith's knees crackled as she went down to his level. Jellyroll wagged his entire back end and licked Edith's face in long laps. She moaned with delight and petted his back. Dwight was smiling with the happiness of it all.

"Edith, goddamnit, take it up!" bellowed the Commander from atop his sub.

"Just a moment"—she winked up at Dwight and added—"Sparky."

Sparky must have thought Edith was still up in the crane. When he looked down and saw her on the float, he did a big take and bellowed, "Goddamnit, Edith, what are you doing!"

"This is the R-r-ruff Dog, dear."

"The R-r-ruff Dog? Celebrity dogs? Do you know what celebrity dogs represent, Edith? A culture in decline! Decline, Edith!"

"Good luck with the launching, Commander," called Dickie.

"You, goddamnit! Are you still alive?"

Dickie wilted.

Edith stood up, with a boost from Dwight. "How's Phyllis?" she asked him.

"Fine. She told me to bring you her best."

"Well," said Edith, "we've been kind of busy what with the launching and . . . all."

"She knows that, Edith. You'll be back in touch soon's it's done."

Edith squeezed Dwight's forearm before she started

up the steps with much less energy than on her descent. Jellyroll looked kind of sad to see her go.

Dwight started the engine after giving it another sniff for my edification. "Well, there you are. Ready to go." He may have sensed my hesitation—the boat was pointing up the Crack; I didn't see how there was room to turn around without hitting the rock or Alistair's boat—because he said, "Hop in. You can save me a trip back up the steps. Plus you want to get your chart off my boat—" He took us backward around Alistair's boat and out where there was room to turn. He brought us up against his boat with the gentlest of taps, my bow pointing out the Crack toward open water. He climbed into his own boat and passed me my chart. "Now you feel okay about the trip back?"

"Oh, sure," I said. Did I?

I cleared the mouth of the Crack feeling good. I felt good all the way back to the cove. I was stoned on crystalline air.

I turned us into the cove. Remember the sunkers, I told myself. I saw them on the chart as well. It took me a couple of tries to pick up the mooring line. I overran it the first time, jerked it out of my hands. But I got it on. I didn't know what kind of knot to tie, so I tied a lot of them.

I didn't notice I was tired until I sat down at the picnic table on the porch at dusk. That long sweep of falling light, lengthening shadows, would have been a time of peace and introspection at the old summerhouse with the loved ones.

I'd brought a cellular phone. I used it to call Clayton to tell him I love it, thanks a lot, but he wasn't home,

and then I remembered he had told me he was going
to California. I left the message on his machine. Then
I called Shelly, but he wasn't home either. And Crystal
was en route to Memphis. Jellyroll, who seemed to
have strong inner resources, had found his place. Dogs
always need a place. His was against the wall near the
bedroom door on a small hook rug with concentric
rings of earthen colors. I unpacked our gear, finished
putting away the food, and explored the boathouse
more closely.

Its internal frames made a lot of horizontal surfaces.
They were used as bookshelves and for displaying
knickknacks. There were guides to reptiles, birds,
mammals, mosses and lichens, mushrooms, butterflies,
tide pools, marine invertebrates, wildflowers; the
knickknacks were mostly things from the sea or from
the woods collected over the years. Sea urchin skele-
tons, glass net floats, horseshoe crabs, round rocks,
flotsam and jetsam. I didn't see much that clearly belonged to Clayton. Guests like me could have collected
these things and left them as thank-yous.

Jellyroll had already gone to sleep. Maybe that was
the key to life, full days, early to bed, early to rise.
Maybe one didn't need extraordinary inner resources
to live in the remote regions, after all. I had a meatloaf
sandwich and went to bed with the wildflower guide.
I didn't get much further than the names, but they were
wonderful. The names could hypnotize: hoary alyssum,
pipsissewa, blind gentian, early saxifrage, pink lady's
slipper, painted touch-me-not, false Solomon's seal,
common fleabane, sandwort, spotted Joe-Pye weed, and
pearly everlasting. . . .

*   *   *

Jellyroll started barking before dawn. I awoke with that odd feeling of not knowing where I was. I had to force myself to remember. Jellyroll pawed at the front door, barked, looked over his shoulder at me, and pawed some more. The rest of the house was pitch dark, and I had no idea where I'd left the matches. One had to remember matches if one lived in a gas house.

I groped into the kitchen for the flashlight I'd seen earlier. I was struck by the night fears, the little-boy fears. I managed to get the flashlight and shine my way to the front door. There was nothing on the porch, nothing lurking against the walls. I went out on the porch.

The dog pack. They stood in a semicircle below, near the foot of the stairs, but none made a move to come up.

"Stay," I told Jellyroll.

We watched each other. I shone the light on them. A couple wagged their tails. Others milled and paced excitedly. Their tongues lolled. Their eyes glowed, startling yellow or green discs.

11

I stayed up for the sake of the sunrise. I sat at the picnic table dressed in everything I owned drinking coffee and watching the sky lighten until I could see the water in Dog Cove, the birds, the geology, and I felt at peace here, in tune with the sad, persistent rhythm at the center of things. Some man-made music, if carefully chosen, might merge with the music of the spheres. I set up my boom box on the railing and played the female vocalists tape I'd made before leaving NYC. I had been neglecting vocalists of late. Billie Holiday sang: "Stormy weather, since my man and I ain't been together—keeps raining all the time."

Suddenly, from nowhere, listening to that haunted voice, I slid back into that state of abject eroticism. I ached for contact. I have sexy thoughts all the time, say riding the IRT or walking Jellyroll in the park or listening to music at home. I assume everyone does. They pass. I move on to other matters, but this was different. This was reminiscent of the mad adolescent lust of last-period civics class in seventh grade. Mrs. Fosdick was telling us about the Russians. The Russians always lie, she was saying. You can *trust* them to lie. In fact, they'll stop at nothing to stomp out America and Jesus, too.

If Mrs. Fosdick had been a Russian and offered me a look at her soft, pendulous, warm, naked flesh, even a fleeting peek from afar, through binoculars, I would have signed myself into slavery.

I went inside and phoned Crystal at the tournament site. I just wanted to hear her voice. Maybe I could catch her before her morning match. When she said hello, I could tell that she wasn't getting the good rolls.

"I'm out," she said. "Eliminated before lunch yesterday. They had me for breakfast."

"Were you missing balls?" I asked.

"No, I was blowing position. Even the easy position. I'd get out of line, and you know what happens then."

"It must have been tough to concentrate."

"You should have seen Gracie Cobb's eyes when she saw I couldn't run balls. Like the eyes on those African scavenger birds. What do you call them? You were watching a nature show on them."

"Vultures?"

"No, the other ones."

"Griffins?"

"Yeah, that's how she looked at me. Like a griffin looking at a dying antelope."

"If you'll come here, I'll pay for the trip, and coddle and cosset you when you arrive."

"Yeah? What's it like there?"

"Warm and moist," I said, and I told her about the

island, about Dwight, the Commander and Edith, the Crack, and about my new boat.

"You? A boat?"

"Hey, I come from a long line of seafarers. My ancestors sailed with Dennis Connor. Maybe you were unaware of that."

She giggled. "How do I get there?"

I told her.

"Why don't I rent a car at the airport? We could drive home slowly, stop at country inns and things. I've always wanted to stop at country inns."

"You have?" I pictured intense Yankee carnality on a creaking four-poster—

Then she asked me about the status of the stalker, and I told her about Rand Dewy at the airport and how he knew not only that Jellyroll was being stalked but that we were leaving New York on that specific day.

"The figure skater?"

"Yeah, he's the on-screen talent for *Celebrity Tonight.*"

"How did he know? . . . Shelly wouldn't let it get out, would he?"

"No."

"What about Clayton Kempshall?"

"No, he'd be afraid of Jellyroll's clout. He'd never work again. He knows that. Besides, he's a nice guy. He just wouldn't do it."

"What about Shelly's detective? Have you talked to him?"

"The detective is Shelly's brother-in-law."

"No."

"Shelly says he's a retired New York homicide detective."

"Do you think we should call in Calabash?"

"I tried him on Poor Joe Cay. His Uncle said he's at sea." Then I told her all about the ax murder that had taken place in Micmac.

"I'm feeling real scared, Artie. Sometimes it comes over me in a wave."

"No wonder you couldn't get any position." I told her I loved her.

"Look, there's not really any point in hanging around here. Maybe I'll head for Micmac right now. Okay? Maybe I can be there by tomorrow."

"I'll pick you up in my boat." That was met with silence. "Don't worry, I'm a master mariner." We made kissing sounds into the receiver and then hung up. I sighed with expectation.

"Let's go for a walk!" I said to Jellyroll. He pronked straight up in the air and bolted out the door. A full day ahead of us, it was time to do some exploring.

There were two hills on our side of the Crack. The view would be worth the trek to the top of either. I could climb the one that crested in the interior of the island; the trail up its steep flank began near Jellyroll's woodpile in back. Or I could climb the hill that crested on the coast above the cove. That trail started right below the porch. Jellyroll sprinted off to the woodpile in the general direction of the former, so I followed. His chipmunk friend didn't make an appearance to taunt him, and he seemed for a moment dispirited, ears dropped. That quickly changed to delight with the new, and he sprinted ahead.

The trail was well beaten, circling the base of the hill on flat ground through a garden of luxurious, leafy ferns. Jellyroll ran through them, leaving a wake of swaying plants. I wished I could do that. Maybe humans have always envied animals their undampened sensuality and absence of clothes. The trail steepened abruptly. Skull-sized rocks made the going precarious, requiring concentration, even for Jellyroll. We were passing through a thick forest of white pines and a few spruce trees with fat burls, like strange tropical fruit, hanging from trunks and limbs. The forest floor was covered with lichens, mosses, and ferns. It was a sweet forest, welcoming, nonthreatening. However, after about half a mile, the trail expired, and the grade steepened radically. Common sense told me to head back down the way I came. But I didn't want to do that. I liked the isolation. I liked that the human presence didn't figure here.

I climbed on, here and there scrambling on all fours. In stretches bipedalism was impossible. There were still trees and shrubs, there was still soil, but mainly it was a realm of rock. The whole island was a gigantic chunk of rock, fissured, broken, and eroded by eons of ice and wind and water. Sometimes spruce trees grew right out of cracks in the granite as if they'd found a vein of nutrients, a marrow, deep down inside the rock itself.

Then we came to a place of upheaval. Some force had dislodged great rocks and strewn them around like a petulant child's toys. Though cracked jaggedly, their sides were often straight. There were cubes and trapezoids, shapes that don't show up naturally, some the size of steamer trunks and some the size of panel trucks. How did the sides get so straight? Quarrying? Tall spruce trees with tendril roots like tropical creepers disappeared into the cracks between the broken boulders and seemed to be holding them together. I paused on top of a flat one and tried to figure out what I was seeing.

Jellyroll didn't care. He was rock hopping, trailing his tongue out the side of his mouth. He yapped at me to hurry up. Dogs are much better equipped for this kind of going. The human center of gravity is too high. A bad step up here, I could break my leg and die of solitude.

We arrived at a plateau . . . at least a wide ledge. The flat ground felt good. I was glad to stand up straight. Jellyroll went sprinting after an imaginary chipmunk. The plateau seemed to originate here at this ledge. To the right it widened and curved around the side of the hill. I followed, turned the bend, and suddenly came upon the remains of the Castle.

It must have been enormous. It was still enormous in a sense. Its shape was outlined by a waist-high foundation wall made of that same round skull-sized rock used in the boathouse foundation. At each of the four corners stood towering rock chimneys, like turrets.

I went in through an empty doorway, but after two steps I retreated. Lichens, mosses, and tiny evergreen saplings covered jagged rubble from the old fire, smoothed it out, making me think I could walk around inside the walls. The rooms were choked with boards and huge hewn beams, congealed ash and charcoal, chunks of black metal, and things that passing winters had turned to black ooze. Flaming, the place had apparently dropped within its own foundation walls and burned itself out. This was where Clayton had grown up. It must have been tough, being the son of the meanest prick in the county.

I climbed up on the wall to see what I could see of
the interior without actually walking in there. The wall
was two feet thick at the top, wider at the base. Some
of the interior walls were also made of the local rock,
in endless supply along the shore. I could count ten
rooms on this level, but I think there were more.

Around front there appeared to have been a sweep-
ing veranda. Its charred frame timbers remained. It
overlooked an open area that, I decided, had once been
a great lawn because the trees were clearly younger
than the forest around it. This might have been a peaceful place to spend one's early years looking out on the
blue-green ocean, but not if the old man was a psycho.

One big room near the front, however, was not
choked with rubble. In that room, the dirt floor was
packed hard and swept clean. Ropes were strung like
clotheslines from wall to wall, and on the ropes hung—
upside down—row after row of fat marijuana plants.
This, I happened to recognize, was top-o'-the-line can-
nabis *sativa*. Somebody had taken great care with this
crop. It had been nurtured and tended and pruned by
hand. I happened to be passingly familiar with the
plant because two old friends of mine are hydroponic
growers in a loft downtown, near the courthouse. Sarah
and Stuart are pros, unapologetic about it, but they'd
never hurt anyone. They keep no weapons. If raided,
they'd go quietly. I'd heard different about some of
these country growers. Some of them held dangerous
views about the individual and society. I'd heard horror stories about booby traps and trip wires and trigger-
happy sociopaths tending their crops in some of the
heavy pot-growing regions like the Hawaiian Islands,
northern California, the Smokey Mountains, etc. Of

course, I'd heard these stories from professional dopers who sometimes tend to exaggerate.

Nonetheless, I did a sharp about-face, slapped my thigh for Jellyroll's attention—I only slap my thigh when it's important, and he knows that. He gobbled in his tongue and snapped his jaw shut. His head darted. So did mine. We backed out the way we came. We made it to the edges of the ex-lawn—

"What say?"

I couldn't see him. . . . "Look," I said to the general environment, "I'm just walking here, you know, hiking, I'm just passing through, I'm a guest at the boathouse—"

"It's okay."

But I still couldn't see him. As far as I knew, he was watching me through cross hairs—

"Most people from away figure we're a bunch of inbred murdering moonshiners out here on the islands."

"Not me, but I'd feel better if you showed yourself."

He stepped out of a thicket on the other side of the collapsed veranda—right where I had been looking without seeing. This guy was part of the environment.

"I saw you come over with Dwight." He was about thirty-five, stocky with thick shoulders and arms that hung away from his sides. "Dwight's functional. Dwight always takes care of Clayton's guests."

"Does he have a lot of guests?"

"Not enough for Dwight to make a handsome livin'. You're from New York, right? Same as Clayton. I'd like to go to New York. I went once when I was a child. Every time I went outside something blew into my eye. Big flecks of black things. I couldn't really identify them." He wore the same work clothes the salts on the

Micmac dock wore—heavy wool pants with suspenders, rubber boots, flannel shirts, with long johns underneath. "I'd like to go back, though."

"Why don't you?"

"Go back? Yeah, I could wear goggles this time. . . . Trouble is, my parole officer don't like me to leave the state."

". . . You're on parole, huh?"

"For takin' a man's life. It was one of those meaningless things. You know the kind of thing, bein' from New York, spur of the moment thing where you take a man's life." He watched me sideways, looking for the effect of that talk. "Once taken, you can't give it back."

"A spontaneous killing," I offered. "You probably didn't have any choice. Sure." I looked straight back at him. "Like I said, I'm just passing through." Jellyroll leaned against my shin and looked warily up at the guy.

"I've known Clayton since childhood," he said. "We were children together. Runnin' wild in the woods. These very woods right here. We ran wild in them."

I nodded.

Something was physically wrong with this guy. He held his head turned to the right in a weird way, as if his neck muscles were dysfunctional, or he had some kind of growth in the way. Not everybody is a psychopath, I reminded myself, even if it seems that way. He had enormous hands with short, thick fingers, which he held as if they were about to pick up a wheelbarrow.

"Well, I guess we'll be strolling on. Let's go, boy."

"Of course we're from different classes, Clayton and I. Where do you know him from?"

"He was in one of my dog's movies."

111

"What do you mean?"

"This dog is in the movies."

"No shit?"

"None. And TV. The R-r-ruff Dog." Ex-R-r-ruff Dog, but it wasn't necessary to go into that.

"Like Rin-Tin-Tin?"

"Yeah." Keep it simple. This guy had never even heard of Jellyroll. I liked that. It's unusual to find someone in the industrialized world who hasn't at least heard of the R-r-ruff Dog. "Was this Kempshall's mansion?" I asked.

"This was the Castle. These movies—your dog is the *star* of these movies?"

I nodded. "Clayton was in one."

"Wow. Who'd he play?"

"An . . . evil high school principal."

"Was he good?"

"Excellent."

He had a far-off look on his face, imagining, I thought, Clayton as an actor, or as a human being in the world, or as an evil high school principal. There had been something between them, running wild in the woods.

"What happened to the Castle?"

"Arson."

It was right about then—"arson"—that I saw the other side of his face. The entire right side—from his hairline down to the hinge of his jaw, including his ear—had been fried. Layer covered layer of scar tissue. It looked like the gold braid naval officers wear, except that it was mostly flesh-colored with vague, thin purple streams running through it. His ear was melted down into a little bud the size of a thumb knuckle. The ear

112

hole was still there. He peered hard at me, as if waiting to see what I was going to make of it.

". . . Did anybody get hurt?"

"Compton Kempshall—Old Man Kempshall—he got killed. 'Course that fucker deserved it."

"Everybody seems to agree on that," I said.

"Yeah? Who? Dwight?"

"Clayton himself said so."

"Really? When was this?"

"Last week. He didn't go into any details, but that's what he said." I was just trying to hold up my end of the conversation.

"The Selfs is the peons, and the Kempshalls is the aristocrats."

"What happened to him?"

"Who? Old Man Kempshall? Fried to a fuckin' crisp."

"He died in the fire?" Hadn't Dwight and Clayton told me his body never was found?

". . . He was dead before the fire got started. At least he looked dead to me. Of course I was just a kid at the time. I'd never really seen a dead guy before. Maybe he was partly alive. Maybe there was like a glimmer of life left. After I whacked him with my trusty Cub Scout hatchet."

I didn't want to know that. Even if it wasn't true. I wanted to keep things light. That's why we were here. We were here to relax and hide out for a couple of weeks or so. We didn't need to get involved in any ancient hatchet murders. Especially not alone out in the woods with the guy confessing to it, the guy drying his dope in the ruins of his victim's castle. Far too weird.

"What's your name?"

"Artie Deemer." Jellyroll was leaning against my leg the way he leans when he's nervous. "What's yours?"

"Hawley Self."

If this were New York I'd naturally assume he'd made that up, but this was not New York. "How do you do, Hawley?"

"Say, Artie?"

"That's your boat in the cove?"

"Yeah, that's where I live. Aboard."

I wondered if he lived in the boathouse when it was guest-free. "Dwight says you're a sea urchin diver."

"It ain't a good time for fishin', but it's a good time for urchins. They're out there by the fuckin' billions. Japs buy from me in Micmac, little peckers. Twelve hours later some electronics magnates is slurpin' them up in Tokyo. Say, let me ask you. You wouldn't have connections in New York who might want to buy top-grade urchins? Like for restaurants, coffee shops?"

"I doubt it."

"Yeah, too bad. I'm lookin' for a wider outlet, since there's so many urchins. It's a problem, though, since they taste like a gob of tuberculosis snot."

"I'll bet the water's cold."

"You think it's cold on the surface. It's fuckin' toasty compared to the bottom." He slid a spliff the size of a toilet paper roller out of his vest pocket and put a match to it. "Smoke?"

"No, thanks." I used to smoke some doo-dah while listening to music or while not listening to music, but I stopped, mostly. It was not making my edge any keener.

"A guy comes and stumbles on your stash and goes, 'No, thanks'? That's opposed to the code."

"The code?"

"Yeah."

"What code?"

"The code."

Okay, so we smoked. It was clearly something special. My friends Sarah and Stuart would speak quietly
in its presence. I sat down on a chunk of round rocks
still cemented in a mass.

"Are you the gardener?" I asked.

"Pretty excellent, wouldn't you agree?"

"I certainly would."

"Yeah, this is the best crop yet, but the pressure's
gettin' too hot. The long dick of the law. Too bad, I
was just learnin' what I was doing. I've always been
interested in growin' things. I see you're interested in
wildflowers."

I was carrying the guide to wildflowers. "I am, but I
don't know anything about them."

"There's a lot of them. My mother cooks with them
sometimes. . . . So is Clayton comin' up?"

"I don't think so. He went to California."

"California, huh? L.A., I suppose. Beverly Hills. So
he just said, 'I got this rustic place on this backward
island, why don't you borrow it, laugh at the locals?' "

"He didn't laugh at the locals. I'm here because
somebody's stalking my dog," I said.

"What do you mean?"

"Do you know what a stalker is?"

"Like a hunter?"

"It has a special meaning. It means a nut who follows
celebrities. Sometimes the nut kills the celebrity."

"No shit? Why?"

"For publicity. It usually doesn't happen with dogs."

115

"Somebody's tryin' to kill this dog?"

"Maybe." I told him about the stalker because I wanted a local ally. Dwight was an ally, but he didn't live on the island itself. Even if this Hawley Self didn't care to be my ally, I wasn't taking much of a risk telling him. A guy who's never even heard of Jellyroll isn't going to call the nearest TV station to sell them the news that Jellyroll has arrived.

"So you mean you're hidin' out here?"

"Yes."

"Well, look, if I see any stalkers, I'll let you know."

"Thanks, I'd appreciate that—"

Hawley saw something in the woods to my left, beyond the front of the ex-Castle. I looked that way. So did Jellyroll. Something had moved over there.

"Dickie, goddamnit, get over here!" Hawley sprang up and started after the apparently universally loathed Dickie. Maybe there's one on every island. "Look, this joker is my partner." He waved an arm that included the entire ruins, but I took the gesture to refer to the curing weed. "Of course, only a total asshole'd have him for a partner. Excuse me, okay, Artie? It was nice meetin' you. I'll see you around. How long are you around for?"

"It's kind of up in the air."

"Well, then I'll see you around." He started off at a jog, but he put on the brakes, turned, paused, then said, "Say, Artie, have you seen Clayton?"

"Seen him? Where?"

"Wherever."

"He's in L.A."

Hawley seemed to ponder some question, but he

didn't pose it. "Well, . . . bye." Off he went after Dickie, his partner.

Jellyroll watched him for a long time after he'd gone. I remained seated until I felt reasonably confident I could walk without herniating any discs. Jellyroll idly licked my cheek.

12

I made it back to the boathouse intact. So did Jellyroll, but then he didn't ingest dangerous doo-dah. He went to his place and waited for food. I fed him, made a cup of coffee, and settled back on the porch. Helen Humes sang the Earl Hines tune "Blue Because of You" as the tide came in, and in and didn't stop until it had reached the foundation of the boathouse.

The phone rang. "Artie, how is it?" Shelly asked.

"It's great, Shelly. Quiet, remote. You'd love it."

"I hate remote. The Upper West Side's too remote for me. Listen, the R-r-ruff idiots have been calling all morning. You ought to hear them. Nobody'll take responsibility. They're making a scapegoat out of that poor fucker who fired you. He's gone. They're implying he had a drug abuse problem. They're so relieved Crystal's a woman, they'll do anything. Guy called to offer you a Mercedes Benz, the big one, four-door. A bonus."

"To do what?"

"To come back, of course. I'd like to let them swing

a little just for fun, then you can decide what you want
to do."

"Okay, Shelly."

"Artie, another bowling sheet arrived today. It was
from the Atomic Bowl in Seabrook, New Hampshire. It
had those TV cartoons. Like the others. The, uh, stalker
was explaining to the interviewer how he loved the
R-r-ruff Dog so much he just had to . . . do it, the
fucker. Do you want me to send it out to you?"

"No. Shelly, you don't think the R-r-ruff people are
behind this somehow, do you?"

"How?"

"Well, like you say, there's no such a thing as bad
publicity."

"I'll get Myron to look into it. He'll lay a cease and
desist on the scumbags, see what they have to say. That
idiot who fired you, he didn't mention stalkers, right?"

"Right."

"Okay, Sid—my brother-in-law—he'll be in touch
with you. I suggest you do whatever he says. He knows
how to handle these things."

"Okay, Shelly."

I drove the boat out around the Dogs and headed
generally south toward open water. I told myself to
notice things that might be useful later as landmarks.
The twin hills on this side of Kempshall Island would
stand out, and so would the Dogs. Visibility was unlim-
ited. I'd never seen such clarity.

Three wooded islands came into view, and I headed
for the middle one, beyond which I think there was no
dry land until Portugal. The sea was flat calm. The
center island was called Hope. Hope Island. Artie

119

Deemer of the Hope Island Deemers. . . . I carefully ran my finger along the chart from Dog Cove to Hope Island. There was nothing to hit. The water was over a hundred feet deep in places.

Jellyroll stood in the bow, ears flapping. I munched some oatmeal cookies the Selfs had made. Suddenly I was in a sea of lobster pots. As far as I could see in all directions, there were markers floating languidly, all colors and combinations of stripes and bands, each trailing ropes that could tangle in my propeller to leave me floating fucked and banjaxed. I put the transmission in neutral and we coasted almost to a stop. Could I pick my way along? They weren't quite as close together as they seemed at first.

Nearby, a lobsterman in a spattered yellow rubber apron aboard a salty green lobster boat worked a row of yellow and black banded floats. I watched through my binoculars. The man had a round face with a spotty, reddish beard. He wore a red plaid hunting hat. He was just a kid, I realized. Seventeen, maybe.

A wire lobster trap popped out of the water and leapt up onto the side rail of his boat. All those old-fashioned values of perseverance, ingenuity, endurance. No one from here lived off their dogs. The guy saluted at us as he dug in his trap with rubber gloves and threw things he didn't like back overboard. I returned the salute, the brotherhood of the waves, here on the way to Hope Island. And suddenly I was out of the crowded lobster fishing grounds. There were no more traps, clear sailing. The traps had been placed in one area about the size of an Upper West Side block. I wondered why, what was there on the bottom that attracted so many lobsters. Baited traps?

Don't Explain

A three-story white frame house with a green roof and a veranda overlooked the water from Hope Island, but it seemed to be boarded up. "Hey, Jellyroll, you want to buy that house?" He looked back at me from the bow and wagged. Sure, he'd be delighted.

I motored down the side of the island as close in as I dared. Hope was typical of this ocean full of islands, wooded, surrounded by rock in piles with a central, rounded peak. I went around behind Hope. There were no other houses visible. Feeling confident, I kept going for a while—

What was that ahead? White. I looked through the binocs. Waves. Big waves were breaking over black saw-toothed rocks in a line across my course. Reflexively, I slowed the boat as if I were about to hit one, and Jellyroll slipped off his feet. I consulted the chart.

The Disappointments.

That's what they were called, this alligator's back of sunkers. It wasn't a wall. The Disappointments consisted of rock in piles, clumps, and pinnacles that were very close together; according to my inexperienced reading of the chart, there were only two places a boat like this could squeeze through in four miles of malevolence. Hope behind—the Disappointments ahead.

There were barely any waves around us, gentle swells, perhaps you'd call them, but big combers crashed over the Disappointments and exploded in glaring white spray—

I saw the white wake while the boat was still far away. Spray flew from its bow. I put the glasses on the boat. It was a sportfisherman type, very modern and expensive with a flying bridge. The hull was black, the deck and all the rest of the stuff above was white. Boats

121

like that were used in the charter fishing business in Florida and the Bahamas. People paid five hundred dollars a day to murder fish. Two men sat side by side at the topmost steering wheel—the flying bridge—under a white canvas top. The boat was still far away, but it was coming very fast right for us.

I looked back at the Disappointments. If the waves broke like this on a calm day, imagine what it would be like in some wind. I felt good. The vicious look of those rocks didn't stiffen me up with indecision. It excited me. I was happy to be out here. I should have done this sooner. Maybe boating would be a new career for me. But I didn't like that black sportfisherman. And it was getting closer by the minute.

I turned around and headed us back toward Hope Island. I had our Hampton boat going as fast as she could. I watched and waited. The sportfisherman's sharp bow was still pointing at us. Maybe that was merely an illusion caused by unfamiliarity with relative speeds and converging courses in clean air. I kept going, and soon it became clear that the black boat was turning at us the whole time. This made me edgy. The sportfisherman began to take on a menacing aspect. . . .

He caught up with us suddenly, it seemed to me. He slowed down and turned parallel to my course. The boat was bigger than I'd thought. I didn't know boat lengths by sight, but it was over twice as long as my boat.

"Hello." The man waved from the bridge. "I tried to call you on the radio—"

"What's wrong?" I shouted back across the water without slowing down.

"Oh, nothing, sorry to alarm you. But my son wanted to meet the R-r-ruff Dog—"

I couldn't see the son's face, because it was completely hidden behind a big camcorder. He was hanging over the side aiming the damn thing at us, getting a shot of me scowling back at him. The father had an oddly elongated face, as if it had just begun to melt, and a long beak of a nose. His eyebrows met in the middle. Everything else being vertical, his smile seemed surrealistically horizontal. He wore a captain's hat with yellow braid on the bill. He sat there rocking atop his enormous gleaming boat, grinning down at Jellyroll and me. We rocked in his waves. Jellyroll scratched for footing on the wooden bottom.

"Where are you headed?" he asked. We were going along slowly side by side now, shouting across the gap.

"Nova Scotia," I said. Jellyroll looked edgy.

"In *that?*" His eyebrows arched sardonically.

"No, I have a mother ship. Waiting for me. A gunboat."

He chuckled and nodded.

I was icy. He was a nosy intrusion on my fantasy of remoteness, a shithead from the world of pop values busting in on my fantasy of connectedness to permanence and peace. Fuck him and his son with the camcorder in my face.

But then the guy said, still grinning, "I heard some bastard's stalking him."

"Wha—? Where? Where'd you hear that?"

"On TV. You know those kind of shows, those celebrity shows. Channel surfing." He made a motion over the side as if flipping a remote. "I can't remember."

All this time, the kid continued to shoot at me. I never did get a look at him.

"Yeah," I said unconvincingly. "We hear that a lot. All kinds of rumors." Everybody in the world knew! "Just rumors."

"Where you headed?"

I waved in mock friendliness as I peeled off and turned back toward the Disappointments, hoping he wouldn't follow. I looked over my shoulder. The guy was watching me, the kid was shooting, but they kept going. The boat was named *Seastar;* there was a home port on the black stern, but I couldn't read it. I leaned back against the wheel and looked through my binoculars.

Boston.

I looked up from the stern to see the guy looking back at me through a pair of binoculars even bigger than mine. The kid kept shooting. I turned away—

The Disappointments were much closer than I thought. I wasn't about to run up on them, but I was close enough to distinguish individual rocks, black, barnacled, weed-covered ship killers. I wanted to get even closer, but I didn't dare. I feared the place, but it fascinated me. Why were waves breaking over them when it was almost dead calm here? I turned parallel to the Disappointments until I couldn't see the black boat anymore, then I turned for home.

Dwight's boat lay against the flat rock when I returned to Dog Cove. He was bending over something at the foot of the stairs. I looked through my binoculars. Five-gallon gas cans. He was leaving me fuel. He heard me coming, straightened creakily, and waved.

Jellyroll saw Dwight and began to bark happily. I managed to pick up the mooring without getting jerked overboard, and we dinghied ashore. Dwight and I shook hands, one seaman to another, while Jellyroll danced around trying to get noticed.

"I met Hawley Self," I said.

"Yeah, it'd be inevitable."

"He said he killed Compton Kempshall with an ax— no, a hatchet—when he was a boy, and then he burned down the Castle."

"Well, he might have."

"He might?"

"Yeah, but Hawley don't go anywhere."

"You mean what difference does it make?"

"Sort of."

"Do you want a beer?"

"Sure."

We sat at the picnic table. Jellyroll barked at the chipmunk. I asked what had happened to Hawley's face.

"Gasoline boat engine blew up. Happened over at Micmac. If it'd happened out in the islands, he'd be dead. And that's why you got to perform the sniff test. You thought maybe it happened while he was burnin' down the Castle? Don't worry about Hawley. Hawley's harmless."

"I saw some unusual boulders up the hill. It looked like a quarry."

"That's wildcat granite. Good granite cuts along the grain real predictable. Wildcat granite cuts straight for a while, then suddenly splinters all to hell. This's all wildcat in through here. Quarryin' goes back to before the Civil War."

"Do people on this island shoot dogs for chasing deer?" I asked.

"There ain't any deer on Teal Island. Why do you ask?"

"Dickie said so. Dickie the Red."

Dwight just shook his head.

Shadows stretched all the way across Dog Cove, the still time of day, but that black boat had jangled my nerves. I asked Dwight if he'd ever seen it before. *"Seastar,* it's called. From Boston."

Dwight rubbed his cheeks thoughtfully.

"Very fancy, high-tech," I prodded.

"Ain't any summer person I know."

Then I told Dwight about the stalkers. Why not? Everybody already knew anyway.

Dwight pondered the whole concept for a long time. His brow knit, his face moved. "So they'll get famous, huh? Is that why they do it?"

"That's about it, I guess."

"So you think it's them in the black boat?"

"No. I have no reason to think so, but they'd heard he was being stalked, perfect strangers. I'm worried that other nuts will get the idea."

"Afraid of the stranger. . . . That'd tend to keep a man near home." He nodded to himself and looked out across the cove. He understood. "You planning a trip over to the mainland?"

"Yes. Tomorrow, I hope."

"On the way over, you just aim for the smoke from the cement plant. Micmac's just to the left of the smoke."

13

I set off early on the Great Crossing of Cabot Strait after performing the sniff test. This was no half-assed embarkation by my dog and me. I'd lain awake last night thinking about how ludicrous it would be to die in a boating accident on the way to pick up my lover. She'd wait on the dock at Micmac, hours, days passing, until they brought my body ashore in a rubber bag. Jellyroll, too, only the bag would be shaped differently. No, wait, I'd forgotten: these waters never gave up their dead, due to the absence of bloating gasses. But the day was perfect, bright and crisp, and I was prepared. I had charts, extra gas, water, dogfood. I'd just follow the smoke from the cement factory. I couldn't go wrong. Hawley's boat was not on his mooring as I passed. Maybe I'd see him out urchining. The tide was ebbing. I let us drift in it for a few boat lengths toward the mouth of the cove.

I also had thought about Crystal herself as I lay awake thinking about the voyage, about the turn of her ankle when she wears these particular open-toed shoes. I thought about fondling her ankles. Not all my thoughts of her were lewd. I thought about the way her face lights up when she's enjoying herself. I mused, for example, on her nine-ball break, that full-bodied snap, all her weight behind it, arm extended. . . . Well, I guess that one was a little lewd, too. Actually, I believe I was grinning with delight as we left the cove to pick up Crystal. I seldom grin with delight on a day-to-day basis, especially when I'm alone.

There was barely any wind. We rounded the point, and Jellyroll took his place in the bow where the wind would flap his ears. There, he could throw up without it sloshing underfoot. Everything seemed shipshape. I turned around the point, and we stepped off into the unknown—

The white smoke, my landmark, hung against the cloudless blue sky. The horizon was empty. I was *offshore*. The compass said we were heading due west. Okay. That seemed fine. The engine ran with a determined, steady sound. I relaxed, had a swig of water and— Wait a minute, the water was moving.

It took me a long time to recognize the meaning of those lobster trap floats lying flat on their sides with water running around them so fast it made a wake. The current ran from right to left. That had to affect my plans. I looked back at the smoke. We were still heading straight for it. I decided to observe for a while.

I thought about the old man I'd seen dead on the subway. Shortly after I'd moved to New York, learning the urban ropes, I was waiting for the downtown local at 103rd Street. I was late, I needed a train—and here it came. Perfect. Not such a hard town after all. Only the train didn't stop. It slowed down, but it didn't stop. The cars were all empty. It slowed still more, and at walking pace passed through the station, car by car. Until the very last car. That's where the dead guy sat, absolutely alone on the Number 1 local. He was old, frail, and bony in a threadbare herringbone sport coat. His bald head bobbed against his chest with the movement of the train. His hands lay in his lap palms up. A violin case leaned against his legs.

I needed to do something about this moving water. I still headed for the smoke, but I was moving sideways as well. I had to compensate. By turning right. Turn right how much? I tried to make the boat go faster, but it wouldn't. I pondered the problem. Jellyroll looked over his shoulder at me a little skeptically, I thought. After all the sea miles we'd covered together. . . .

So I decided the thing to do was to keep pointing at the smoke until I arrived at the coast—then I would know I had to turn right to get to Micmac. But what about going back, without smoke? I'd worry about that later. Besides, Crystal knew about boats; she grew up on Sheepshead Bay. With her aboard, I could share the loneliness of command.

Land. I first saw a wooded hill with a cone of bare rock at the top. Soon I saw the shoreline itself. It was wild and stern, rocky shelves that offered no safety, but it was beautiful and serene. As I turned right, I began to see white frame houses overlooking the water, and soon I came to Round Island. My first trip was over. I'd crossed. I was grinning, but I still needed to dock without making a spectacle of myself.

There was plenty of room at the dock forward of the Belgian's boat. I turned around and came up dead slow beside it, caught hold of its rail, and carefully walked us hand over hand along its side. That was a conservative way of getting to the dock, but there I was without incident. I stepped ashore and tied us on.

There were twice as many people on the hillside as when I left. They sat or stood in clots, idly. Some were cooking breakfast over outdoor stoves, others were eating out of bags with their fingers. Many, apparently, had slept up there. Some were still doing it on fold-out cots, cameras dangling on lanyards from their limp wrists. A few kids were trying to play, but now the hill was too crowded for frivolity. The kids tripped over supine adults. Had they lost hope?

I climbed up on the dock. Jellyroll hopped up behind me. "Hey, Jellyroll," I said in a special voice. He snapped around to attention, his lip caught on a canine. "Do you want to see Crystal?"

His head spun, looking for her. I leaned down to pat his side. "Later," I said quietly. Later is a hard concept for dogs. Expectancy. Maybe it's hard for all creatures. I always feel guilty when I do that, but I love to see his delight. I hauled out the disguise one more time, and he rolled his eyes as I put it on him.

We walked out to the road. Pilgrims were still coming, but they were coming by foot, because the road was now closed. Approaching, couples lugged blue plastic coolers while their children stumbled along behind with stuffed animals trailing. Where would Crystal have to park? I sat down on a planter box in front of the Cod End to wait. Jellyroll sat beside me. By the time I straightened out my legs, somebody had recognized him.

As usual in crowds, it began with a twitter of recognition. One person over here recognizes him, another over there independently recognizes him, and they make eye contact.

"Huh? Am I right?"

"Naww—"

"It *is!*"

". . . You're right! It *is!*"

Soon everybody knows.

"It's the goddamn R-r-ruff Dog!"

That opens the gates to a crowd. Crowds like that make me edgy. My smile gets tired as I scan the crowd for the one—or more—with crazy eyes.

"Hey, what's that on his back?"

"Some kind of pelt."

"Some kind of coat."

"Must be hot in a pelt coat in goddamn August."

"Yeah, look how hot he is—panting, even."

They began to compress in on us. I stood up. Jelly-roll, who was not panting, didn't mind a bit that his fans had gathered. Jellyroll was wagging his rump and smiling—but then suddenly without warning or direct provocation, he began to retch. His tail plunged down as if that were the lever that started the hooping machine. His whole body began to heave. When the effluvient reached his throat, he seemed to yawn. He then curled back his lips and expelled a gob of yellow bile.

The crowd gave out a collective "Ugghhh—" and recoiled. The last of the bile hung in a string from his lower lip. I wondered if I could *teach* him to do that as a method of crowd control.

A large woman with thick ankles snapped his picture, though she didn't reapproach us.

I retreated into the marine hardware store and shut

the door, but I knew that would never stop them, not after they got over the initial shock of seeing the R-r-ruff Dog blow lunch right before their very eyes. They hesitated for a little while, gathering at the door, peering in. I pretended to examine some enormous anchors.

The door opened. They were coming in.

But someone behind me, someone I hadn't seen, planted his foot in front of it. The crowd came up hard against it. As they recoiled, the stranger footed the door shut, locked it, and turned the sign on a string from OPEN to CLOSED—

It was the guy from the sportfisherman— His face was odd. I hadn't just imagined it out in the boat. It really was odd. It was elongated, as if drawn on a balloon and stretched. He looked like a caricature of himself. Even his eyebrows arched like upside down V's. I had seen that face before yesterday. Where?

He was tall and lanky, and he had an expensive haircut. He wore fresh khakis, a crisp denim shirt, a maroon pullover draped around his shoulders with the arms tied together at his sternum. He looked like an aging Gap model on location. There were streaks of gray at his sideburns.

He offered me his hand. "Richard," he said. He had a sonorous voice.

Richard? I peered into his eyes for a sign, for some knowing glance between us, but he introduced himself like a boring guy named Richard.

"Artie," I said.

He turned to the owner, who sat on his stool behind the glass counter. "You don't mind closing for a few minutes, let this man catch his breath."

"They weren't buyin' anyhow," said the owner.

" 'Mornin', Cap'n," he said to me. "How do you like them binoculars?"

"Excellent binoculars," I said.

"You've been buying, too?" said Richard to me. "That's the fact of life afloat. Buy, buy, buy." He chuckled, shook the shopping bag he held.

"Where's your boat?" I asked, still watching him closely for some indication of something.

"Out at the end of the dock. My son's taking some local-color footage in the village. How about that murder? Happened right out here, you know. I guess it doesn't only happen in your large metropolitan areas these days. Violent death happens everywhere, I guess. But senseless, really senseless."

I nodded, looking to extricate myself—

"So this is the R-r-ruff Dog—" He knelt face-to-face with Jellyroll. Jellyroll licked his cheek.

"Are you the cutest dog in the world? Yes, you are. Are you the most famous dog in the world? Hmm? I didn't mean to disturb you about the stalker out there in our boats," said Richard without looking up, as if he were talking to Jellyroll.

"Oh, that's all right. You didn't." I turned to the man behind the counter. "Excuse me, but do you have a back way out?"

He pointed over his shoulder with his thumb— "Out that way'll put you on the Cod End porch or the dock. Depends which way you turn. The Cod End's closed, of course."

"What is this," said Richard, "a disguise?"

"He gets cold. Chilly out on the water. Well, listen, thanks a lot, and take care. Boat'll leave without me." I headed for the back exit, whistled, and Jellyroll trotted

133

behind me. The door opened onto a catwalk. The porch was empty, but there it was—the cubicle-like john where the young woman was chopped. Several strands of yellow crime-scene tape were wrapped around it.

I hurried down the ramp toward the Hampton boat. I nodded at a small convocation of old salts dressed exactly alike.

"Say, Cap'n," said one in a friendly manner.

"Say, Captains," I said.

I climbed aboard my boat and sat on the engine box to wait. So did Jellyroll. I poured him some water in a bowl I'd brought, and I had a cup of lukewarm coffee from the thermos.

A man appeared above me at the dock dressed entirely in black. His long hair was slicked back and tied in a stubby ponytail. This guy looked like an East Village club hopper. What the hell was he doing here? He had a hard set to his face behind black Ray-Bans. He just stood there staring down at me.

"What?" I demanded.

"Is that the R-r-ruff Dog?"

"No."

"That's what I thought," he said slowly. Then he walked away.

My hands were trembling. Jellyroll was watching me nervously.

"Artie—"

"Crystal!"

I generally try to avoid the mushy, but I *felt* mushy at that moment, choked up at the sight of her standing up there on the edge of the dock where an instant ago a possible psycho had stood. She blew me a kiss. She looked tired from travel, but I could tell she was glad to see me, too. Jellyroll and I sprinted slowly up the steep ramp. He was yapping in frustration at the delay this ramp was causing him.

Crystal and I hugged while Jellyroll hopped about on his hind legs to be noticed. I didn't see the man in black anywhere on the dock.

"I've been feeling very funny since I got out of the car back there," she said in my ear.

"Funny? What do you mean, funny?"

"You know, *funny*."

"Really!" She felt it, too! Hurray! "Let's go, then. I've got a very fast boat." I wanted to hear some whoop-di-do songs. Or maybe sing some.

"I remember feeling like this in seventh grade."

I imagined the raw carnality of Crystal lowering a refrigerator to the deck. Panting, I shouldered up her stuff. She was traveling light compared to Jellyroll and me. Reduced weight would aid in speed to coitus.

"Is this where it happened, Artie? The killing?"

"You heard about that already?"

"I had to park way down the road, and people were talking about it as we walked."

"It happened in the rest room on that porch right over there."

We paused a moment to look before going down the ramp.

"Was it political?"

"What? Political?" I looked at her profile. She was looking at the Cod End rest room.

"I walked from the car with two women, sociologists from UCLA, who came to study this whole thing."

"What thing? The murder?"

"No, the expectation. That's what they call them. Expectations. Remember when all those people gathered in somebody's backyard in New Jersey? That was an expectation, as opposed to a visitation. I'm just telling you what they told me. They said if the expectation doesn't become a visitation in a reasonable length of time, people begin to factionalize. That was the word. Factionalize."

"You mean like left and right?"

"I guess. Conservatives and liberals. Sometimes they turn violent. But nobody's ever been murdered before."

"What would the factions want? I mean what's their objective?'"

"That's not clear."

We went down the ramp to my new boat. "How do you like her?" I asked proudly.

"It's wonderful!"

"Got to have a boat if you live on an island."

"Okay, Captain."

I gave her a hand coming aboard. She kissed me. "I don't think we'll factionalize, do you?"

14

We stood side by side at the wheel. The sea was flat and friendly. Jellyroll stood in the bow, ears flapping.

"Gorgeous," Crystal said of Cabot Strait. Her face was alight. "Does anybody swim here?"

"It's pretty cold." That was cant. It was bloody freezing. Briefly dunking my hand caused great throbbing, but maybe I was being wimpy. I didn't want to discourage Crystal. Crystal loved to swim. And I could then strive to warm her up.

"Would you like to go to the submarine launching?" I asked. I had told Crystal by phone about Commander Hickle and Edith and the orange submarine.

"This is the guy who abuses his wife?"

"Well, maybe he's just an asshole."

"What's the difference?"

"You don't want to go?"

"Whatever you want, Captain." She smiled at me lasciviously. I loved it when she smiled lasciviously. It wasn't exactly a smile. It was barely even a grin. The corners of her lips turned upward, and her eyes glistened. That was the most erotic thing about it to me, her glistening eyes. However, I still needed to hit the island. There was still that. There was no smoke beacon going this way, and I hadn't been paying attention to anything but Crystal. The wages of lust claim another small craft. I studied the lobster pots to see what the water was doing.

"What's the matter?" Crystal asked.

"Oh, nothing. Us seamanly fellows are attuned to our environment. The minutest thing has meaning to us."

"Oh."

The lobster pots stood straight up, which meant that there was little current. I could see the smoke behind us. I looked at the compass. It said we were going in the correct general direction, but it didn't feel right. Had I gotten turned around? Should I turn around? People who know more than their compass are never seen again. I had read books about it. That would be a drag.

"Would you like some water?" I asked.

"Water? No thanks."

"Don't want to get dehydrated."

"Oh, look," said Crystal. "Land."

"Land?"

"Isn't that land?"

Sure enough, land. Dead ahead, a hill just above the horizon. It was probably the hill the Castle used to stand on.

"Wow, Captain, well done," enthused Crystal.

I supposed it was unseemly for a captain to glow like

a boy of ten at the World Series in Ebbetts Field. Perhaps I could work up a stolid visage, exuding nautical confidence, jaw set. Perhaps I'd look for some sort of salty hat. Maybe a blue wool watch cap like the locals wore.

I showed Crystal the islands of Dog and Outer Dog, and she sighed with contentment. She said she loved Dog Cove. I pointed out the rocks awash in Dog Cove. "Dwight calls those sunkers."

"I can see why."

"There it is, the boathouse. Well, it's not really a boathouse, but that's what Clayton always called it."

"Where?"

"I know. It's hard to see. It blends with the surroundings."

I docked us with some dignity, even some aplomb, against the flat rock, where we unloaded Crystal's stuff. Then I put the boat on the mooring and dinghied back in.

Crystal loved the boathouse, too. We took a quick tour. I showed her all the food the Selfs had sent. And then we sort of dove out of our clothing. Perhaps we should just move here and live in sexual splendor for the rest of our days. I watched a single bead of sweat roll down the inside slope of Crystal's right breast toward the sweet valley floor. I envisaged myself in lilliputian scale wallowing in bliss between the mounds.

Crystal heard it first. She stiffened, a move that would have sent the miniature me bouncing down her belly. "Hear that?"

"Dogs," I said.

"What dogs?"

"Jellyroll, stay," I said. "This pack of dogs runs wild. I don't think they do any harm, but he wants to run with them, and I don't want him to."

"He's the boss," said Crystal to Jellyroll, who at the sound of the dogs had stood up at Crystal's side of the bed and stared at her as if requesting that she intercede. "I can't help you, pal."

"Do you think I'm cruel?"

"He's a city dog. He could run off a cliff."

We went out on the porch naked. I thought of Clayton, who'd said we could do that. He was right. Hawley's boat was gone, there was no one else around. It felt wonderful to be outside naked in the sun.

"Why don't you take Jellyroll and me for a boat ride instead, Captain?"

"Really? You want to?"

"Yes, that was fun."

"I'll show you the Crack," I said.

"What are you trying to say, Captain?"

"That's what they call it. . . . No, it *is*."

"Look at this place—" said Crystal after a short gasp of amazement as we entered the Crack. The light dimmed, the cliffs loomed. Crystal moved from side to side to see each in turn. A few people looked over the edge on the left side, but I didn't know any of them. A line of boats was tied nose to tail on moorings down the center of the Crack, a crowd for these parts, here to see the launching, I assumed.

The submarine still sat on its cradle halfway up the cliff at the apex of the Crack. I could see Commander Hickle atop his steed. He fidgeted from thing to thing, tightening, adjusting, moving in sharp jerks almost like someone in strobe light. He wore rubber flip-flops and a yellow slicker that fell just below his knees with nothing visible underneath. His naked legs scurried like a little shore bird's. Commander Hickle looked like a flasher. There had been a flasher disturbing the dog walkers in Riverside Park a while back. In the middle of a pizza-oven heat wave, he wore about ten layers of jackets and coats. It took him so long to flash that most people just walked off. Those who stuck around, for reasons of their own, said it was a frightening sight.

I was a little excited by the submarine. It touched a boyish chord. It could probably go deep without getting crushed like a Dixie cup. And maybe Dickie was right, maybe the Commander was some kind of genius mad scientist. What else could possibly explain building such a thing in isolation on an island without electricity?

But Crystal didn't give a shit about any of that. I had told her on the phone that Hickle was mean to his wife, and that cooked his goose with Crystal. She hates all spouse abuse. There could be no redemption for Hickle, certainly not through technology. But cruelty notwithstanding, I liked the old coot's contrariness, even though you could tell by watching him work up there that he was a wacko. The launching, apparently, had been delayed.

I stopped with reasonable accuracy at the Hampton boat's old dock. As I did so, Crystal looked up—almost directly up—at the submarine on its rack of creosote railroad ties. I loved the curve of her neck seen from that angle and those two bones on either side of the indentation at the base of her throat.

Commander Hickle lifted a round hatch, dropped on

his butt, and shimmied, hands overhead, down into the bowels of his submarine. He next appeared in the nose bubble. He had a walkie-talkie in his hand, and though we could hear none of it, we could tell he was screaming at Edith, out of sight on the cliff top, at the controls of the crane.

"Afternoon, Artie." It was Alistair sitting in his boat with his feet propped on the transom as if he hadn't moved since yesterday.

"Oh, hello, Alistair," I said. "I didn't see you there."

"Man's got to pay attention to his pilotin'. Woman, too, for that matter."

I introduced Crystal to Alistair. He actually stood up and bowed slightly with a lecherous glimmer in his old eyes, which amused Crystal.

"You sell lobsters?" she asked.

"Why, I certainly do. I take pride in my lobsters. Between you and me, there are those who'll sell you a soleless boot and call it a lobster, but I won't accept that. And that's why I can guarantee your satisfaction on every lobster." He never took his old but twinkling eyes off Crystal through all that bullshit.

"Let's get some, Artie," enthused Crystal, making eyes at Alistair.

"Sure."

His jaw bobbed twice before he could speak. "Tell you what I'll do. Since you are new visitors to Teal Island, I'd like to welcome you with two nice ones free of charge."

"Aww, that's so nice," said Crystal. "But I thought this was Kempshall Island."

"Yes, that's a common misconception. It's always been Teal Island. Why don't I hold onto your lobsters in their natural habitat until after the launchin'. 'Course that could take a couple of years."

"So there have been other launchings?" asked Crystal.

"Many launchin's," said Alistair, "many, many launchin's."

"What happened?"

"Nothin'."

Jellyroll started up the steps, and we followed. I found Crystal's ass as she climbed as aesthetically pleasing as the environment itself. So did Alistair, I'd bet. On the way I told Crystal what happens in the winter when the northeast winds blow and people take everything apart and leave the Crack to nature. I told her why there were no trees around the Crack, and she said that it was hard to imagine waves breaking up here.

We sat down on a shallow dome of rock near the edge.

Then the black-hulled sportfisherman entered the Crack. Richard steered from up on the flying bridge. His son shot videotape from the low, open stern. They slowly made their way along the moored boats down the middle.

"See that boat?"

"The black one?"

I told her about how they'd made a beeline at us yesterday out by the Disappointments. "See the skinny guy at the wheel? He said he'd heard on TV that Jellyroll was being stalked."

"On TV?"

"That's what he said. That's his son taking pictures."

"Can I use your binoculars?" She looked at the father and then at the son as they passed directly below us, but there was nothing to be seen of Sonny's face except for the camcorder.

"Everybody's watching us," Crystal whispered. Crystal and I hadn't been together long enough for her to grow used to Jellyroll's notoriety. For me, it's been a way of life, and I'm still not used to it. In this country, pop culture makes you famous and fortunate, and then it kills you if you're not constantly vigilant. Even if you are.

"Is that his wife?" Crystal nodded toward the woman sitting at the crane controls.

Since I'd last seen it, the crane had been reinforced with a wooden A-frame structure that was guyed by thick cables anchored with bolts and turnbuckles into the rock—so the weight of the submarine wouldn't pull the crane off the cliff. Edith sat slouched in the seat under the A-frame and stared out across the Crack to the northeast. She seemed to be nodding every now and then at the invective coming in over her headphones. She glanced over to her right, in our direction.

"Look at that!" snapped Crystal. "She's got a black eye—" Crystal was outspoken on the subject of female battery and abuse. She informed me early on in our relationship that if I ever belted her, I'd meet with an abrupt end. Something about an icepick thrust through my eye socket into my braincase while I slept. I would never belt her, but I didn't doubt she'd do that if I ever did.

"Pardon us, but could we meet him? You probably hate people asking."

"No, it's okay. This is Jellyroll."

Two women of about forty sat down on the rock

across from Crystal and me. Jellyroll went to be petted, as was the routine. He smiled and wagged his tail as they fondled and rubbed him, making the usual sounds.

The woman who'd asked to meet him was stocky and muscular. She wore a halter top, an unbuttoned denim shirt over it, Bermuda shorts, and clogs. She might have been the star sculler in her day on the Vassar four. "Would you like some lemonade?" she asked.

Sure we would, and she withdrew a plaid thermos from the wicker picnic basket hanging on her arm. "I'm Eunice and this is Lois. We live over on the east end. We heard the R-r-ruff Dog was staying at the boathouse, and we couldn't resist." She had an endearing toothy smile.

The lemonade was homemade.

Lois was birdlike, light, angular. Who was she? I knew her face from somewhere. I remembered the long fingers with which, one hand at a time, she constantly touched her face as if she weren't certain that it was firmly rooted and wouldn't go careening off into the audience. She wore a bulky knit wool sweater with a high shawl collar much too warm for the weather. I wondered if she were ill, and that's when I recognized her. I tried not to stare, but I'd definitely seen her before—

"Lois Lane?" I said.

"Yep, that was me. Way back when."

"I thought you were brilliant." She performed these wild theatrical pieces back in the late seventies, and I saw two early ones in Brooklyn. Both were on the same subject—a young woman's relationship to her schizo-

145

phrenia. She addressed it, her disease, as if it were another figure on stage, called it Carl. As she did so, she broke up Saltine crackers without remarking on the fact and dropped them on the stage until it was completely covered with crackers. Each step she took crunched.

"Do you live here year round?" Crystal asked.

"We have for the last two years," said Eunice.

"I went insane," said Lois matter-of-factly. "Eunice is hiding me out here."

"We were having breakfast on the porch at the Cod End when that poor woman was murdered," Eunice said.

"You saw her?" asked Crystal.

"When someone opened the door, there she was, sitting against the sink." They both nodded silently. "Brains actually are gray. I always thought that was just a figure of speech, gray matter. Hers were, anyhow," Lois said.

The sportfisherman had turned around and was now heading back out the Crack. I nodded at it. "Have you ever seen those guys before?"

"We saw them in Micmac the other day," said Eunice. "Hard to miss on that big fancy boat. Lois thinks that's Dick Desmond."

"It *is* Dick Desmond."

"What do you think?" Eunice asked Crystal.

"I never heard of Dick Desmond."

I thought I remembered the name, an actor—

"The *Ten Pins,*" said Lois. "Remember that show?"

A chill went through me. The *Ten Pins*— It was a TV series, a naked rip-off of *The Waltons,* but cutesier,

full of cheap sentiment. Instead of a farm, the family
owned a bowling alley!

"Pins? Like *bowling* pins?" asked Crystal.

"Sure, bowling," said Lois. "He was a star for a minute or two back then. I saw him close up in Micmac.
I'm certain it's him."

"Did you talk to him?" I asked.

They shook their heads.

"The other guy is his son," I said.

"Really?" asked Lois. "He looked about fifty to me."

"You saw him without the camera?"

"Briefly."

"Yeah, but that's not Dick Desmond," insisted
Eunice.

"I'll bet you a hundred dollars."

"You're crazy."

"What's that got to do with it?"

"Hey, look—" said Eunice, nodding toward the crane
and nearly whispering. "There's Roxy. That's quite a
rare sighting, Roxanne Self in the flesh. She's nearly
a hermit."

"Why?" Crystal asked.

"Nobody really knows, but some people think because she's atoning for the murder of Compton
Kempshall."

"I met Hawley Self, and he told me he killed
Kempshall."

They nodded. Hawley apparently told everyone
that.

"They never found the old man's body," said Lois.

"No," said Eunice. "In fact, some people say he
planned his own disappearance. He was about to be
indicted for selling defective stuff to the navy during

World War Two. There's no reason to believe Roxanne killed him, or that there ever was a murder."

"That's her husband over there, a tough old bird named Arno Self. His family's been here since before this was a country."

I briefly put the binoculars on Arno Self. He was an old salt with a big gray beard. He was watching Roxanne talk to Edith Hickle.

The crane whirred, the cable came taut on the sub and twittered vertically. The cables and rock anchors counterbalancing the submarine creaked and strained. You could *see* the strain in the cables. But nothing moved. That would be a crashing anticlimax. No, it was lifting the sub. The railroad-tie rack moved first, then the sub itself visibly rose but only slightly at first. The crane whirred louder, and then the sub rose off the rack. People applauded nervously. Edith looked tense. I'd look tense, too, sitting under all those desperately straining cables. She hunched her shoulders, but that would have done her no good had one of them snapped. I'd read in books about that happening on ships. The cable snaps back with force enough to cut a man in half. We all hunched our shoulders for Edith. Roxanne Self stood near the crane and watched the proceedings sourly.

Then the sub eased away from the cliff and out over the water. Nothing snapped. Hickle's island engineering had held. When Edith stopped the outward movement, the suspended sub swung gently back and forth and began to pivot slowly. As it came around, sunlight glinted cheerfully off the bubble canopy. Hickle was crouched inside, but he was clearly unhappy about something.

I looked with my binoculars. Joystick in hand, the bony, nearly naked old commander crouched on a bicycle seat, his face twisted with hostility, screaming silently at Edith over the earphones. The cords in his neck were yanked as tight as the cable that supported him. He repeatedly pounded his knee with his fist. Up on the crane seat, risking decapitation, Edith nodded regularly, calmly. The sub's bubble nose pivoted slowly away from us.

Then the sub started down at a controlled rate. We all applauded—there weren't that many of us. But again we applauded as concentric rings rolled out languidly when the bottom of the sub touched the water. Was that the actual moment of launching, I wondered?

The sub never actually paused to float on its own, but we figured that was probably in the nature of submarine launchings. Undramatically, it went right under. We hustled toward the edge to see. It looked like some extinct benthic giant as it submerged, as it broke apart into orange slivers and finally disappeared completely.

Now what? How long does a sub need to stay down to be considered launched? One wondered about the protocol of submarine launchings. As far as we knew, the commander could stay down for days. Edith gave no hint. She was leaning over the edge of the crane listening to Roxanne, who was tapping the palm of her hand with the back of her other hand, making serious points. After a while, Edith shook her head no, sat up straight behind her levers, and folded her arms.

I'm not certain how much time passed before the

crane whirred again, long enough for the spectators to straggle back to the places they had occupied before the launching. We all looked toward Edith, who was taking up the slack in the cable, which when it came taut transferred its load back to the crane, the scaffold, and the cables anchored into the rock. They creaked and cracked. Edith cringed, but again Hickle's engineering held fast. The sub was surfacing.

We gathered again at the cliff side to watch the orange flecks dance abstractly, then leap together into a vague sub shape—but something was wrong. The sub was surfacing tail first. A murmur ran through the spectators. We shifted closer to the edge as the tail fins broke the surface.

The sub had been launched suspended from its balance point, but now that point had changed. Now the sub was nose-heavy. What would change the balance point of a sub after submerging? There was only one answer to that, clear even to us low-tech lubbers. The sub broke free of the water entirely, and it didn't stop until it came almost level with the top of the Crack. And there it hung, cascades of water pouring, pivoting torpidly around its new balance point.

At first we were silent. Immediate realization was unavailable to us. We saw it, our jaws gaped, we reached for each other's arms, but it took a while to realize that the sub had suffered the most fundamental of submarine breakdowns. It had leaked. Bad.

The big bubble nose was filled with water, and Commander Hickle sloshed around inside like a dead guppy. He floated upside down, arms and legs akimbo like a skydiver, fingers splayed. His eyes were bugged, bloodshot, slightly crossed, and his lips were pursed in a cruel parody of a fish. He'd probably died sucking the last draft from the exhausted air trapped at the top of the bubble. I could almost hear that fatal, futile sucking.

15

"D o you think Edith did it?" Crystal asked me in the boat on the way home.

The notion had flitted across my mind, but so does a lot of baseless stuff. "You mean intentionally?"

"Sabotage."

"Do you?"

"Well, she had a funny look on her face as he was sloshing around in there. She didn't look surprised. I don't know these people, of course, and maybe she was in shock, but she didn't look surprised."

I gave that some thought. . . . Two dead in three days. New York pace. I supposed Sheriff Kelso would investigate, but he probably didn't know submarines, couldn't tell if this one had been sabotaged or not. "Didn't you feel a little sorry for him floating around in there spread-eagled in his Speedo?"

"Sure, but I feel sorry for Edith, too."

It seemed odd that Edith would endure a decade of shit from him, if that was the case, while he built the damn thing, then drown him in it on the day it was launched, at the very climax, didn't it? On the other hand, maybe the timing was all the more reason to suspect Edith; but the truth of the matter no doubt was that Commander Hickle was a crank and a shitty submarine builder.

"Tell me more about Clayton's father," Crystal said.

I didn't want to become enmeshed in local legend.

"So what does everybody think? That he took a powder?"

"I love it when you talk like that." But it was no use. Crystal was interested. When she gets interested in a thing, she seldom lets go of it.

"Do we know for sure that he wasn't burned up in the fire?"

"They had experts in. I guess it's hard to burn up all traces of a human body."

After a time, we stopped talking about Kempshall and put our arms around each other. She laid her head over on my shoulder. Jellyroll looked back at us from the bow. He was smiling contentedly. This is what I wanted. Was it wrong to want contentment and safety, or just unrealistic?

Suddenly he began to retch. The whole routine: the full-body heaving, the hideous yawn, veined lips curled inside out at the moment of expulsion. Crystal had seen it before. She knew to avert her eyes when the climax came.

There was a man in a dark suit sitting on our porch. He heard us turn around the rocky point at the mouth of the cove, and he stood up, waved. I slowed down and put the binoculars on him. Crystal took the wheel. He was burly and barrel-chested. I really didn't expect to find the stalker waiting on our porch in a suit. It shouldn't happen like that. But psychos are not predictable. His light hair was chopped militarily close, his suit blue and crumpled. He had loosened his styleless tie and unbuttoned the collar of his white shirt. He looked like the kind of guy who'd bite your ear off.

"Shelly's brother-in-law?" said Crystal.

Our detective? He looked more like a detective than Shelly's brother-in-law. "Do you think we should go on in?"

"What does he look like through the binoculars?"

I handed them to her. She focused. "Tough," she said.

He took something out of a briefcase at his feet. I couldn't see what because the picnic table was in the way. He was writing something. He finished and held up the *Cabot County Swapper,* the local want ads. Across the center fold, he'd penned: SHELLY SENT ME.

I had a little trouble docking the boat against the flat rock this time. While I was back and forthing, Shelly's brother-in-law grabbed the side of the boat and pulled us in. His wrists were as thick as my ankles.

"I'm Sid Detweiler," he said. "I thought it was time we met. So I came out. It's more remote than I thought."

I could see then that he had been a New York cop, just as Shelly had said. Though they're of all races and both sexes, New York cops share an aspect, a certain seen-it-all look in their eyes. Maybe they teach it in cop school. It says, I'm a cop, and you're not, you're a crime waiting to happen. Even the little cops look the look, but in a big man it's viscerally intimidating. NYPD's aspect and attitude are probably not best for the commonweal, but on your side they can be comforting. Sid was comforting. I introduced him to Crystal.

"I saw you play about a year ago, Ms. Spivey, at Amsterdam Billiards. You beat Jimmie Renzi."

"Call me Crystal." Crystal was brilliant that night. She beat Renzi for high stakes on pure heart. He was the better player, but Crystal safed him to distraction, then ran balls whenever she had a chance.

"And this is the dog himself. God, he's cute, all right." Sid went down to Jellyroll's level, and they nuzzled. I noticed a faint scar on his cheek that pulled the corner of his mouth downward, making him look sad from that perspective.

But I wondered why he was here. Wouldn't his time be better spent tracing the stalkers? Unless—he'd traced the stalkers here. . . . I put the question to Sid Detweiler.

"No. At least not that I know of. Why? Do you think they're here?"

"Not necessarily. Coffee?"

We walked up on the porch, and I went in to brew some coffee, while Crystal told Sid about the launching. After I put the water on, I went back out on the porch in time to hear Detweiler say, "Did she do it?"

After I'd brought the coffee and distributed utensils, Sid said, "I want us to call Shelly right now to verify I am who I say I am. Do you believe I'm Sid Detweiler?"

Crystal said she did.

"Don't," Sid said. "I'm a stranger. I came up here by seaplane. That was Shelly's idea, a good one. It's at our

service on the mainland, if we need it. I've been looking around from the air a little bit. It's remote as hell.
I thought it was gonna be like a small town, but it ain't.
It's damn near wilderness. This is all good, unless you
think one of the locals is the stalker. Do you?"

"No. Many of the locals have never even heard of Jellyroll." Where was he, by the way? He'd left the porch to
chase the chipmunk around the woodpile. At least that's
what I'd assumed. . . . I called him. He came around and
looked up at me, What did I want that was so important?
"Good dog," I said.

"So we can isolate the strangers. That's what's good
about being here as opposed to NYC, where most everybody on the street's a stranger. Here strangers stand
right out, you don't confuse them with the locals, and
that's good." He dialed Shelly on his own cellular
phone, which he took from his beat-up leather briefcase. I saw inside as he did so. There was a black handgun in there. "Shel, it's me. Yeah, how's it going? I'm
here. Yeah. Shelly, you recognize my voice, don't you?
Security, that's why. Tell Mr. Deemer—"

I liked this guy Sid. I was glad he'd come. If we
couldn't have Calabash by our side, Sid would do. He
handed me the phone.

"Hello, Shelly. Anything up?"

"Did Sid tell you?"

"Tell me what? Did you get another bowling sheet?"

"No. Hype. The stalker story, Artie, it's out. Nobody
knows who got it first or how, but now it's common
knowledge. The tabloid-TV idiots, they're hysterical.
It's not just that smarmy figure skater. I don't know
how it got out, but it's out. I got networks calling about
movies of the week, already!"

That's the part that had always frightened me most. Maybe there never was a real stalker; maybe the asshole that sent the bowling sheets was a harmless crank. But now there would have to be a stalker. In America publicity is powerful incentive to kill.

"*Celebrity Sleuth* called me," Shelly said. "They offered ten grand for the stalker's phone number. They said we could keep the ten grand even if they didn't get the stalker at that number."

That caused spider-foot chills to run up my spine. "Shelly, what do you know about Dick Desmond?"

"Who? Dick Desmond? Dick Des— Oh yeah, it's coming back to me. He was a tiny talent, a mediocrity, tall, blond hair, had a series— Aw, shit, Artie, the series was about bowling!"

"*Ten Pins.*"

"Yes! Bowling! Is it him? Is he the stalker?"

"He's here. At least he might be here." I told him about my encounters with Dick Desmond.

Shelly waited for more.

"That's it, Shelly."

"Tell me again."

I did. I told him about the encounter out by the Disappointments, in the marine supply store, and in the Crack when Lois Lane had insisted the boatman was Dick Desmond.

"Wait a minute, this isn't Lois Lane, the weirdo?"

"She's not a weirdo. She's a brilliant performer." But it was no use arguing with Shelly about taste.

"She may be a brilliant performer, but she's still a weirdo. The part I don't like about Dick Desmond, besides the bowling connection, is the kid taking video of you and Jellyroll."

I didn't like that part, either. What good does it do if you kill the cutest dog in the world if nobody knows you do it? There has to be video. "Shelly, do they know where we are, the media?"

"I don't think so, Artie. I think they'd be there if they did. How's Crystal?"

"Fine."

"Give her a hug for me. Look, I'm telling everybody, What the fuck is the fuss? There is no stalker, you're in New Zealand to help with kangaroo conversation. I'll call in an hour."

"Shelly, there are no kangaroos in New Zealand."

"They don't know that, the ignorant geeks."

I returned the phone to Sid, who said, "Okay, tell me all about this Dick Desmond character," and I repeated what I'd just said. "That's it?" he said.

"Artie," said Crystal, "what about the timing?"

"What timing?"

"You saw them out in the water the day after you arrived, right? That was yesterday, right?"

"Yes."

"Then they couldn't have followed you here," Crystal pointed out. "If Desmond and the kid with the video camera are the stalkers, they had to know you were coming here before you got here."

I thought about that.

But Sid wasn't ready to jump to conclusions yet. He opened his briefcase and removed an Oglevie flight schedule. "What time did you arrive at the airport?"

"About nine," I said.

He ran a stubby finger down a column. "There were no incoming flights after that. . . . This Desmond is a stranger to you? Your paths have never crossed in show business? Who knew about the threatening bowling sheets besides the three of us and Shelly?"

"Clayton Kempshall. He owns this place."

"Who else?"

"Nobody else," I said.

He looked to Crystal, and she shook her head. "Have you spoken to Clayton Kempshall since you've been here?"

"No. He said he was going to Los Angeles. I've left messages for him."

"Where?"

"In New York and L.A."

He nodded as he jotted something in his notebook. "Is Clayton Kempshall a special friend?"

"No, in fact, we don't know him very well."

He glanced at me, then jotted some more. "The point about strangers is still true. They're gonna stand out, and that's good. The problem is the Jesus people. They're *all* strangers, and what with the murder, there's a press presence, but that seems limited to the mainland. The islands seem to be another world altogether." He consulted his notebook. "You mentioned that Dick Desmond and his son were on a boat. Did you happen to notice the name of this boat?"

"Seastar. From Boston."

He wrote that down. "How old would you say Desmond's son is?"

I told him I really couldn't tell because of the camcorder in front of his face.

Dwight's boat came around the point.

"Here comes my ride. I like this guy. You told him about the stalker, and he's looking out for you. This is a straight-ahead guy. You can depend on guys like him. Oh, coincidence. Turns out I know the local law. He retired from the force about the same time I did. This is all good. Don't you worry. The stalker always has the element of surprise on his side, but he's going to be fish out of water up here. He'll stand out like shit in the shower. Well, excuse me, but you know what I mean. This is all good."

As we went downstairs, Crystal asked Sid what he was going to do now. Sid said he wanted to talk to Sheriff Kelso in person, and he might try to trace *Seastar,* because then "at least we'd know if this guy really was Dick Desmond. Oh, I almost forgot. Step around here, please." He led us behind the house near Jellyroll's woodpile.

Sid pulled the black handgun from his briefcase. But it wasn't a handgun. My dog danced with joy as if to share his chipmunk game with us. It was a shotgun sawed off short enough to fit in a briefcase. Heartless and black, it had a pistol grip and a single purpose. "I don't think you'll need it or anything, but I want you to have this. Just cock it, point, and shoot. Accuracy is not an issue. Thirteen-year-old pulled this on the IRT. And here's a box of shells."

I didn't believe that Sid had forgotten about the gun. I think he meant to size us up before he gave it to us. What did that say about Crystal and me? That we were responsible adults capable of bloody slaughter at short range?

"Are you being well paid, Sid?"

"Shelly's taking good care of me."

I put the gun inside the back door, and we went to say hello to Dwight.

"Well," he said, "we got the sub drained out and back on its stand. And we got the Commander out of there."

"How's Edith?" Crystal asked.

"I don't exactly know. She went off with Roxanne
Self. Frankly, it wasn't a thing she should've seen, getting him out of there."

"Crystal," I said after we'd eaten dinner and drunk
a glass of the wine Crystal had brought, "What would
you think if I murdered them? In cold blood. Say it
was Dick Desmond, or say it was anybody. Say we
knew they meant to harm Jellyroll, but they hadn't
done anything yet. Those are the circumstances."

"Okay."

"Then say I killed them both."

"Before they actually did anything you killed them?"

"Right. Not in a passion of dog defense, but in a
calculated, premeditative way, covering my tracks so I
wouldn't get caught."

"You'd have to dispose of their bodies."

"That's right, I would. I could put the bodies in the
boat, tie rocks around their necks, and drop them in a
hundred feet of water. Bodies never come up around
here."

"They don't?"

"No."

"Why?"

"The water's too cold for gasses to form?"

"What gasses?"

"The gasses of decomposition."

"Oh . . . so are you planning to kill them, or is this
hypothetical?"

"I don't know. I was just thinking about what murder
would do to our relationship."

16

*T*here were no strangers to shoot at next morning, so I left the cannon under the bed and joined Crystal on the porch. She was sitting on the railing still in her nightgown.

"Look at the colors," she said about Dog Cove. "They're so bright they sting my eyes. I like it here, Artie, but then I'm trying to run away, too."

"From what?"

"I dreamed last night that I was playing Gracie Cobb on ESPN. Gracie was wearing a tux, but I was naked except for a pair of tennis shoes. When I leaned down to shoot, people made remarks about my ass."

"Aww." I sat beside her, put my arm around her shoulders. "That's awful."

"Would you mind if I lived off Jellyroll for a while, I mean if it came to that?"

"No, I wouldn't. Do you mean you're quitting?"

"Thinking about it. I've been playing bad for six months. But I wouldn't really live off Jellyroll."

"No, that would be immoral. I could probably exploit some connections and get you a job loading concrete blocks over in Jersey. Come on, it's just a bad time. You've got the talent. You'll come back." But I knew what she was fearing. Her mind wasn't right just now, and maybe it never would be. If so, I hoped it wouldn't be because she lived with me.

"Look!" She pointed over my head toward the coastal hill at Jellyroll.

He was sprinting full tilt up the trail on the heels of the pack. We didn't exactly see whole dogs, just parts, a swish of tail, rustling ferns and bushes, a flash of fur. They must have skulked silently down here to pick him up—

"Jellyroll, you stop! Bad!"

But he didn't. He chose the pack, the wild. They sprinted together up the trail, barking and baying, taking themselves very seriously, like predators on the tundra with survival at stake. I'll admit that hurt my feelings a little.

"Wow," said Crystal. "Has he ever done that before?"

"Never."

"I'll go get some clothes on, we can go after him."

"We'll never catch him if he doesn't want to be caught."

"I know."

Nevertheless, we hustled up the trail. In places it grew too steep to walk upright without a handhold, in others it turned rocky and precarious, threatened to dump us over the edge. We didn't have the shoes for this kind of going, but the view was exquisite. We looked back on the boathouse nestled so sweetly in the crotch of the cove. We saw two ospreys circling at eye level. Looking the other way, we could see the Dogs. Out on the ocean, a brisk wind seemed to be kicking up whitecaps. The air was as clear as any air I'd ever breathed. My eyes, like Crystal's, stung with the unaccustomed transparency of it.

All during the hike, we heard the dogs whooping and laughing in the distance. Maybe he was now a feral thing. An island dog. Maybe Jellyroll'd never mind me again. We'd eye each other nervously across the gulf of natural selection. Then the sound stopped abruptly.

We hurried on. We got close enough to see the underbrush moving, but we couldn't see any actual dogs until we climbed a steep, rocky stretch, rounded a bend, and came upon a swirling mass of them, undifferentiated, tails flashing, nails skittering on a bald dome of granite rock in a little clearing. Jellyroll was in the thick of it, eyes wide with pack energy. When they saw us, the other dogs bolted, and Jellyroll made to go with them—

"You stay!"

He did, and I was relieved. I wasn't sure he would. But he wouldn't look around at me.

"Hi, Jellyroll," said Crystal, but he still didn't turn around.

His back was hunched, his head and tail lowered. That posture meant only one thing. He had something in his mouth. Jellyroll is an eater. I've taken hideous things out of his craw in the park, on the street, at the beach, things I wouldn't even want to mention. Chicken bones, petrified pizza crusts, things like that are typical fare. Without constant vigilance, he'll ingest anything that isn't a mineral. And since he has that weak stomach, his scavenging results in unspeakable expulsions.

"What's he got?" Crystal wondered.

He still didn't turn around. I approached him. "You better stay," I said in my serious dog handler voice. "Crystal, watch the look I get: *Drop.*" He dropped, the thing clattered, and then slowly he looked back at me with a smoldering stink eye.

"Oh, nasty," she giggled.

Clattered? What had clattered? He stood over the thing motionlessly, guarding it like a hyena. A deer femur, I decided. That would clatter when dropped. Jellyroll doesn't find many dead deer in Riverside Park. He would love a good femur. Or it could be that other part of the mammalian leg bone? What was that part called? But wait a minute, hadn't Dwight told me that there were no deer on Kempshall Island?

Crystal saw it first. She gasped urgently. Crystal had one hand slapped across her mouth, the other pointed at the thing. "A hand," she said in a tense, even voice.

We bent from the waist, heads together, watching it. That's what it was, all right. A hand. The hand was barely attached by dried, black gristle to an arm bone. We stood over it timidly, as if it would leap at our throats like the hand of the Mummy. Okay, what were the rational possibilities here, if we dismissed the Mummy? That this was an ancient Indian burial ground, and the dogs, or something, had disturbed it. This region was probably alive with Native American burial sites—

Birch tree trunks creaked together overhead, but no cooling breeze made it down to us on the granite dome. I knelt beside the arm. Crystal squatted on her haunches. We peered at the bones. They did not look like those on a stand in my chiropractor's office. These bones were not white and they were not clean. They were brown like roots or things of the earth. Dust-to-dust things. They looked like the bones you see exhumed on ITN reports about death-squad massacres. The flesh was not entirely gone, but the desiccated leathery patches clinging to the bone had nothing to do with living flesh. On some spots, as between the first and second knuckles, hair still clung to the flesh.

"Do you want to look for the rest of him? Or do you not want to look for the rest of him?" Crystal asked.

"I guess it's that simple."

"I don't see how we can not look, do you?"

"Yes."

The arm lay at the outer slope of the shallow dome, which was about half the size of a tennis court. Crystal went one way around, I went the other. I didn't want to find him. Why was I searching?

Cracks and fissures ran through the rock. Probably about four hundred million years ago it was molten matter pressing upward at the cooler crust of the earth. This is where it came to rest, at least as far as human time is concerned. Trees blotted out our view of all but the sky directly above. While I circled, Jellyroll guarded his find, still hoping I'd change my mind. There were dog tracks around the edges of the dome where boulders and pine needles gave way to brown dirt, the same color brown as the arm and hand bones.

I had done half a lap when I saw the next piece of him. A foot and shinbone, including knee, stuck up from a crack between two big boulders. There was a sickly comic quality about the way it stuck up like that, as if its owner, sensing mortality, had tried to hide by ostriching himself down the hole. Part of a sock was still visible around the ankle. Had the dogs done this, spread him out like this?

"Artie," called Crystal in a fading voice, "over here." She was ninety degrees away from me. "I found some more of him. Christ."

I went to her.

The pelvis lay flat in the dirt. His thighbones spread out from it at obscene angles. His spine lay visible, curled like a snake under a delicate fern leaf. The cushioning material between the vertebrae had turned black.

"I think I've seen enough. How about you?"

"Me too—" Then she gave out with a high whine of a sound that ran down my spine like icy rain, the kind of sound one might make as a sharp, thin blade penetrated one's belly. She pointed at the guy's skull.

He was staring at the sky, and we were looking up into his braincase from under his chin, through the arch of his lower jaw, which wasn't there. I was soaked with sweat. I touched Crystal's back as we moved three steps toward the thing. Her shirt was plastered to her spine. Sweat was a sign of life here in the leafy charnel house. Her shoulders were hunched, and she grasped her cheeks with both hands.

The skull was lying on brown earth at the edge of a small cave. It was the same kind of cave I'd seen on the other hill, where the granite was wildcat, as Dwight had called it. Five vertebrae trailed the skull, but they were nearly buried in the dirt.

"You don't think this is some kind of practical joke on the city slickers, do you?" asked Crystal quietly.

"No."

"I don't either."

We stepped closer. . . .

"Aw, Jesus, Artie, he's been murdered!"

"Yeah," I mouthed dryly.

You didn't need to be a pathologist to know that this guy didn't die of old age. His skull was split from the top of the crown to the bridge of the nose. Earth nearly filled the brain cavity. Cracks spiderwebbed out from the ragged edge. Had he seen the blow coming and screamed in terror? Had it hurt? There were dog tracks all around in the soft brown dirt of the forest floor. Crystal and I leaned over and peered down at his hollow eye sockets as though he had something to impart to us, but he was eloquently silent.

I suddenly felt like an intruder, but it wasn't our fault. This rude intimacy had been forced on us. We didn't want it. Dogs will be dogs. I felt like apologizing to the poor soul for seeing him that ultimately naked. But at the same time something else was bothering me—

Why now? If this person had been dead long enough to decompose this thoroughly, why only now were the dogs finding his bones? Or could it be that they had dug him out of his wildcat crypt generations ago, and they took visitors to see their bones like the siblings in *To Kill a Mockingbird* take the new boy to see Boo Radley's house? That was probably it. Dogs dug the poor bastard up ages ago. . . . If so, wouldn't some person have found them by now?

"Artie, do you think it's Kempshall?"

I envisioned calling Clayton: "We sure enjoy your place, met your dad."

"Artie—?"

"Hmmm?"

"I think I'd like to get out of here right now."

"Sounds good to me."

"I feel like we're being watched."

"You do? You mean figuratively?"

"No, I mean literally."

I circled in place. I didn't see anything except trees and sky. And bones.

"It's probably just a feeling, though," she said stiffly. "I'm sure we're not *really* being watched."

"Naa, who'd be watching us?"

I slapped my thigh. Hard. Jellyroll appeared at it. I looked down at him, he up at me. He was looking a little edgy himself. His ears were flat against his skull. His upper lip stuck to a canine. The three of us started backing toward the trail down the hill.

"I still feel it—" said Crystal.

We went slowly at first, but with quickening pace. Soon we were hotfooting it down that path. We didn't exactly run, but we didn't slow down until the trail leveled out along the shore. It felt better to have the water nearby. Without trying, I could smell myself, the stink of mortal fear. Jellyroll walked at my ankles, peering up into my face. He doesn't have much feeling for human remains, but he knows when I'm shook. It undermines his faith in the order of things. Sometimes I find the responsibility burdensome.

"I'm sorry," said Crystal.

"What? Why?"

"For scaring us. I just felt creepy."

"Understandable."

"Does anybody ever swim here?"

"Walrus, maybe."

Unseen birds twittered sweetly. They didn't give a shit about human business.

"I want to."

"I think people die of exposure in that water, Crystal."

"I want that feeling off of me." She stripped off her shirt. Leaning against a white pine tree trunk, she removed her jeans. In a pair of powder-blue panties alone, she padded down to the rocks. I looked both ways. There were no boats except ours at anchor in the bay. She covered her breasts with her forearms as if that would protect them from the searing cold, and in she went. It took her breath away. Watching her it took mine, too.

She gasped and hissed and screamed all at once. I wanted her suddenly, deeply, but I wasn't willing to enter that water. She swam a few strokes out into the cove. Then she turned and raced ashore. I met her on the rocks with her shirt. I rubbed her body with it as she gasped in my arms. I wanted to make love, and further, I thought it was important that we do so. Even before we called the police.

I mentioned that to Crystal as we hustled toward the house.

It sounded good to her, she said.

17

*T*he skull was gone. The spine was gone, and so were the ribs. There was no pelvis, no arm or leg bones. Even the dog tracks were gone. There was no sign that bones or dogs—or Crystal and I—had ever been anywhere near this particular location.

Sweaty and dirty, Cabot County Sheriff Theodore Kelso climbed out of the ex-crypt. Almost three hours had passed since our last trip up here. It had taken that long to get the message to Kelso and for him to come to Kempshall Island. Crystal, who had made the call, did not mention the bones on the telephone. We didn't say a word about bones until Kelso arrived in person. But now the bones were gone without a trace. Someone had obviously been here in the last three hours. The killer? And whose bones were they? And did Kelso think we were bullshitting him?

He leaned his ass against a fallen tree trunk, wiped his face with a white handkerchief, sighed. His uniform was informal. The khaki shirt had epaulets on the shoulders and flaps over the pockets. That was about it for uniform, except for the silver badge over his heart. He sighed again, looked skyward as if for guidance. Or patience.

Crystal and I stood around waiting for him to decide something. I admit I have a problem with authority. Crystal has an open and trusting nature, so she has no problem with authority. I tend to assume those in authority are all Nazis.

"I heard from your friend Detweiler," said Kelso, neither here nor there. "He left me a professional courtesy message. He said he was working on a matter for you. 'Matter,' that's what he called it. What would be the nature of that matter?"

I told him that someone was stalking my dog, or more precisely that someone had claimed to be stalking my dog.

He peered at me. "A nut?"

"I guess so."

Then he peered at Crystal. She peered right back at him. "You mean to say you're hiding out here?"

"Sort of, yes."

He didn't like that idea, you could tell. Maybe I wouldn't like it either if I were him and some outlander brought psycho bait into my community. Besides, he had a vicious and very public human killing in Micmac to deal with. "Do you and Sid Detweiler know the stalker's identity?"

"No. We've been getting anonymous letters."

"Did you actually see the dogs spread the skeleton around?"

We said no.

Kelso pushed absently at a flat stone with his toe. "I

172

wouldn't like it if you and Sid Detweiler took measures against the stalker, should one show up here."

I said I understood.

"I wouldn't like it if you were luring him out here."

"What? Luring? Absolutely not. Is that what you think?"

"I don't know. You tell me what I should think." He looked to Crystal.

"We're here for the solitude," said Crystal. "Luring crazy people is the last thing we want to do."

"So then if you identify the stalker, what are you going to do?"

"Call you," I said right on cue.

"I knew Sid Detweiler in New York. Well, by reputation. He solved the Ramirez case. Family of twelve shot to death execution style, including two infants. 1985. He solved it singlehanded."

I was sorry we didn't remember the Ramirez case. Seemed families were being murdered execution style every couple of weeks back during the Reagan years.

Kelso pushed himself away from the log and unpacked his Polaroid after rummaging for it in his nylon duffel bag. He asked us to point to the precise spots where we'd found the bones. We did, and he photographed each one. Then he labeled the photos on the back: "Arm and hand," "leg w/foot," "pelvis w/upper legs," and so forth. I couldn't see how the photographs would be of any use.

We stood around waiting as he worked. I was ready to get out of that place before it tainted my view of the whole island. I liked the rest of the island. I wanted to stay a while and have nice sex without old corpses turning up.

"Well, I guess you've heard about the night the Castle burned and Kempshall disappeared."

We said we had.

"Yeah, you got to be in Cabot County at least fifteen minutes before you hear about that." Kelso's jowls hung, his trunk was thickening, but he was the same kind of urban hardass as his retired colleague Sid. "Tell me about the condition of the skull one more time."

Crystal told him this time.

He took notes. "What sort of object would you say might cause a wound like that? Obviously, you can't make an informed judgment, and I'm not expecting one. I'd just like to hear your opinion. Like an ax?"

We nodded, looked at each other. "Or a hatchet," Crystal said. "Or a meat cleaver."

"Or a sword?"

Crystal agreed. "A machete, maybe."

It was the same general kind of weapon as killed that woman in the rest room at the Cod End. I'll bet that's what he was thinking, but he didn't say anything. "Are you close friends of Clayton Kempshall's?" he asked instead.

I said no, we were more casual friends, business friends.

"Would you have a number where he can be reached?"

I had numbers. "He's in California."

"Are you going to tell him?" Crystal asked.

"I'm not sure," said the sheriff. "Depends on how this plays out. He closed his notebook, paused. "I guess you see my problem. There still ain't any remains. It's tough to investigate a murder without remains." But it wasn't that cut and dried for him. He was troubled by something.

"So what'll happen, Sheriff?" Crystal asked.

"Things are different here in Cabot County. In New York, there'd be supervisors and procedures. Things are different here in ways I couldn't even imagine before I spent a couple winters. One of the ways things are different here is that what *I* think matters. By the way, Ms. Spivey, the wife and I are big fans of yours."

"You are?"

"We installed a Brunswick Gold Crown in the basement a couple of years ago. Oh, we're not good players or anything, but we enjoy the game. The wife just taped you on ESPN last month against Norma Jean Garth."

Crystal moaned. "I was awful."

"Well, you got a couple bad rolls. There's of course nothing to say you found old Kempshall's bones. Nothing to say he's even dead. Now I could make a big thing of it, shake the trees, I might come up with something, but I'm not going to do that. This is on the assumption that we don't ever see the bones again. A skeleton with its skull split open, you got to think homicide. I'd have to take steps, but not without the actual bones. However, there's something you ought to know. Most of the people from around here already know about your find."

"They do? How?"

"How could they?" said Crystal.

"I don't know how. But I know from experience it's true. I'm from away. My wife grew up here, but not out here in the islands. It's different in the islands. Maybe you hear the rocks talk if you were born here, the waves tell you everything, I don't know."

"This just applies to people who live here?" asked Crystal.

"Yeah."

"Then we're talking abut the Selfs, aren't we?" I asked.

"Mainly, yes," said Kelso.

"How about a cup of coffee, Sheriff?" I offered, ready to get off that hill.

"Sounds good," Kelso said. "Incidently, I'm deputy sheriff. But I'm the law here."

The day was still exquisite, the air pure and undamaged. Birds sang. Small animals, much to Jellyroll's delight, scurried and scratched in the brush as we passed. What did nature need with people?

I brewed up a pot of Zabar's extra good, and we sat at the picnic table drinking it. Kelso seemed distracted, even morose, and I thought he was thinking about the bones up on the hill, but he wasn't. We sipped in silence for a while, then he said, "In New York when something really savage happened, well, like the Ramirez case, I began to think it changed people for the worse. Not just the people directly involved or the dead people, but everybody in the whole city. At first I thought it was just us cops it changed, because we're the guys who pick up the shit. But I think everybody changed because of the killing. Now this killing in Micmac—it's going to change people."

We sat in silence and watched the harmony of Dog Cove.

Then Crystal said, "Why now?"

"I beg your pardon."

"Why did the dogs only now find the bones?"

His beeper went off.

"Do you need a phone?" I asked.

"You brought one?"

"Yes. Come on in." I showed him the phone, then went back out on the porch.

Crystal nodded toward the shore trail.

It was Dickie shambling along, pretending to be all loosey-goosey casual, looking around, as he headed our way. Jellyroll barked at him. Dickie walked to the foundation of the boathouse, stopped, looked up at us. Then like a Hollywood Indian he raised his right hand and said "How." Jellyroll poked his nose through the railing. And Dickie said "How" to him.

Crystal had that "asshole" look on her face.

Dickie said, "Say, I was having a chat with my employee Hawley Self. Hawley says you enjoyed our product, and you seem like a man who appreciates plain speaking, so I wondered if you'd be interested in purchasing—"

All along I'd been pointing to the boat plainly marked POLICE resting against the flat rock twenty feet over his right shoulder blade, but he didn't catch on.

Crystal could only shake her head.

"Wow!" exclaimed Dickie as it finally caught his eye. "Here? Shhh! Kelso's *here?* Now? What is this? Some kind of setup?" Dickie started backing away. He stumbled, spun, caught himself, and began to flee headlong.

Kelso stepped out on the porch. He said, "Thanks for the phone. If you'll excuse me, I'm going to shout at this fool. Dickie, *halt!*"

Dickie halted.

"You wait right there. I want a word with you." He turned around to Crystal and me. "This could prove to be a case of police brutality, so you better look the other way, could get real ugly. It's an interesting question you ask, Crystal. I've been asking myself that same question. It just doesn't seem reasonable that human remains have been laying around in the open all these years."

"So what do you think?" she asked. She was getting interested. I wished she wouldn't.

"You brought it up," said Kelso. "What do you think?"

"The only thing I can think of is that somebody was interrupted in the middle of digging them up."

"Interrupted by what?"

"Maybe by us coming up the trail, maybe by the dogs."

Kelso nodded thoughtfully. "These two idiots—Hawley and Dickie—think they can grow dope right under my eyes without me knowing about it. That's always pissed me off, even back in New York, they think I'm stupid as they are."

Dickie had gotten tired of standing and had sat on a rock. He chucked pebbles into the water like a little boy waiting for punishment after school.

"Crystal—" I said after Kelso had gone after Dickie, "remember I told you I met Hawley up the hill and he said he'd killed Compton Kempshall?"

"Sure."

"Did I mention that the weapon he used for the job was a hatchet?"

"No."

Late that night after Crystal had unpacked her things in the bedroom—I was in the living room listening to

Mingus's "No Private Income Blues," the 1959 scorcher, not missing the irony—she appeared in the bedroom doorway and said, "Look what I found."

Crystal was naked beneath the soft flannel shirt she slept in, and it was breezing open as she approached, distracting me from what she'd found.

"This was in the bottom drawer in a shoe box. The box was falling apart. Look how sad it is."

It was a tan teddy bear. The fur was ratty, bald in patches, faded in others. The sad thing about this teddy bear was that it had been ripped down the front, torn or cut from under its chin down to its crotch. Someone—a child?—had attempted to patch the wound by lacing it closed. But in places the shoelace had torn through the teddy bear's skin, and time-browned cotton stuffing protruded from its thoracic region.

"Aww," said Crystal. "Do you think it was Clayton's?"

18

"Artie—!" Crystal hissed. "Somebody's out there!"

I must have heard it in my sleep, before Crystal shook my shoulder, because I was dreaming about a screen door, white paint peeling, slap-slapping in a desiccating wind that blew across an arid, cactus landscape I'd never seen before. I snapped bolt upright, but the distinction between that dreamy desert and reality was still fuzzy.

Jellyroll was barking his alarm bark—

Was this a job for the shotgun? You didn't even have to aim to change the world. . . .

There was enough light to see Crystal pulling a shirt over her breasts. I saw, also, that her eyes were flashing, and that argued for hauling out the firepower. Unarmed, I followed Crystal to the front door. She peeked out one corner, I peeked out the other.

"It's me! It's Hawley!" He proved it by shining a powerful flashlight under his chin. His scarred face looked horror-movie hideous in that light. Rainwater puddled in the scar tissue. Rain? I didn't know it was raining, but it was. And it was windy—

I told Jellyroll to stop barking, and I opened the door. The wind yanked it out of my hands and slammed it against my bare toe. The pain paralyzed me. I waddled backward as Hawley entered.

He was bundled in black rubber boots, stiff yellow foul weather gear, and one of those *Captains Courageous* hats. Water still sluiced off it. He had to lean against the door to get it closed. The wind howled.

"The old man called on the radio. Comin' back from Micmac in the slop, his engine quit on him. Old man's needed a valve job since way last summer. I told him. Anyway, he got the hook down, but somehow got all twisted up in the rope and, pop, snapped his arm. So he had to cut the anchor away. He's driftin' for the Disappointments right now."

I didn't quite grasp the message here. What did he want from us? "Ah, did you call the Coast Guard? Do you want to use my phone?"

"I need to get a man aboard his boat to take a line."

"A man?" He couldn't be proposing that we go out there and get him near the Disappointments in the dark on a night like this? Nah. "You mean me?" My voice cracked a little. My toe throbbed. I tried vainly to dampen the throbbing with the instep of my other foot.

"Look, you don't have to. I just thought—"

". . . I don't have any experience."

"It's not too hard," he said.

"I'm going, too," said Crystal.

"Excuse me," I said to Hawley and turned to Crystal. "Jesus, I'd love to have you along. But please stay here

181

with Jellyroll. Can you picture him out there in that? I can't leave him alone under the circumstances. I'd never forgive myself—" He knew we were talking about him, deciding something. He listened, cocking his head from side to side.

"Okay," she said, but her grave look accelerated my dread. And the caring I saw in her eyes made me even less enthusiastic about the trip. What the hell was Hawley's old man to me? I'd never even met the geezer. Saw him through binoculars—that's not exactly intimacy. And besides, these old salts weren't supposed to get caught out in storms like a lubber from away.

And what about Hawley himself, for that matter? Hawley was no friend of mine. He was a mere acquaintance. I would probably go out there on a night like this for kith and/or kin, but to die for some old coot I didn't know in a place I might never return to, that was sheer stupidity. You'd have to be a chump, you'd have to be suffering from some delusion of indestructibility to go out there and *take lines,* whatever the hell that meant, anyway. Jesus. I'd just tell him, "Look, pal, I'm no seaman, I don't know from lines, I rent boats. Besides that, I'm in love, and I just don't want to drown my hapless ass right at this stage of my life—"

It wasn't as bad as I had feared—until we rounded the point. Until then, I had been inclined to consider the proud maritime heritage of these rockbound coasts, generations of stalwart sailors, stout lads, who met the sea in all its fury. Now I—from away—would join that band of brothers to rescue one of our own in peril on the deep. That was the kind of ignorant twaddle that crossed my mind—before we rounded the point.

Once around, thought became impossible. Thought

had no place out here. This sea was prethought. This was the primordial sea. Nothing had evolved from it as yet, no terrestrial life at all, certainly no thinkers.

The boat went over on her side when the wind hit us on the outside of the point. I couldn't even see the Dogs. The wind blew insanely out of utter darkness, no difference between air and water. And the fog was thicker than when we went to sleep. I thought wind blew fog away.

Heavy things crashed and clattered on the floor below. Hawley's boat was thirty-eight feet long, heavy and powerful, but it got blown down like a rubber duckie in a typhoon. I held on to some handles, but I felt the freezing seawater wash around my thighs. . . . Is this how it happens? The boat goes over, fills, and sinks like a Brunswick Gold Crown pool table.

It's easy to drown, anyone can do it admirably well the first time out. I remembered seeing a nature program about the deep ocean. Most of the dead things that drift down to the bottom of the abyssal darkness are consumed by the hagfish. The hagfish is a hideous beast, eel-like, colorless, so primitive it has evolved no jaws, just a gaping mouth ringed with sharp teeth. They suck that ring of teeth into the dead flesh of the dog owners who drop in, and they spin to dislodge the soft tissue, which they then suck on down their gullets.

At least I'd be dead by then. Probably of hypothermia. I remembered reading somewhere that death by hypothermia was painless, even peaceful. You don't feel cold anymore, you just drift off to everlasting sleep. There was that on the plus side. At least it didn't hurt as the hagfish drilled out your flesh.

I glanced at Hawley. He was doing things. Wedged

securely in place, he was turning the steering wheel this way and that, adjusting the throttle, taking measures. He wasn't giving up. In fact, he didn't look all that shook.

The boat came up, shouldered aside a lot of water, and moved forward as if nothing had happened to it. We were climbing the fronts of big waves and crashing over their backs with an explosion of spray, the only white in the world, and it glowed eerily. I looked back. The land was gone. There was no light except for the green glow on the face of Hawley's compass.

How the hell did he know where he was going? Maybe he didn't. I had had my suspicions about the guy's sanity from day one, skulking around in the ruins. Maybe this was his idea of a kick, one of those live-and-die-on-the-edge sort of doper psycho assholes. Yet he certainly looked like he knew what he was doing. He looked like he'd been doing this out here since infancy. But how could *anyone* know where they were going? There's better visibility in the small intestine. . . . Maybe it wasn't a matter of seeing. Maybe some other sense got employed.

I listened to myself every now and then to make sure I wasn't whimpering. My toe throbbed resolutely inside my borrowed rubber boots, a size and a half too big. Hawley still hadn't explained what exactly I was supposed to do once we got to the Disappointments. I visualized those savage rock pinnacles sticking up from the hagfish floor of an icy ocean somewhere out there in the darkness. I had seen no sign of Hope Island.

Hawley was pointing down the companionway with stabbing gestures. "Harness!" I thought he said.

Harness? I looked below, found the harness. It was

made of stout green webbing and heavy rings, like a
parachute harness with a long tether attached. Either
that, or some kind of bondage device. I went quickly
back up into the wind with it. Hawley didn't say anything, but, steering with one hand, he pulled off my
life jacket, put me into the harness, cinched it up
around my chest, and put my life jacket back on.

"This line right here—" Fat, dirty rope lay coiled at
our feet. "You take this line aboard the old man's
boat—I'll put you right into position—You step right
up on his bow—He's got these big bitts—You just drop
this loop over them bitts—It'll hold—I guarantee it."

I was afraid of that. I was going to *change* boats. I
began to experience some queasiness. . . . I looked out
into the dead black night and thought of Crystal. A
dumb fuck but true, he drowned like a rat thinking
of you.

"Listen, I'll put you right up alongside—You ain't
gonna jump, you're gonna step. If you can't step, then
we just go around again. It'll be my fault. Don't be no
brave hero."

"Don't worry about that."

He clapped me on the shoulder and went back to his
steering into the blackness.

Maybe I felt a little better now that I had the harness
and the life jacket. If I went in the drink, Hawley could
reel me in, and if I didn't get crushed like a grape
between the two boats, I might survive the immersion.

A light! "I just saw a light!" I shouted.

Hawley wasn't surprised. He nodded. He spoke into
the radio, listened for a while, said something, then he
hung up. "Let's take a practice turn. Stand over there
where you'll board from and I'll show you how it'll

be." He pointed to the side of the boat, where the wheelhouse began, basically beside the steering wheel.

Suddenly the old man's boat rose up on a big one and loomed over us—then it vanished. One didn't normally see boats from below when they were in the water. I tried to take deep breaths. While I still had some air to breathe. . . . Miserable hagfish sensing dinner—

Steering in a circle, Hawley had to turn sideways to the wind and seas again, and they knocked us over. Water came aboard, but I was used to that. Hawley pointed—

I spun.

There it was! The bow of the old man's boat! Brightly lighted by an enormous spotlight shining from the stubby mast. Hell, it looked cheery and welcoming, like the first fires in the ancient caves of winter. We almost touched, but if we had, contact would have been nothing worse than a gentle bump. I could have stepped aboard a half a dozen times before we came separate again. I began to feel some hope. We went around again.

"What's that noise?" I shouted.

"Breakers."

"Breakers!"

"The Disappointments get right up in a blow," he drawled.

I could see them now. Explosions of merciless white water over terrible black rocks. I couldn't exactly see, but I could feel them crash. No boat in the world could survive that, no *ship* ever built—

I was sweating like a rubber enthusiast in my foul weather gear. My arms ached from holding on. . . . It was coming around again, I could see the lights aboard the old man's boat rocking crazily.

"One more thing—" said Hawley.

"What!"

"Cut the old man's anchor line. He's sayin' now maybe he didn't cut it away, after all. I'll come back for the gear later. Out here's where I urchin."

For cutting, I had this capable serrated knife that Hawley had duct-taped in its sheath to my safety harness job. Armed, I was ready to go into harm's way. I positioned myself, stiffly waiting for the old man's bow to loom, testing my footing on the deck, locating my handholds. My toe had stopped throbbing, the body's way, perhaps, of focusing attention in the face of serious mortal threat away from a stubbed toe. I was ready to go. I was in position, poised to take the big step.

"Uh, Artie, don't forget to take the towline." He pointed to the loop lying at our feet.

". . . Right," I mumbled and picked up the purpose of our trip this night.

I stepped across the carnivorous chasm between the boats. It was easy. He put me into perfect position.

I sat on the flat deck at the bow as it went way up, then way down, but I was safe. Well, not safe, but not dead yet either. The wooden deck flexed beneath me as I dropped to my knees and scuttled toward the bitt. This must be the bitt—fat black pipes welded in the shape of a squatty cross. I dropped the loop over it. I waved at Hawley, who was still very close, leaning outboard, watching.

He waved back. Embracing the bitts, I drew my knife. I couldn't see too well through my salty glasses, so it took me a while to cut the right line. The severed end of the anchor line snapped over the side and vanished. I waved again, and I saw Hawley reach for his throttle. He brought the line taut gently, gradually. Then the strain came on it, and it stretched as Hawley accelerated. We were under control.

I slid on my ass four feet aft and leaned back against the windshield. The boat was roofed over from there almost to the stern, just like Hawley's. To get into the cockpit I would have to walk a narrow side deck holding onto the roof, with my butt hanging four feet above the waves, before I could actually come aboard. I wasn't quite ready for that trip, but that wasn't the whole reason I lingered. I wanted to take a minute on that plunging bow to savor my success and my adrenaline. However, I began to get sick. It came on suddenly. I needed shelter. I stood up and made the trip aft, hand over hand, three-point contact at all times, slowly, without going overboard—

The old man was at the wheel—

I swung inboard and stood holding on silently for a while. My vision was blurred. I licked instead of wiped my salty glasses, an old trick I learned on the Murmansk Run, and replaced them—

Arno Self was ashen-faced, his head lolled. He looked about a hundred years old. "Evenin'," he said, nonetheless.

"Evenin'," I found myself saying. "I'm Artie Deemer."

"You're the one who found the bones."

"Ah—"

"Thank you for coming. I couldn't've took no line. I'm grateful."

"I just stepped aboard."

"I broke my arm deployin' my anchor. Never would've done that before. . . . Before World War One. Fuck."

He was leaning over the wooden dashboard where the wheel was mounted, resting his arm on a flat place. I hadn't noticed it before. Six inches up from his thick wrist, the arm bone took a ninety-degree hard right. The middle two fingers on that hand twitched like a deranged castanet player's. "Maybe you could take the wheel."

I took it. Isolated in the blackness was the bouncing light on Hawley's stern. Violent lurching and jerking, rising and dropping had become commonplace.

Arno Self bowed his head and shivered as a wave of pain overcame him, then he looked up at me and said, "Them is old Kempshall's bones you found. I killed Compton Kempshall." He nodded once as if to lock it in. That was that. The wind and sea raged behind his head as I looked into his face. Kelso was right. Things and people are different out here.

"Why did you do it?"

"Because he was evil."

"Did you take the bones away?"

"Huh?"

I repeated my question.

But he didn't answer. His eyes rolled back, and he wavered. I let go of the wheel and grabbed the front of his slicker. He cried out, I guess because his sagging body put weight on his right-angled arm. His one-note moan tore through me like a hook and ladder siren speeding up Broadway as he cradled his grotesque arm from its resting place on the dashboard and moved aft with it. Legs wide, he took little mincing steps as if on ice. He sagged down on the deck and leaned his back against the engine box.

I began to shiver when I saw that he was shivering, or maybe I'd been shivering all along.

"Yep. I strangled the bastard. With a piece of old pot warp. Strangled him 'til his eyes bugged out."

19

I was hearing voices! I'd read a book about a guy adrift in a life raft in the middle of the ocean who after several weeks began to hear the sharks talking to him, trying to make a deal for his thigh. Maybe it was happening to me, only quicker, because I was unused to the ways of the sea. But it turned out only to be the radio. The radio was mounted on the dashboard beside the steering wheel. The mouthpiece part, suspended by a helix of black cord, was bouncing on the deck. I picked it up.

"Artie! Artie! Come back! This is Hawley! Over—"

I studied the thing for a moment. I depressed the lever and said, "I'm here." And I released the lever. Nothing. Fuck, I didn't say over. I knew you were supposed to say over. "Over!"

"Everything okay back there? How is he? Over."

"The arm's definitely broken. He's cold." I'd seen a documentary on hypothermia, and I was pretty sure Arno's body core was going that way. I knelt down to

look into his face. His eyes were distant. His head
lolled, but every time he passed out, he'd drop his broken arm, and the pain would wake him with a moan.
"I don't know whether to get him below or not. Depends how far we are from wherever we're going.
Over." I looked outboard into primordial, permanent
night.

"A crossin' to Micmac would be cruel on the old
bastard. Over."

"Where are we now?" I was sick of this "over."

"About fifteen minutes from the Dogs."

How'd he *know?* I looked out again to see if I'd
missed something, some mark that might mean something to a local. But there was nothing. Absolute darkness. I could barely see Hawley's light at the end of
the towline. There was no other beacon of civilized
humanity visible.

"Then let's take him to the boathouse." I looked
down at Arno to see if he'd heard his son call him an
old bastard. Hell, maybe he was an old bastard, but I
felt a little protective of him sitting there against the
roaring engine box. "Over."

"Okay, thanks a lot."

I went down below to find something warm, but it
was pitch dark down there. I tried the usual places
for a light switch, but I came up empty. The cabin
was tiny, hot, and stuffy. I began to spin. I didn't
have long down here before I'd start retching like Jellyroll. I felt around on my knees. A bed. I could feel
that it was neatly made. I tore the blanket off and
took it up to Arno. But Arno was unconscious. I put
it around him as best I could without touching that
contorted arm.

And then it dawned on me—we weren't slamming into the waves anymore. The water was relatively calm. Did that mean we were being sheltered by the Dogs or were we already in the cove? I looked outboard. Only darkness—

Hawley came on the radio to say that he was going to cast off the towline and come up on our port side.

"What do I have to do? Over."

"Nothin'. Out."

Good.

He tied the two boats side by side quickly and efficiently. We proceeded slowly. "Turn the wheel a little to the left," he instructed. "There, hold that. Thanks, Artie." He began his approach to the flat rock—

Suddenly I could see lights in the boathouse. Crystal. Lights. Jellyroll. Hearth and home. The sweets of civilization, doubly so to us stalwart, square-jawed types just back from the savage sea, timbers shivered.

Crystal! I could see her now on the porch waving both hands over her head. Jellyroll was up there, too, swirling with excitement. She ran inside and immediately back out, now wearing a raincoat. Crystal and Jellyroll headed down the stairs and out of sight. After that dark, I took deep pleasure in mere illumination.

With the boats mated like a motorcycle and sidecar, Hawley placed his father's boat gently against the flat rock, where Crystal waited. She bounced with excitement on the balls of her feet, a sweet, girlish trait of hers I find deeply touching. Jellyroll barked with high-pitched urgency. He wouldn't stop until I'd greeted him. I climbed ashore and hugged Crystal. Then I petted Jellyroll.

Hawley and Crystal were leaning over Arno. I joined them after I'd finished tying the boat to the rings in the rock.

Arno looked up at us gratefully. "Don't want to be no imposition. You folks is on vacation," I actually heard him say.

Crystal rolled her eyes. "You can use the bathroom, but then you have to go."

He stood up. Cradling his angled arm, he stepped over the side of his boat onto the rock, and under his own steam, with hardly a grimace walked toward the boathouse steps. Hawley and Crystal went with him, guarding him like basketball players, not daring to touch him.

Crystal, deciding he didn't need help, turned back to me. Rain ran off the brims of our hats. The wind still howled through the trees. Their tops whipped, but that was barely a hint of what I'd seen—or not seen—out there. Feeling very salty, I removed my safety harness and life jacket, and I liked that Crystal stood watching me do it. We kissed, while Jellyroll danced around on his hind legs to get into the act. We knelt down to his level so he could.

"Was it scary?"

"Naa. Walk in the park."

"Well, I was scared. I thought you'd never come back."

"Did you pace?" I tried to picture it.

She pulled my hat off because it was in the way and kissed me wetly. This was romance. Without the stalker business, we would have been free of cares and woe. For a while, anyway.

I whispered in Crystal's ear, "The old man said he killed Kempshall," as we went up the steps.

"He *did?*"

"Yep, strangled him. With something."

I put the water on to boil and assembled the coffee gear, while Crystal examined Arno like she knew what she was doing. She sat him on the wicker couch and knelt to look clinically into his eyes. She cocked her head like Jellyroll, scrutinizing. "My name is Crystal, Mr. Self."

"You're the pool player."

"Right."

"Ditn't know they had lady pool players."

"We'd better get that raincoat off, Mr. Self. You're too cold."

"I once saw Ralph Greenleaf play down in New Hampshire when I was a boy. Now could you give him a game?"

"Nope, not him, not even with the added advantage of being alive."

Crystal went to work removing his foul weather gear. It must have been excruciating. After the first two layers, Arno was panting, and they gave up. Crystal cut off Arno's sweater and his flannel shirt with a pair of shears. As they did that dreadful tugging and coaxing, Arno didn't make a sound, but from time to time his eyes rolled back in his head. As the layers fell away and the end neared, we gathered around to see. Even Jellyroll gathered with us. He sat down and waited.

All four of us gave little simultaneous groans, different in pitch and tone according to our wont. It made me think of a twisted doo-wop group. The skin around the break was purple and pulpy. It bulged in unnatural places. You could see sharp points pressing on the skin. If you touched it, even gently, it seemed to me, you would leave fingerprints in the flesh, a little more firmly and you would puncture it like something swollen by the gasses of putrescence.

Crystal said, "There's a lot of subcutaneous bleeding, but the skin's not broken, and you don't seem to be in shock, Mr. Self."

"Well, then I guess I better be runnin' along."

"Right. . . . This is a complicated break. I'm going to immobilize it, and we'll get you to the hospital as soon as the storm ends."

Maybe the ministration by a beautiful woman had softened the craggy edges of his features somewhat.

"I wish we had some real painkillers," said Crystal to no one in particular.

"Oh, the old man don't take pain pills. He's too tough," Hawley said. I glanced at him. It wasn't a joke, he wasn't smiling.

"Hell I don't, boy." Neither was Arno. "You get them, I'll do the rest."

"Mare-o-wanna, Dad. That's all I got."

"Does it work?"

"Hell yes, it does."

"Go get it."

He rummaged through his layers to get to his shirt pocket, from which he withdrew a fat spliff and held it up beside his face. "I already got it."

"My son, the drug czar, the great shame and sadness of my life." Was this a routine? "Have you met Dickie yet? Dickie is his partner in crime. Dickie."

Delighted, Hawley was lighting up under clouds of

cloying smoke. "First one's free, Dad. Then when you're hooked, you'll have to sell your soul to Dickie." He handed it to the old man.

Arno puffed away, then stared out, apparently waiting for some effect to hit.

I looked at Crystal. Did she think it was a routine or was it real? I guess you can't tell if you're from away.

Crystal went into the bedroom and came back with a pillowcase. She began to make a sling out of it. She *did* know what she was doing.

"Psst," said Hawley, flicking his head in an unsubtle high sign toward the door. He wanted to talk to me. I asked Crystal if she needed anything. She said she didn't.

Hawley Self and I stood under the eave of the roof; the rain that drummed on the porch touched only our boot toes.

"Wind's layin' down some now," he said. "But that was a mean little front. I appreciate you goin'. . . . What'd the old man have to say? Did he talk on the way back?"

"What?"

"Did he tell you things?"

"Like what?"

"Like did he tell you he killed Kempshall?"

"Yes."

"How?"

"By what means?"

"Yeah."

"He said he strangled him."

"Bullshit."

"With pot warp."

"Pot warp, my ass. He didn't strangle nobody."

197

"What's pot warp?"

"That's the line you tie on to the lobster trap to pull it up with. Pot warp was not the murder weapon. Right here, *this* was the murder weapon—" Hawley had in his hand a beat-up canvas gym bag with broken handles. I had wondered why. He zipped it open with a flourish and pulled out a hatchet. "Here, this is what killed Kempshall, this right here." Hawley hefted the thing to show me. "He was scum. He stole people's lives. That's why I killed him with a blow from this. You saw the bones, right? You tell me. Does this fit what you saw?"

". . . Yes."

"Well then, there you have it."

"Okay." What did he want from me? We looked at each other for a while, the raindrops splashing off our toes. "Why are you telling me this, Hawley?"

"Well, let's just say something happens. You know, a thing we couldn't even imagine at this point in time. The unexpected."

"Like what?"

"Like maybe the bones turn up again. God knows where, but let's say they do. Let's say the cops or somebody comes up to you and wants to talk about the Kempshall killing."

"Why would they do that? I'm from away."

"I *know* you are, but we're just saying here, okay? The cops ask you about the killing, like what you've heard about it. You might say, 'Hawley Self told me he did it.' "

"No, I wouldn't."

"You wouldn't?"

"No, I promise."

Hawley looked disappointed. "What if I wanted you to?"

"Oh. You want me to? Okay, then I will."

Hawley looked at me. "Anything, right, as long as it doesn't fuck you up?"

"Right. See, I think you have a beautiful place to live here, and I'd like to get to know it a little. I got a psycho on my dog's ass. I don't want stress, and I don't want to cause stress. It's stressful uncovering dark secrets of the past. I only did so by accident. As far as Kempshall's murder is concerned, you can have it any way you want it. Let me ask you this, Hawley, out of curiosity. Did you dispose of the bones?"

". . . Yeah."

"After Crystal and I saw them, after the dogs got to them?"

"Sure."

"What did you do with them?"

"In the drink. Deep fucking six."

"So they'll never be seen again, right?"

"I shouldn't think so."

"Then what difference does it make? The law isn't going to do anything without a body. Sheriff Kelso said so. None of you need to confess yet."

"Kelso said that?"

"Yep."

He blinked twice in a comic sort of way and said, "Then what the fuck is the problem?"

"No problem," I said.

He produced and lit another spliff, as if in celebration. Under a cloud of smoke too thick to blow away in the diminished wind, he said, "We solved that matter. The bone matter. Then let's turn to another matter. Let's turn to the matter of this stalker. You think it's those assholes in the black sportfisherman, don't you?"

"Yeah, it's possible. There's circumstantial evidence." I didn't want to get into *Ten Pins* and the threatening bowling sheets. "They're the only strangers around right now."

"So why don't we have a word with them?"

"Say what?"

"Say like, 'Get the fuck out of Cabot County with the next tide, or I hack your nuts off into the bait sock.' Something along them lines."

Frankly, that sounded good to me.

"Hawley Self!" It was a woman's voice.

Hawley jumped at the sound of it—

"Will you quit smoking that devil weed!"

Hawley was pushing forty, but he jerked that spliff out of his mouth and hid it behind his back. "Mom!"

She was standing on the rocky shore squinting up at us. Raindrops struck her face.

"What are you doin' here? You heard about the old man?"

"Of course I did. I was up the east side with Edith. Don't call him that."

"You mean you walked all the way over here?"

"No, I got high on your weed and floated. Are you Mr. Deemer?"

"Artie."

"How do you do, Artie? I'm Roxanne Self. Thank

you for what you did out there," she said in a clear, accentless voice.

"You're welcome. His arm is broken."

"Hey, what about me?" said Hawley. "I did it, too."

"Yes, Hawley, you did," said Roxanne gently, sincerely. "And you did it good."

"Thanks, Mom."

20

"I didn't know you knew first aid," I said to Crystal when we were by ourselves out on the porch.

"I don't. Not really."

We leaned side by side against the railing. The underbellies of the black clouds in the eastern sky were tinted russet, but it was still dark in Dog Cove. I put my face close and breathed the scent of her hair from behind her ear. She knew first aid. There were so many things still to learn about her. "Say, would you be interested in a little carnal knowledge?"

"Sure, but we have guests."

"Presumably they'll leave."

"While I was fitting his sling, Arno told me he killed Compton Kempshall. He sort of whispered it in my ear. What are they doing? Who are they trying to protect? . . . You don't care, you just want to satisfy your throbbing lust."

Was that so bad? "Hawley told me *he* killed Kempshall. He had the murder weapon to prove it."

"What? He carries it with him?"

"A Cub Scout hatchet. He had it in that gym bag. He had it to prove his point. And if the sheriff investigates, Hawley wants me to say he did it."

"It's fascinating, don't you think? . . . You don't, do you?"

"It's making me edgy, all these people confessing to murder."

"Under normal circumstances, yes, but this is an old murder. It's not so real. Bones and bodies aren't the same." She was making certain wanton moves with her left hand. "Can't you think of it as the vacation mystery?"

"If you put it like that, I'll agree to anything."

"These folks think you're a hero. Are you aware of that?"

"They do?"

"They said so. Hawley said it was very bad out there. He said you stood up and stepped right onto the other boat. I've always imagined since I was a little girl what it would be like to have carnal knowledge with a hero."

Wow. If it hadn't been raining, I might have suggested we avail ourselves of the privacy of the woods, roll around in a bed of ferns like our indigenous progenitors. I think Crystal felt it, too. I could see it in her eyes.

"Did you really want to have carnal knowledge with heroes or were you just being facetious?"

"No, it was a true fantasy. Now I will."

"Tell me about the fantasy. I mean about sex with heros like me."

"No."

Then I saw Roxanne, apparently heading our way, hesitate on the other side of the French doors, not wanting to intrude. I invited her out. Her face was tired, drawn, and old, but it was also strong and elegant, like one of those black-and-white photographs of Depression women who hold the family together, Ma Joad types. She had narrow features and a tall forehead. Hatless, her hair was pure white and long. She moved lightly, despite her age and what must have been a tough slog on foot over the hill from the Crack in the middle of the storm.

"I want to thank you again, dear," she said to me.

"I was glad to help, Ms. Self."

"Call me Roxanne." She touched Crystal's forearm. "And thank you, too, dear. You two are in love, aren't you?"

Crystal patted Roxanne's hand and said yes, we were.

"That's good. I'm glad you're here. The boathouse has been lonely for a long time." It was all very maternal, familial, old-fashioned—until Roxanne said, "I'm told you found bones."

"Accidentally," I mentioned. "We weren't looking."

"Where?"

Crystal pointed off to the top of the hill, obliterated now in low cloud and fog.

"Out in the open?"

Crystal told her about the dogs.

". . . Dwight is on his way over from the Crack," she said distractedly. "He thinks we can cross the strait. We'll be leaving you in peace soon." She turned her back on the cove and leaned against the rail. "Clayton—Do you know how to get in touch with Clayton?"

"I have his New York number, but I believe he's still in California."

"California? He is? Oh, that's wonderful!"

What? Wonderful?

"Why wonderful, Roxanne?" Crystal comes right out and asks. It's one of the things I love about her.

Hawley was standing in the threshold between the French front doors. "Are you telling it?"

"I was about to."

"Can I listen?"

She didn't say yes and she didn't say no. "He's in California," she said.

"He is? No kiddin'? For sure?"

Crystal and I watched them blankly. Why was that such good news, Clayton in California? Hawley ducked back in to tell his father that Clayton was in California.

Roxanne looked at us. "There's been another murder in town," she said. "One of the pilgrims or a tourist. They don't know yet. Teddy Kelso thinks it's a psychopath. The man was murdered the same way as the young woman was. His head was split down the middle. . . ."

"Maybe you'd better tell us, Roxanne," suggested Crystal.

Hawley returned and stood against the outside wall like a little boy trying not to be noticed.

"Back that night—the night of the fire—Clayton Kempshall knocked on our door. He was about ten. We lived over on the other side of the island. It was blowing a gale of wind and cold that night. The kind of wind and cold that kills. We didn't expect visitors. He must have been out there a long time, knocking, but we didn't hear him because of the wind. We might not

have seen him at all, except we began to notice a pale
glare at first, like ice in the sea from a long distance
off, then a flickering light, and that brought us to the
door. There stood little Clayton on the step. He had on
white pajamas—they were soaked in blood from top
to hem.''

Crystal gasped.

"Yes. And he had his Cub Scout hatchet in his
hand."

Oh Jesus, it dawned on me. She meant to connect
murders—the old one and the new ones—

His face pale and drawn, Arno appeared in the doorway, just stood there, head bowed listening,
remembering.

"We warmed him, comforted him," Roxanne continued. "Pretty soon, we became aware he didn't know
how he came to be running the island in a winter storm
in blood-soaked pajamas. Like he was out of his head
with fever. He seemed to know about the fire, but he
didn't know where his father was. He didn't remember.
Took a day and a half before the Castle burned itself
out.

"Police came, experts, and poked around in the
ashes. We were sure they'd find his father's corpse. But
we never questioned Clayton about the bloody pajamas, we just stayed with him and waited for him to
tell us. But the experts found nothing. They said if
there was remains in the ruins, they'd have found
them. Even now I don't know for certain what happened in the Castle that night. Did Clayton kill his father with that little boy's hatchet and drag his corpse
through the storm all the way up there—?"

We looked up the hill; it seemed to be scudding

along with the windblown clouds. We tried to imagine the scene that night. Gale wind and rain like last night, only cold, December. Clayton dragging the freshly killed corpse of his father over the rocks, through the undergrowth, brains running out on his pajamas. How could you forget a trip like that? But of course maybe the opposite is true.

"The police came and questioned Clayton. They were very suspicious. They suspected that Compton Kempshall faked it all so he could disappear. He was under investigation for all sorts of frauds and crimes. They thought Kempshall burned the Castle himself. But Clayton didn't seem to know anything.

"Arno and me, we'd made a decision. We discussed it, before the police came. We decided not to tell anybody about the bloody pajamas or the hatchet, if Clayton didn't tell them himself. I don't know if that was a good decision or bad, we only wanted it to be best for him. If he didn't remember then, maybe he'd never remember ever. I don't know about that, I mean, whether the mind can work that way. But the fact was that boy did not remember. We burned the bloody pajamas." She fell silent.

"Are you saying you think Clayton killed those people in Micmac?" Crystal asked.

She didn't respond immediately. She looked down at the boards beneath our feet. "I think I hear Dwight's boat coming."

Crystal and I listened. We heard nothing.

"I believe you met Eunice and Lois?" said Roxanne.

"Yes," said Crystal.

"Lois said she saw Clayton."

"Here?"

207

"Lois said she saw him out in a little boat off the north end. Lois is a dear. I love her. But she's . . . subject to fits. So that's why we'd be ever so grateful if you could get in touch with Clayton in California. Just to be sure."

"I bet Shelly could track him down," said Crystal.

"Shelly?"

"Jellyroll's agent." Jellyroll sat listening to the whole thing. When we looked at him, his tail thumped the deck. "I'll call right now. All agents get up with the crack of dawn." I called him. He was up. He said he'd get right on it. I told him thanks for sending Sid. Sid seemed perfect for the job.

Dwight came around the point. Hawley moved the boats away from the flat rock, so Dwight could dock there. We carefully put Arno aboard. He looked terrible, but he managed a nod to me and a faint grin as he went over the rail.

Hawley put his father's boat on the mooring and in his own followed Dwight out of sight around the point.

Crystal and I went to bed.

21

rtie—somebody's calling." Crystal was pulling
on a sweatshirt, shimmying into a pair of
jeans. Jellyroll was barking. I was trying to regain consciousness. I studied the clock. It was late afternoon.
We had slept all day.

Crystal looked out the small, high bedroom window.
"It's Hawley," she said.

"What's he want?"

She didn't know. I joined her at the window.

Hawley was docking his boat against the flat rock.
He shouted and waved his arm excitedly as he did so.

We went out on the porch to see. The air was cool
and damp. Jellyroll, turning circles, was charging up
on human excitement.

"I got 'em! C'mere, I got 'em!" Hawley vaulted over
the side of the boat with docking lines in hand. He was
vibrating. Jellyroll sprinted down the steps and jumped
at him. "I got the bastards in the boat right now! Hi,
Jellyroll!"

"Who?"

"Who? The stalkers, that's who! I got 'em!"

"You mean you—?"

"Damn right, I do!" He pointed into the cabin of his boat.

Uh-oh. Crystal and I looked at each other, down at Hawley and his boat, then back at each other.

Crystal clambered aboard Hawley's boat, but she didn't look down the companionway that led below until I came aboard. Side by side we bent at the waist and looked in. Hawley, grinning proudly like a suburbanite showing off his new hatchback, flooded the place with powerful bright light—

They were stuffed back to back down there on the floor and chained together by the necks.

Cabin wasn't really the right word for the place in which they were chained. The Belgian's boat in Micmac had a cabin, but not this one. It was a dark pit full of gear. There were a couple of anchors, scuba tanks, fins, weight belts, welding equipment, miles of coiled rope and chain, a pile of lobster buoy floats, and a lot of arcane urchining paraphernalia. For amenities, he had a lopsided bed frame of naked plywood with a deflated air mattress and a grimy sleeping bag. For a galley he had a blackened single-burner camp stove, a crusted plastic coffee mug, and a Swiss Army knife. Hawley's home stank of mildew, sweat, and dead fish. There was no standing headroom. There was barely sitting headroom.

It was Dick Desmond, all right. He even looked TV-familiar to me at that moment, something about his lower face, despite the raw terror that distorted it. He squinted and covered his eyes with the crook of his arm, and with the other hand he clutched the chain links that dug into his throat. A line of spittle spilled from the corner of his mouth. "Please," he pleaded, "I have money. I can pay! Cash!"

We couldn't see his son, the videographer, because he was facing forward, but I could hear him whimper as he tried to turn his head our way within the strict confines.

Jellyroll tried to squeeze his snout into the hatchway to see what the attraction was.

"Dick Desmond?" I said just to be sure.

"Y-y-yes."

"Ten Pins, right?"

"Are you a . . . fan? Wait. It's you, with the R-r-ruff Dog. I met you, remember? In the town."

"Who's with you?"

"That's my son."

"What are you doing here?"

"Doing? This—this madman kidnapped us at gunpoint!"

"Look who's talking," said Hawley, "a fucking dog stalker."

"No, I mean, why are you here in the first place?"

"Vacation, we're on vacation, that's all, a father-and-son vacation. He's a film student at NYU. He wanted to get some moody coastal material, you know. We're just cruising the coast!

". . . Have you been stalking my dog?" I demanded, but there was no heft behind it, no commitment. It was barely a demand. I was beginning to feel like a cruel asshole. "You were sending us threatening bowling sheets!" I tried to sound like a man full of conviction.

The son moaned.

"No, please," said Dick, "I don't bowl. I loathe bowling. Even on the show, I never bowled." He was babbling now, trying to talk death away. "You never once saw me bowl. I don't even know how to keep score! Look, I know how you feel. If somebody was stalking my dog, I'd be upset, too. And I wouldn't blame you if you hurt them. But it's just that we're not them. I swear! Please! We're choking to death down here!" I could see the mortal fear etched on his face like old age. "Plus it stinks!"

"Excuse me," I said, and straightened up.

So did Crystal and Hawley. We stepped astern to talk it over.

"Well, what do you think?" Hawley asked, puffed with pride.

"I don't know, Hawley. I appreciate the thought, but this might not be them."

"What do you mean? Why? Because they *say* they aren't?"

"Well, we don't know. Look at them down there. . . . We'd have to prove it and all. I can't prove it."

"Yeah, well, one way to prove it would be to dump them out to seaward of the Disappointments with an anchor each. Glub, glub. If Jellyroll stops being stalked, then you could be pretty certain you got the right fuckers."

That contained a certain dreadful logic I found attractive. Hawley was clearly ready to go. All I needed to say was okay. They'd be gone. Granted there could be complications, but they'd still be irrevocably gone. Bodies never come up to haunt one. . . . No, I couldn't do it under the circumstances. Maybe if I could have been sure these two were guilty, if I had had clear evidence, but of course I didn't. I had a bowling motif.

And I had the only strangers on the island. The bowling motif would blow away with the first stiff breeze. And I couldn't go around killing people for the crime of being unknown to me. What an insular lifestyle.

"You *said* this was them," Hawley pointed out.

I felt Crystal's face spin around toward me. She didn't know I'd said that. But how could I deny it? "Yeah, but I didn't think you were going to go straight out and kidnap them," I heard myself muttering like a Milquetoast.

Hawley thrust his hands into his pockets and looked at his black rubber boots. He was embarrassed. "Okay, so I take them back to the Crack, give them some free seafood, and say, 'Ooops.' What's the worse that could happen? They could sue me, I guess."

"It was my fault." I could feel Crystal beside me readily nodding agreement. "If they sue or press charges, I'll own up to it."

"You did me a good turn, I wanted to do you one. I guess I got carried away. What do you call it? Hasty," Hawley said. "I got hasty."

Then we heard the siren echoing around the hills, coming fast.

"Oh, shit," said Hawley. "Kelso. Somebody must've ratted. There was a lot of goings-on up at the Crack because of the Commander drowning and all. Somebody must've seen me snatch them and ratted."

"You snatched them from the Crack?"

"That's where they were."

"How could you snatch somebody in the Crack and expect not to be seen?"

"I told you, I got hasty. Gimme a break, okay?"

"I'm sorry."

Kelso skidded around the corner with the whole side of his boat out of water, spray flying, siren and light pulsing, shaving a sunker close. There were two men in the boat. Kelso wasn't driving. A skinny kid with a blue wool watch cap pulled down low over his brow was behind the wheel. Kelso held on tight in the turn. I'd never seen a boat go that fast in Dog Cove, and its wake was beginning to bounce back and forth between the sides. The urgency of the sheriff's approach did not bode well for us kidnappers.

The skinny guy slowed as soon as he completed the turn, but the waves were still reverberating, seemingly gaining energy with each wash across the narrow cove. Hawley's boat began to pound against the flat rock. Dick Desmond and his son screamed from below.

The police boat skidded to a stop rail to rail against Hawley's boat, and the rocking and rolling increased. Everybody on both boats gripped things to keep their feet. Hawley's boat thudded harder against the rock. There were grinding sounds. It must have been hell down there in the brig.

"Jesus, Earl," said Hawley to Kelso's driver, "you're fuckin' up my entire starboard chine."

"Sorry, Hawley," said Earl, who was trying to grow a beard. " 'Full speed ahead.' That was the sheriff's orders." The wake still bounced chaotically.

The red light was still flashing—

"Sheriff? Is that police? Help! Help! Down here, help!"

There was a third person in the police boat. Edith Hickle sat on a seat in the back grinning sweetly at us. She wore the same print shift as at the launching under a thin nylon windbreaker, sneakers with the pom-pom socks. Her hands looked white and cold as she held on—

After the boats stopped bouncing against each other, Sheriff Kelso slung his leg over the rail and followed it aboard. He shoved Hawley aside and looked below. "Jesus," he muttered to himself. "Excuse me," he said to Dick and Dick Junior, "I'll be right with you." Then he turned on Hawley and said, "Have you lost your mind?"

"These fuckers've been stalking his dog!"

"No, he kidnapped us off the street!"

"Look at that dog," insisted Hawley. "The cutest fucking dog in the world. They meant to *kill* that dog! They came out here to do it!"

Now Kelso turned on me. "Is that true?"

"Ah, yes, well, it sure could be—"

"Why?" Kelso wanted to know. "What makes you think so?"

I was afraid he'd want to know that. All eyes fell upon me. "Well, you see, we've, uh, been getting these threatening notes written on bowling sheets . . . score sheets, you know? Strikes and spares?" He glared at me, that withering New York–cop look that seems to assume you're insane, and I began to babble. "That's Dick Desmond down there, and he used to be on a TV show about a bowling alley. Bowling. You put that together with them being the only strangers on the island, and, uh, there you have it."

"Okay, you're under arrest. You, too, Hawley."

"Aww, come on, Teddy—"

Eyes burning, Kelso shoved Hawley by the chest. "Get those people out of there, Hawley, right now."

Earl let slip a giggle, and Kelso spun on him—"You

like driving boats, Earl, or you want to go back to rehab?"

"Uh, no sir."

"Then get over here and help."

"Hello, Ms. Hickle," said Crystal.

"Hello, dear."

"I'm Crystal Spivey."

"Yes, I know. You could call me Edith."

When Jellyroll saw Edith, to whom he'd taken a shine back at the Crack, he leapt over the rail and sat down at her feet.

"Awww," she said cuddling and hugging, "he's smiling at me!"

Kelso turned on Crystal and me. "I'll thank you to get off this boat and wait in the house."

He politely fetched Edith, assisted her ashore, and told her to go with us. As Crystal and I were helping Edith toward the steps, she said to Crystal, "I've confessed, you know."

"You have? To what, Edith?"

"I drowned him, you know. It was sabotage. J undid a bolt. That's all it takes in a submarine, you know."

"Don't confess," said Crystal. "Don't ever confess. Do you have a lawyer?"

"A lawyer?" Her right eye was clouded with a cataract.

"He habitually abused you, didn't he?"

"How do you mean?"

We helped her up the steps. As we climbed, I heard this exchange from aboard Hawley's boat:

"What's the holdup?" Kelso demanded down the companionway.

"Lock's all seized up. I gotta get some WD-40 in there."

There was a pause, but it didn't last long. Dick Desmond and his boy screamed and coughed and sputtered. "He's drowning us in oil! Help!"

Hawley came topside: "Gotta let that *penetrate*."

How quickly things can go absurd on you. . . .

It turned out to be a delicate procedure, getting two people of such size discrepancy chained closely by the neck back to back out of a space that small. After I put water on to boil, I went out on the porch to watch, while Crystal made Edith comfortable on the wicker sofa. I knew Crystal would be giving her an earful about her rights.

Dick Desmond's face was screwed up, teeth bared in a kind of rictus grin as he emerged first from below. His fingers clawed at the chain tightening around his esophagus. Desmond sort of crawled out of there with his son almost riding on his back like a papoose, Kelso supporting him from under his butt. It was an ugly scene. Earl helped, with a smartass smirk on his narrow face, as Hawley fiddled fruitlessly with the lock.

"Little more WD-40 ought to do it—"

"No! No more, please!" screamed Junior.

"Get him away from us!" screamed Dick Desmond.

Now that father and son were out of the hole, Kelso tried to figure out what to do with them while the oil penetrated. He suggested they sit down on the engine box. As he manipulated the duo, he looked up and caught me watching. I braced myself for hostility, but the look on his face reflected stress, exhaustion, and sadness. He stuck a rubber bumper under Master Desmond's ass to even things out.

Now I saw the son for the first time without a camera in front of his face. He was small, but he didn't look young enough to be Dick Desmond's son. Of course, he had a chain locked tightly around his trachea, and that tends to alter the set of one's features, but from up here on the porch, he looked like he was over forty-five; he looked like a retired jockey who hadn't ridden a lot of winners. His hair was jet black, combed straight back, but it was thinning. His face was wrinkled, and his left eye drooped at the outer edge.

Kelso yanked the key away from Hawley, and now he tried to get it to open the lock. This caused the boy to look up. Our eyes locked. . . . I'd be pissed, too, if I had just gotten a faceful of propelled lubricant while chained by the neck to my old man. But this guy looked at me with mortal malice. If I saw a stranger looking at me like that on the street, I'd duck into the nearest doorman building and ask for a phone to call 911. His black eyes burned with hatred, yet at the same time the look was glacially cold. His eyes frightened me, even from that distance. I avoided them, turned, and went inside.

"Crystal, look at the son. The son's visible. Come see—" I importuned. I held the door for her, and we went to the rail to see. But now Kelso, working on the lock, blocked our view of the fruit of Desmond's loins.

She looked at me. "What's wrong, Artie?"

"I don't know, he *looked* like a psycho killer."

"Didn't he have a chain locked around his neck?"

"I know, I know, but still—"

"Just because a person looks like a psycho doesn't mean he is a psycho. Just look at our neighborhood."

"But most of the people in our neighborhood are psychos."

"You didn't plan this kidnapping job, right?"

"Absolutely not. Hawley just went and did it. All I did was shoot my mouth off."

"I just wanted to know for sure. We don't want to let the stalker business get us nuts."

"No, you're right."

She took my hand, and we watched the operation continuing below, but we never saw Sonny's face.

"They'll probably sue you. I would."

"Me, too."

The oil penetrated, but it took an uncomfortably long time. I made sure I was not visible when release came for the Desmonds. They left quietly with Earl in the police boat. He was going to take them to the Crack and their boat, then return for Kelso. I didn't incur any shit face-to-face with the Desmonds, but I wouldn't be so lucky with the sheriff. Kelso was heading for the stairs. He climbed heavily.

We were standing in a line across the living room—Hawley, whom Kelso had sent up here before the penetrating oil had finished its work, Crystal, Jellyroll, and I. Who would take the fall?

Kelso entered without knocking, but he didn't look threatening. He looked distracted, just as before, and sad. He looked up at us and stopped in his tracks.

"It was all my fault, Teddy. Artie didn't tell me to do it or anything like that," Hawley insisted. "Why, I just went and did it. Artie and Crystal, they did my family a good turn, and well, I got hasty."

"It was my fault," I said. "I told him they were the stalkers."

Kelso looked from one to another, even down at Jellyroll, who cocked his head from side to side. "Do you folks have anything to eat?" he asked.

"Sure!"

"Does that mean they ain't pressin' charges?" Hawley asked.

"No, it doesn't mean that at all. It means I'm hungry."

"How about a meat-loaf sandwich and some chowder?" Crystal proposed.

"Terrific."

Jellyroll strolled into the bedroom to visit Edith.

Everybody liked the idea of food. Crystal and I hadn't eaten anything yet. I sliced the Selfs' meatloaf, Crystal slathered on the mustard, and Hawley formed them into sandwiches. I set a table, but we didn't use it. Instead we stood around in the kitchen eating sandwiches and drinking beer. Teddy Kelso wasn't nearly as pissed as I feared. Maybe this kind of thing happened a lot. I felt disoriented by the weird hours and events.

Jellyroll came back when he got a whiff of the meatloaf and planted himself in position to intimidate Hawley, whom he'd judged to be the easiest mark. I told him no begging, and he slunk off, giving me the starving-pariah-dog look as he went.

"Sheriff Kelso?" said Crystal.

"Call me Ted. Don't call me Teddy."

"She's taking her confession back, Ted."

"Oh yeah? Okay."

"You aren't angry?"

"At you for butting in?"

"Yes."

"I don't believe she did what she says she did. Dwight and a couple of the other guys looked the sub over. They're no submarine experts, but they're experienced mechanics. They found no obvious sabotage. It looked to them like it leaked along a weld between two metal plates."

"You mean she's not under arrest?" Crystal asked.

"Hell no, I'm taking her around to my wife's sister's place."

"Your wife's sister?"

"My mother," Hawley clarified. "Roxanne Self. The sheriff is kin." Hawley grinned.

"By marriage," Kelso emphasized. "By marriage."

"Roxanne told us there was another killing in Micmac," said Crystal.

"It's true. A man this time, about forty-five. Money in his wallet, watch on his wrist. One of the lobstermen spotted him bobbing on the bottom under the pier. The crabs had been at him, but it was still clear what killed him. Same thing that killed the girl from Hartford. This is going to start attracting some nasty attention if I don't close it quick."

We ate our sandwiches in silence.

22

rystal, Jellyroll, and I watched them leave from the porch. Hawley had volunteered to take Edith to his parents' place on the other side of the island. His boat turned right at the mouth of the cove and vanished behind Dog Island. Sheriff Kelso's, with Earl at the helm, turned left for the mainland to continue. The wakes sluiced with a whispering sound back and forth in the round dark stones along the shore and then fell silent. We were alone again. I was feeling woozy and disoriented. Maybe Crystal was feeling the same, because we stood there for a while staring out across the cove. Maybe Jellyroll felt woozy, too. He sat on his haunches staring out and did not chase the chipmunk.

I brooded about the Jesus people. I tried to imagine them not as a faceless flock in windbreakers, white socks, and plaid polyester peering up at the fungus, but as individuals each with personal hopes and dreams, memories, a childhood. What had they expected when they came here? Roxanne Self had called them pilgrims. But that implied a specific objective. Would it suffice simply to glimpse the face in the lichens? Or did the Savior actually have to show up and make their lives beautiful for their pilgrimage to be fulfilled? I wished I had actually seen the face. I could understand their pain and their anxiety easier than I could their faith. Maybe I would know better what they'd come for if I'd looked on the face.

Crystal had been brooding about Clayton. "Do you think it works that way? The mind. Could Clayton have killed his father with a hatchet when he was ten and not remember it for the rest of his life?"

I didn't know.

"And instead of remembering, he starts killing strangers at random with hatchets. Do you think that's possible?"

"For all I really know, he's been killing people with hatchets all his life," I said.

"You don't really think so, do you?"

"No, I don't, but it makes me nervous that Roxanne did. . . . Things have gotten complicated around here."

"Yeah."

"I was thinking of calling Calabash again. Instead of asking him to come here, maybe we'd go there. It'd be hot on Poor Joe Cay in August, but nobody would find us."

Jellyroll was watching us, looking one to the other, as if understanding every word.

"Do you want to see Calabash?" I asked him.

He loves Calabash. His head pivoted side to side, expecting Calabash's instantaneous arrival. Expectancy again. It's not fair of me to do that.

"Artie, I don't want to keep running." Crystal stared

out with a sad look on her face. "Coming here wasn't exactly running, it was more like a little vacation. But if we have to start actually running . . ."

"Yeah." We would live a shadowy existence in an angular urban landscape. It would rain all the time, gutter grates smoking, rubbish tumbleweeding down dead streets discordant with shrieks and sirens, plastic bags blown against our shins. We'd deal in cash and promises with men holding toothpicks in the corners of their mouths. . . . But what could we do but run if there really was a determined stalker? I feared the necessity. So did Crystal. Life on the run would not nurture our relationship. I guessed we could kill him. I wondered where Sid Detweiler was.

A rumbling speedboat rounded the point. We heard it before we saw it. This was not a local boat. It even sounded different from the local boats. It was a long, lean Cigarette boat about forty feet long with a fire-engine red hull, a high, sharp bow to sever the waves, and a menacing black wraparound windshield. We couldn't see the driver, or even if there was one. The boat approached dead slow, at a swimmer's pace. Crystal, Jellyroll, and I watched motionlessly. Fear of strangers would quickly turn a person into an eccentric hermit.

Someone climbed out from behind the black windshield and stood on the deck. I put the binoculars on him. Dressed completely in black, silk shirt buttoned up around his throat, crease in his black jeans, black pointy cowboy boots with upcurled toes, this guy was as out of place as his boat. Wait, I'd seen him before! Yes, in Micmac, looking down at me from the dock.

He'd asked me about Jellyroll. It was just after the murder. . . .

"I think they're going to hit the sunker," I said.

"Can you warn them away?"

"Fuck 'em."

"Now we don't want to get like that, Artie. Besides, if they sink, we'll just have to rescue them. I mean, you couldn't stand up here and watch them drown like rats, could you?"

I wasn't absolutely certain. Maybe I'd avert my eyes. But still, Crystal had a point. I didn't want them around even if they weren't stalkers. I started signaling urgently, waving my arms, to indicate a left turn. Crystal joined in.

The guy in black pointed to us, then leaned down to discuss it with the person at the wheel. At least I assumed that was what he was doing. He completely vanished behind the smoked windshield. But there was no time for talk. If he didn't turn immediately— The boat swerved hard to the left. They couldn't have missed the thing by an inch.

The red speedboat made a slow turn near the boathouse and stopped. Jellyroll pricked up his ears. The guy in black stood up again. "Rocks," he said to Crystal and me. "Rocks, rocks, rocks. This place is solid rocks, rocks everywhere you turn, the Land of Rocks."

"Yeah," I said.

"Kempshall Island, right?"

"Most folks from here call it Teal Island," I said. "Who you lookin' for?"

"Are there any other houses around here? I mean, I heard people live on this island. In houses." He had jet-black hair combed straight back, slicked down with some foreign substance. This guy looked like a lounge lizard from Avenue A. "In tepees, I don't know, yurts," he said. "Caves. Where do the people *live* around here?"

"Got several houses on the other side. Who you lookin' for?"

He didn't answer.

"I pretty much know everybody in the county. Lived here all my life. The wife, too. She's lived here all her life. Who you lookin' for? We're sure to know 'em."

The boat continued its turn. The guy in black turned his back on us. . . . Who was this fucker! Some media-wise hipster who meant to kill my dog because his career was on the skids and he could use the publicity?

"Rock!" he shouted at the driver. "Don't hit the rock! Turn, turn! No, the other way!" The boat swerved away from a nonexistent sunker. "Jesus, you about hit that fucking rock head on. . . . No, you did! I'm tellin' you! I *saw* it, okay. I'm watchin' my life flash before my eyes!" The guy in black went back under the cover. We watched him nestle into a white Naugahyde bucket seat beside the driver, an elegant, dour woman with bare shoulders and long, black, shiny hair that cascaded over the seat back onto the deck. The engines roared to the pain level and beyond, and the boat tore out of the cove under a rooster tail of white water.

Was that them? "I hope they hit a sunker and drown like rats," I said.

"What, you know them?"

"No."

"You mean just because they're strangers?"

"Why didn't they say what they wanted?"

The roar of their engines echoed around the hilltops long after they'd disappeared around the point.

"Look at that!" Crystal pointed seaward—

A mountainside of fog was rolling in. Ledges, plateaus, and pinnacles of fog formed on the fore slope and then were swallowed up in the roiling murk that abolished all in its path.

"Jesus," Crystal muttered.

First the sea, then the Dogs and the rocky points that marked the mouth of the cove vanished from the face of the earth. The Hampton boat on its mooring went monochromatic before it disappeared altogether. On the porch, Crystal and I stepped back instinctively—a thing that big moving that fast, a thing with the power to wipe away geological features, had to arrive with corporeal impact. . . .

After the fog had avalanched over the boathouse and climbed the hill behind, Crystal and I couldn't see the water's edge from the porch. We stood speechless. We could hardly see each other. The air was half water. Fat beads of liquid buzzed around on the gentle breeze. Small animals could drown in air this wet. Jellyroll's nose was going a mile a minute. He'd never seen fog either, not real fog, anyway, not like this. We were wet in minutes, but we stayed and stared into the opaqueness, fascinated and expectant. The phone rang, and we retreated inside.

It would be Shelly calling, I assumed, with word from Clayton in California, but that wasn't why he called. "Did Sid get you?" he asked without pausing for niceties.

"No."

"Sid traced the boat. That *Seastar* boat. It's registered in Boston, all right—to Kevin James."

"Kevin James," I mouthed. The connection. Desmond wasn't here by coincidence. Kevin was there on Pier Twelve when Clayton invited me. Kevin had said, "Clayton's island was one of the world's beautiful places." He'd encouraged me to accept the invitation.

"He's directing the evil high school principal thing, right?" said Shelly.

". . . Yeah."

"What?" Crystal said. She knew it was going to be bad—

I told her. She sagged onto the couch.

That's how they knew. Kevin told them. They knew Kevin well enough to use his boat, and he told them, maybe only in passing; there would be no reason to keep it secret. I suddenly felt sick and frightened. I tasted meat-loaf bile at the back of my throat.

"What's it mean, Artie?" Shelly asked.

"Shelly, did Sid talk to Kevin?"

"No. He tried. I tried, too. We left messages."

I tried to think. What did that really mean? Removing fear and any other emotion with the power to deflect us from the literal, what did it mean? Everybody in the business knows everybody else. It could be pure coincidence that Kevin loaned his boat to Dick Desmond and his son, who just happened to be coming up this way. Sure, easy. Stranger coincidences happen every day in New York. Sure. "Where's Sid now?"

"He's on his way to you. He'll be there any time."

"Good." What about the fog? "Did you get Clayton in L.A.?"

"I found his place in Santa Monica, left a message.

I'm trying to find out where he's working, if he's working. He didn't say, did he?"

"No."

"Are you okay, Artie?"

"Yeah."

"You don't sound okay. What about just getting the fuck out of there? Sid's got a seaplane somewhere up there. We'll get the best seaplane pilot in the region, swoop down, and pull you out, okay?"

"Okay, Shelly. That's what we'll do."

"Also I got an all-points bulletin out on Dick Desmond. People'll start calling any time now. Then we'll know better. Okay?"

"Okay, Shelly, thanks."

"You kiss that dog of mine."

I promised Shelly we'd call him as soon as Sid arrived. But what do we do until then?

"It doesn't mean that Dick Desmond and his son are the stalkers," Crystal said. "It just doesn't mean that, at least not necessarily."

"No, it doesn't. You're absolutely right."

". . . Just because you and Desmond have a mutual friend with a boat."

"Yeah."

We stood silently at the French doors looking out at the nothingness. We couldn't even see the railings on the porch.

"Scary how quickly it came in," said Crystal. "Kind of makes you nervous."

We stared at the water running down the pane of glass nearest to our noses.

"Crystal . . . ?"

"What?"

"Sid's gun. I was thinking about it."

"Funny, so was I."

"Were you thinking about, uh, familiarizing our-selves with it?"

She nodded. "We don't even know if it's loaded."

"I'm gonna go get it, okay?"

"Okay."

I placed the short black shotgun and the box of shells on the table. We sat down around them as if they were a totem of empowerment. This was the sort of gun lusted after by crazed paramilitary psychos holed up in stinking hotels wearing Nazi regalia and watching the roaches race across the wall. It was just what I wanted. I picked it up, gripping the snub little handle, avoiding the trigger. The handle was made of plastic. The whole thing except for the barrel was made of plas-tic. I pointed it vertically, pulled the slide back, and a heavy red shell jumped out, clattered on the table. "It's loaded."

"Wait a minute," she said. "Doesn't that mean it's now cocked?"

We stared at it. I kept it pointed at the ceiling, won-dering. "Maybe we should find out."

The back door barely cleared the abruptly climbing hillside when full open. Jellyroll squeezed out. Crystal and I stood waiting for him while he peed. He headed off to chase the chipmunk, but the utter absence of visibility stopped him short. He looked back at us, then in the general direction of the woodpile, deciding. He barked once at the chipmunk's woodpile before he joined us in the doorway. Bangs and explosions don't bother him, he's used to them in our neighborhood.

Nonetheless, I petted his side and told him it was okay in advance.

I pointed the shotgun at the hillside and pulled the trigger. The gun almost flew from my hands as it discharged its load. Jellyroll froze, so did Crystal. Me, too. The fog swirled around the short, smoking barrel. Our bodies rocked back and forth in the reverberating waves of concussion.

"Christ, look at the hole," said Crystal.

The sound was still bouncing around the hills as we went to look. There was a hole in the slope you could stick your head in without getting your ears muddy. That's why it's so hard to banish guns; they turn the hopeless and the helpless omnipotent. With one of these jewels folded into the crook of your arm, there's nobody to fuck with your lifestyle. The delusion is easy to cleave to.

"I hope this isn't like Ibsen," I said.

"What do you mean Ibsen?"

"Maybe it was Chekhov. One or the other said that if you show a gun in act one, you've got to use it in act three."

". . . What act are we in?"

"Good question."

The phone rang. It was Shelly. "Artie! Artie!"

"What!" My skin crawled with fear when I heard the brittle quaver in his voice.

"I just got a bad call, Artie!"

"Tell me, Shelly!"

"Kevin James! He's dead! Murdered! In the Boston morgue—they just identified him."

I told Crystal. Telling took my breath away.

"The Boston police—" said Shelly, also gasping.

231

"Sid left word. He had a friend on the force. Kevin James turned up in the morgue. Where's Sid? Don't worry about a thing when Sid gets there. You'll be hearing a seaplane overhead any time now. Also, Sid is very heavily armed, Artie."

"We're having a little fog, Shelly."

"Fog? Fuck!"

"Shelly—what happened to Kevin?"

"You mean how was he . . . ?"

"Yeah."

"His head was split right down the middle. Like with an ax, Artie."

In common with so many of our fellow citizens, we retired that night with a gun by the bedside. Lock and load, say your prayers, hit the hay. We lay there stiffly side by side holding hands, listening. I'm not sure if I slept or not, so I'm not sure when I heard the first noise. I strained to concentrate. Was I conscious? Does a gun beside the bed engender intruders? But where did the noise, if there really was one, originate? That was what I strained to understand.

"Artie—!" Crystal hissed.

Damn. It was real. She'd heard it, too.

Jellyroll barked twice before I told him to hush. What to do? My heart was pounding. I could see my feet bouncing with it. I dropped my hand over the side of the bed and felt for the stock of the shotgun—

Something thudded in the other room. Someone was moving around out there in the dark. The bedroom door was ajar. I could see only half the living room.

"Let's get off the bed, Artie—" Crystal whispered in

my ear. She rolled off. She meant to place the bed between us and the door.

I followed her with the shotgun. "Jellyroll, come—"
He did so, nestling between us.

We hunched behind the battlements, panting with
terror. There wasn't enough oxygen on the island to
accommodate my sudden increased need. Yet the edges
of things were very crisp in my vision, even in the near
absence of light. The adrenaline was pumping, and
things moved more slowly than normal.

Someone was on the porch. Someone *else?* Or the
same as in the living room? The house creaked with
the fulcrum weight out there. I could feel Crystal
trembling, even though our bodies were a foot apart,
but I couldn't comfort her, not yet. I was riding this
wave of atavistic purity, protecting, to the death if necessary, my loved ones and myself from—

"Maybe it's Sid," said Crystal in a tight whisper.

"Think I should call out?"

"Yes."

"Sid! Sid, is that you?"

No response. No movement.

"Hawley! That you!" Nope. "We're armed!" I
squeaked. I got a hold of my voice and screamed,
"We're armed! And I'm gonna fucking kill you if you
don't get out of this house!" I was working myself into
a rage, and it took little effort. Like when I kicked that
guy's lunch. I was atwitch with the impulse to kick
open the door and fire, screaming, like in some jack-
off G.I. Joe fantasy. I did, however, decide: If someone
appears in the doorway, I will shoot him without a
word of warning. That decision was clear and unequiv-

ocal. I cocked the gun and braced it on the bed. I couldn't miss.

We waited. Silence. . . . Had we scared them off? I couldn't sustain this level of readiness over the long haul. . . .

"You think I should go out and see?" I asked.

"Hell, no," she said.

"What if they're gone?"

"Then what difference will it make?"

Jellyroll was trembling so hard it looked like he was running in place.

Then, suddenly, it was dawn, a gray pasty one, but we had made it through the night. Everything is easier in the daylight. We must have slept, at least periodically, at our stations, but now we were both awake. Crystal, I noticed for the first time, was wearing only a pair of green bikini panties and I only a T-shirt. I hugged her close. And then we went into the living room together, but I led the way as the designated shooter. The boathouse was empty.

Jellyroll sniffed the edges of the floor. He knew someone had been here. I went out on the porch. I peered over the railing down to seaweed-covered rocks. No one was lurking down there. From the porch, I looked along the sides of the house. No one was hiding there, either.

Then I realized there was a stiff wind blowing, not so much down in the cove, but the tops of the tall pines were swaying, and the fog had dissipated but not lifted. I still couldn't see the mouth of the cove, but I could see fifty feet in that direction, and I felt a vague disquiet as I looked. Something was different out there. Something was wrong. What?

The boat.

"Crystal, the boat's gone!"

She came out, Jellyroll trailing. She had a grim look on her face. "Artie, where did you leave the telephone?"

"Right on the table."

"In clear sight?"

"Why?"

"It's gone."

23

"T hey took our phone *and* our boat?"

We stared out dispiritedly. We were too tired to fight anymore. The psychos had taken our only means of communication and our only means of transportation.

"Wait a minute," said Crystal, pointing out into the murk. Maybe her gaze hadn't been blank and helpless, maybe only mine had. "See out there? Isn't that the boat? I can't see it if I look right at it, but if I look to one side or the other . . . I see a shape."

I looked out the corner of my eye. I saw it. I got the binoculars, but they didn't work in the fog, magnifying obscurity. "I'll go see," I said.

"How?"

"In the dinghy."

"No, Artie, suppose it's a setup," she said, squeezing my forearm so hard it hurt. "Suppose they're waiting out there in the boat. Suppose that's how they planned it all along. You come rowing up, and pow." She made a fatal chopping motion with the side of her hand.

That was a factor, all right, the chop. But what if the boat had come loose because I didn't tie it on very well? The tide was ebbing. In a little while our boat would be irretrievable, and we'd have no way out except by foot along a rocky trail ripe for ambush. *That* could have been the setup.

"Then we'll go together," said Crystal.

"I couldn't row the dinghy fast enough with all of us in it." We argued briefly over who'd take the shotgun. She insisted I take it.

"Do you have a life jacket?"

"Yes, but it's in the boat. Crystal, maybe you ought to pack a few essentials while I'm gone. Maybe we should get out as soon as I bring the boat back."

"Okay," she said grimly.

It began to rain fat, heavy drops. The sky was black and low. There was another storm coming.

It was a hard row. The wind kept blowing me off course. In the gusts, the raindrops stung when they hit my face. Water ran freely over my glasses. I was almost blind now. . . . I could see why the Indians invented the canoe. This facing backward was a drag. Looking over my shoulder, I feared I wasn't gaining on the shape. Maybe the tide was carrying us out of the cove even now. Maybe I'd never catch up. Maybe I'd soon look around and realize I was alone on a gray sea. In a dinghy. In a building storm. With no idea where I was, and my body would never come up.

No, I was making progress. I was rowing marginally faster than the Hampton boat was drifting. The next time I looked around, I could see I was actually closing on it. I could distinguish bow from stern.

I couldn't detect any activity aboard, but then if they were lying in wait for me in the bottom of the boat, they wouldn't show themselves yet. They'd wait until I was closer, within ax range, maybe when I was trying to climb aboard. Thwack. Five minutes later I had pulled within two dinghy lengths of the Hampton boat. I put the shotgun in my lap and gave two final, straining pulls on the oars to get up some momentum. Then I slid off the seat, crouched in the bottom, and let the nose of the dinghy hit the bigger boat, but I didn't look up over the gunwale. Not yet. We drifted together for a while. I listened . . . silence.

There was no one aboard, I decided, but I still didn't risk it. I grabbed the side of the Hampton boat so we wouldn't separate, waited still longer, before, gun first, I peered over the rail. There was, in fact, no one there, but I got a scare climbing aboard. I did one of those Buster Keaton splits between two quickly separating boats, and I nearly went in the drink. I always expect the ludicrous, even in extremis. On the second go I got aboard.

I tied the dinghy to the cleat in the stern. I retrieved my keys from under the seat cushion where I kept them, but I stopped myself before starting the engine. The sniff test. I wouldn't even feel the explosion, a flash of white light, then nothing. Atomized within sight of the boathouse. Maybe little bits of me would drop into Crystal's hair with the rain. Jellyroll would eat the bigger parts when they came down. I'd been noticing an increased stink lately. I raised the engine box. It reeked of gasoline, but the wind quickly blew the fumes away. Did I have a gas leak or was that normal? I started the motor with the cover open. Then I headed for home—

I hadn't gone more than two boat lengths before I hit something. I put the transmission back into neutral. It wasn't a rock—I was well clear of the sunkers. It felt like a rotten tree trunk or something. I looked into the water, saw nothing unusual, so, gingerly, I put the lever forward and we began to move. . . . No problem dead slow. Everything felt fine. I sped up—and I hit it again with the same thunk.

I yanked the lever to neutral and stood there frozen, my shoulder bones pressing against my ears, water running down my spine. I went back to look over the stern, because it felt like only the propeller or the rear part of the boat had hit the thing. I watched the water longer this time. Twice I checked my position. Was I way off course? No. There was still fog, but it wasn't opaque anymore. I could see the boathouse ahead. I could make out landmarks, a dead tree hanging over the water on the right, the big round boulder cracked in half on the left. I knew exactly where the sunkers were—

Something pale was rising slowly from the green, turgid water. I had read somewhere that cold northern waters are murky because of the rich plankton and other minute marine organisms in suspension, and tropical waters are clear because they are relatively barren. This water was rich in life; I couldn't identify the pale thing until it was about to break the surface.

It was a man's naked leg.

It floated up right under my nose as I leaned over the stern. The leg was pudgy. It had been severed at the hip. The sickening white cartilaginous ball remained intact as if the propeller had wrenched, not chopped, the ball out of the socket. Two parallel bone-deep gashes in the calf streamed raggedy red tissue. Little black hairs danced on the pale flesh as water sloshed over it. His forlorn foot still wore a brown-and-white argyle crumpled around the ankle.

Where was the rest of him? In a kind of trance, I circled my boat looking—

There was a line hanging over the bow. I hadn't noticed that before. It was taut. That meant there was something on the other end of it, some weight. The anchor? No, I was standing on the anchor. I knew it wasn't the anchor, anyway. I knew what it was.

I untied the line and held the end in my hand, felt the weight, while I decided what to do with it. After all, I could just cast the line overboard and not pull on it at all—

An empty shoe, an oxblood wingtip, surfaced languidly. It bobbed upright but awash. I knew that shoe. That was Sid's shoe. Then Sid himself surfaced. I hadn't consciously pulled on the rope.

"Crystal!" I screamed at the top of my lungs. Again. But I knew in a wave of despair that it was futile; she'd never hear me in the wind. "Crystal!" I screamed again, nonetheless.

They had tied the rope around Sid's waist, and his body had bent around it. He surfaced in that attitude. He had hung straight down until the boat moved forward, and then the force of water had brought him up right into the propeller. His pants had been ripped off his body, his shirt and jacket rumpled under his armpits. I never saw Sid's face, but I saw the back of his head. It was stove in, and triangular chunks of his skull had floated away. I heard myself whimpering, but I couldn't stop. I didn't want to stop. Sid had tried to help us. Sid sank back, opening up as he did so, arms and legs akimbo like a skydiver's. I had let his body pull the end of the rope from my hands before I clearly understood that was happening.

I shoved the throttle forward hard. The engine roared, but it seemed to take two days for us to pick up any speed. I strained to see Crystal on the porch as I drew near, but she wasn't there. Neither was Jellyroll—

I hit the flat rock a glancing blow that drove my knee against the steering console. Blades of sick pain stabbed up my leg. I threw the bow line ashore, but I didn't take time to tie it onto anything. I leapt off the boat and hobbled to the stairs—

"Crystal!" No answer from the house! "Jellyroll!" I ran around back, past Jellyroll's woodpile, screaming their names, but they didn't answer. I went up the steps three at a time, though I knew neither Crystal nor Jellyroll would be there—

No phone! I was on my own. Where would they take Crystal and Jellyroll? That's what I needed to think about. Where would I take them if I were a psycho stalker? I realized that I had the shotgun clutched so tightly my fingers throbbed. Where!

They had no choice on foot. They had to take either the back trail toward the Castle or the coastal trail leading toward Kempshall's crypt. I ran down the steps, skidded around the corner in the mud, and went down hard on my left hip. I heard myself moan. There was the woodpile. Jellyroll's woodpile. Somewhere inside was his chipmunk.

I crawled in the mud past the woodpile toward the Castle trail, looking for tracks. Wouldn't I see tracks? If they'd just come this way— But what if they went the other way?

Christ, tracks everywhere! Waffle-soled boots, dog tracks, and barefoot tracks. Crystal's tracks. The imprint of her instep could break my heart. The wind howled. I was shivering.

The tracks led unmistakably toward the Castle trail. I ran as fast as I could under the conditions. My pain—I could feel it—was focusing down into a hot, lethal rage. I was glad. I felt calm now. I loved my gun and the death it would deal. No matter what, the Desmonds would never leave the island alive. I skidded to a stop before I knew why. Had I heard something? I was gasping too loudly to hear anything. I held my breath. . . .

Crystal! She was calling my name! From where? Was it a trap? I ran along the flat part of the trail where the undergrowth thickened. I slowed. I couldn't see around the next bend. Anything could be waiting.

I turned a corner, and there she was—

She was leaning against a tree. Waving her arms overhead. Was she unhurt? But why didn't she come toward me? She was crying and holding her arms out to me, but she didn't come to me. Why? She was naked from the waist up—

They had chained her by the neck to the trunk of a fat spruce tree. I held her as best I could. I'd worn extra layers for the row. I peeled off my slicker and then my fleece jacket, which I wrapped around her.

"It was Desmond! Desmond and that little fucker!

His name is really Perry. It was his idea to strip me like this before chaining me—to slow you down. They're going to the Crack to get their boat. They mean to take Jellyroll to the mainland because that's where the press is, covering the murders. Hurry, you might be able to catch them!"

"I can't leave you like—"

"Yes, you can! Go!" They had wrapped the chain twice around her neck and then locked it behind the tree, so there was no chance she could duck out of it even with my help.

"What are they going to do to Jellyroll on the mainland?"

"You know what they'll do. They'll do what they threatened to do. They killed Sid, Artie. That little fucker was laughing about it!"

". . . Is that strangling you?"

"No. But I'm not going anywhere." Her wet hair streaked over her brow. I pushed it out of her eyes.

"Was Jellyroll terrified?"

She cried. "It was the saddest thing I've ever seen. He kept looking back over his shoulder at me as they dragged him off." She collected herself and whispered, "Go."

I turned and ran. I ran hard, sometimes leaping obstructions, jinking around holes. I wanted to make time here on the flat ground, because I wouldn't be able to run once the trail climbed near the patch of wildcat granite on the way up to the Castle.

I was near full speed when I saw the boots, the legs of someone lying face down across the trail. I saw this lower half of what I assumed was a dead man; it registered in my brain—look, there's a corpse in the ferns—but my body couldn't respond. I tripped on his feet, and went airborne. The gun flew from my hands as I threw them out to break my landing—

Sharp pain. Something bad had happened to my left hand, but the pain didn't have any specificity yet. I rolled on my side and cradled my hand against my chest as if it were a baby bird fallen from the nest. I didn't want to look at it yet. I shimmied back on my ass in the mud and the rain to see who was dead.

Perry was dead. Dick Desmond's phony son from hell had left this life, and that was fine with me. Save ammo. His head was turned sideways—we were almost face-to-face before I realized my glasses were gone. His eyes were open, but they were milky. They didn't blink when raindrops struck them. His lips were pursed as if he'd been slurping blood juice off his empty plate when the blow fell.

The blade had hit him smack in the left ear. There was a deep puddle of half-coagulated blood beneath his head but curiously little on the point of impact. The guy's ear was split in half horizontally, and most of the two halves had followed the blade into the black wound. What remained of his ear looked like a spring bud on a certain cherry tree in Riverside Park.

A sweet little patch of wildflowers grew among the ferns near Perry's crown, but I didn't know what they were. Were they pearly everlasting? It seemed sad that my study of wildflowers had come to nothing before the corpses started showing up. A single mosquito landed on Perry's brow near his wound, wiggled a couple of times getting set and plowed her thing through his skin. I could see it penetrate. I watched it with a terrible concentration. Oddly, I found the juxtaposition, the incongruity (or something) hilarious. I didn't exactly laugh. I made some kind of noise, but it wasn't exactly laughter. And I still hadn't looked at my hand.

24

I was about ready to look. I sat in the mud with my knees drawn up, my back turned on the corpse. If the corpse came here to harm Jellyroll, then he got what he deserved, tough shit. I wondered who turned him into a corpse, but I didn't have time to speculate; I had to get running again. So I'd just take a quick look at the old digit, a glance, and get moving again. I didn't need to dwell on it, to make myself sick with it—

I flashed it up in front of my face. There was a clear problem with my pinkie. My pinkie flopped over at a grotesque angle like a fallen soldier behind its fellows. I moved it gently. I could see the socket gophering beneath the skin. I reached around behind my normal fingers, took hold of the errant one, and tried to lever it back into position. I yelped in pain, but I accomplished nothing. It wouldn't go unless I wrenched it. Christ, I hated the thought of wrenching it. Maybe I would wrench it clean off; maybe only skin held it on.

I began to sob. My shoulders bounced uncontrollably with it. I had reached the end of my rope. My dog was probably already dead. My lover was chained to a tree by her neck. Sid was murdered. What hope was there? None. I stopped sobbing abruptly without decision. I just stopped. I don't know precisely why.

I'd leave my finger like that for now—I could shoot the gun one-handed—but it would be better if I could cover the hand in something so it wouldn't catch on objects as I ran through the woods. I still had a long way to go. I hadn't even reached the Castle ruins yet, not nearly. How far was the Crack from the Castle? I didn't really know, I'd never been from the Castle to the Crack. Why exactly was I going there, anyway? What was the point of fighting psychos if they just keep coming at you? Sooner or later you'd run out of will, energy, ammo. I clenched my jaw against that kind of hamstrung despair. My finger throbbed maddeningly, my dog was probably dead, but, goddamnit, I would keep struggling for the terrible retribution I would inflict, for the pleasure of rollicking in their spurting, arterial blood. The wind keened in the treetops. Or was I making that noise?

I located my glasses after only a brief search. They listed badly to starboard, but they were intact. I could see. I'd missed vision. Things don't seem quite so dreadful when you can see them, even if they are exactly that dreadful. I went crawling around after my shotgun—

Somebody was coming my way on the trail! I couldn't see anybody, but I could hear rocks clunking together. I couldn't find my shotgun. If I had found it, I can't say with confidence that I wouldn't have used

247

it on sight, just started blasting away, no questions asked. But I had to abandon the search for the gun and crawl off the trail into the fern forest to hide. The ferns felt good against my face, like lace, but I remembered the visible wake Jellyroll had left when he'd passed through them, so I didn't go in very far before lying motionless. I felt no wind down there, stillness, the small sound of my breathing, of rain droplets against my face. I could *feel* the stranger's approach, a soft thudding in my chest.

I peeked up. His back was to me—this is when I might have shot him. He was bending over Perry's body. Returning, maybe, to the scene of the crime. He wore brown woolen pants, lace-up rubber boots with leather tops, a dirty white sweater, and a yellow slicker with the hood drawn up. A local. He nudged the body with his toe. Perry would never move again. The stranger straightened, looked around as if surprised, frightened by the corpse in the ferns.

I ducked flat and held my breath. . . .

He dressed just like Hawley, but he was too small to be Hawley. Yet he was carrying that same canvas gym bag, the one Hawley had carried his hatchet in. But then I remembered something—Hawley's gym bag had broken handles. These handles were not broken. His hood was drawn tight around his face, and I had only caught a glimpse of it when he turned my way. What had I seen? There was something wrong with the face, I couldn't tell exactly what, but it had looked familiar, and it did not belong to Dick Desmond. Maybe it belonged to a friend, an ally. I could have used either. I craned my neck to look up. Our eyes met—

It was Clayton Kempshall!

"Artie!" he said. "Artie, is that you?"

"Hello, Clayton." I stood up in the ferns.

"Did you kill this guy, Artie?"

I giggled mirthlessly, hysteria tickling the edges of my mind. "No, Clay, I didn't. I thought maybe you'd killed him."

Clayton giggled, too. He also sounded a little hysterical. He pulled back his hood. His face was streaked with grime; his matted hair stuck straight out on the sides. His hands, too, were caked with dirt. Clayton edged some ferns aside with his boot to see the dead guy's face and said, "No, I didn't kill *him*. I don't even know him. Who was he?"

"He was one of the stalkers. Dick Desmond is the other stalker."

"Dick Desmond? Not Dick Desmond from *Ten Pins?*"

"Yeah. Do you know him?"

"Not personally. You know who knows him? Kevin James knows him."

". . . Desmond has Jellyroll now. I think he's taking him to the Crack. I've got to go after him, Clay." I pointed up the trail toward the Castle.

"He's got Jellyroll—? Want me to go with you? I know this island. Teal Island. I grew up here, you know?"

"Sure—"

"Well, you don't want to go that way. Come this way. This is a shortcut." He stepped over the corpse and headed off into the ferns. I followed. The Castle ruins seemed to be somewhere up on the left. We appeared to be going around the hill rather than over it. When I caught up, he said, "You haven't been having a very relaxing stay, have you?"

I giggled again. Maybe there was a little more hysteria in this giggle.

"I'm sorry."

"It's not your fault." Off the beaten track, I was already disoriented, but I followed. I watched the back of his head and wondered if he'd killed anybody recently. I wondered how to approach the question before I became totally lost. Clumsily, I decided: "What have you been doing, Clay?"

He waved his arm vaguely as if to take in the entire island. "I've been pondering things. The past. Trying to remember. I thought if I came back here, I might discover something. I've been living up in the ruins."

"You've been here on the island the whole time? I mean, you haven't gone to the mainland?"

"No, staying here was the point. I thought if I immersed myself in the past, I'd remember something about it. Actually, it was my analyst's idea."

"How did it work?"

"I don't want to evaluate it too much yet, but one thing seems clear, Artie. I killed my father." With that he held the gym bag out at eye level and gave it a shake. It rattled like—well, bones.

"You mean, he's . . . in there?"

Clayton nodded slowly. "Remember that day on the pier you were telling me about the stalkers, and I invited you to the boathouse? You said there was a cartoon about Jellyroll. The stalker killed him with a hatchet, remember?"

The wind blew the rain against our faces; I staggered. "Yes," I squeaked.

"Such a horrible thought, it struck me. I kept thinking about it all that night and the next day, I couldn't get it out of my mind. I began to think it had something to do with me personally. . . . Artie, I knew exactly where he was buried. I don't know—I don't remember anything else, but I knew just where my father was buried. Nobody else knew. I went and dug him up. Twisted, huh? Well, I thought it would help me remember, sort of like a talisman." He stopped, turned, and looked at me to see how I was reacting.

"Did the dogs disturb you?" I asked.

"Yes!" He patted his chest as though his heart were still pounding. "Those dogs. Here I was all alone, except for the skeleton of my own father which I'd just dug up, and suddenly it's the hounds from hell! I ran. I just freaked and ran until I couldn't run anymore."

"That must have been terrifying, Clayton," I said lamely.

Poor Clayton began to cry. "Maybe he wasn't such a bad man. Maybe it was just me."

I hugged him, tried to comfort him. I patted his back. It was all I had to offer under the circumstances.

"Artie," he said after a while, "how do you know Dick Desmond was heading for the Crack?"

I told him about Crystal and how even now she was standing chained by the neck to a tree.

"Come on, Artie, let's go, this is a great shortcut—"

"Thanks, Clay." And off we went as fast as we could.

The ferns were nearly head high now, like a stunted rain forest.

"You don't feel it down here," he said hustling, without turning around, "but there's a lot of wind blowing, and I think it's blowing from the northeast."

I jogged to catch up. Dwight had said it never blew

from the northeast in the summer. "What about boats in the Crack, Clayton?"

"I'm not sure. I've never seen it, because it never blows from the northeast in the summer, and I've never been here any other time. But I've heard people talk about it. It sounds bad."

We stopped abruptly at the edge of a swamp.

"This is the only trouble with the shortcut, right here," said Clayton.

It wasn't a huge swamp. In fact, it was sort of a miniature swamp, but it still had all the impediments for travelers of full-sized swamps. There was brown water of unknown depth. Lily pads with stiff yellow flowers on short stalks grew in it along with other aquatic vegetation. Dead tree trunks festered in it, and there was a coating of green scum over everything. It was just vegetable matter, but it still looked uninviting, like plutonium waste.

"It's not too deep. At least it didn't used to be too deep."

I looked down at my shoes. I was sinking even as I stood there. Tannin-dark water lapped over my shoelaces.

"But you'll be amazed at what a good shortcut it is." And he stepped into the swamp, immediately plunging to his thighs in black mud and detritus the consistency of oatmeal.

I waded in after him. The swamp sucked at me, tried to claim my shoes; I curled my toes to keep them.

I lost my balance and went down thickly on my hands and knees. The swamp tried to keep my vulnerable finger. I snarled as I withdrew it. Now, dripping

black ooze, it stuck straight out in the opposite direction from before and hurt like hell. It was making me
mean.

"Christ!" said Clay. "You broke your finger!"

"I broke it before. I tripped over the dead guy." That
can happen when there are a lot of dead guys lying
around.

"Let's see," Clayton asked, concerned.

We stopped waist-deep in the swamp, and I showed
him. Maybe he knew what to do.

"Jesus, it's kind of sickening, isn't it? Is there anything we can do?"

"No, let's keep going." We did. We surged on
through the viscosity, and sooner than it seemed, we
emerged and climbed onto rocky ground. "Clayton, I
think Desmond and that dead guy back there killed
Kevin James."

"What! Kevin's dead—?"

"Murdered. In Boston. His head was split by a blow
from an ax or something like that, a hatchet. Just like
the guy back there. Just like the people in Micmac."

"Just like my father," he said.

"Desmond and the dead guy came here in Kevin's
boat."

"What, that big black fishing boat?"

"You know it?"

"I've seen it from the Castle."

"They knew Jellyroll was coming here. They showed
up the next day. How long's it take to get from Boston
to here in a boat? Days, right?"

"I should think so, sure. Do you mean they killed
Kevin to find out where you were going?"

"Could be."

"And Kevin knew because I told him that day on the pier? Jesus. Dick Desmond, imagine! I did a *Murder, She Wrote* with him about a hundred years ago. . . . You never know."

The trees thinned. Were we there already? We both quickened our pace. Then we heard the noise—it stopped us in our tracks. Wind roared through the branches overhead. But there was another component to the noise, a water sound, as loud as a big waterfall, but not consistent like that, more of a staccato rhythm, like artillery salvoes. Surely the *sea* wasn't making that sound—

I could see the clearing ahead, the old railroad station. The wind blew so hard we couldn't look into it. I put my good hand over my eyes, peeked through the chinks between my fingers. Then as I stepped out into that clearing around the Crack, the wind stopped me in midstride, one foot off the ground, like a sight gag. It unnerves me, sometimes, to see how often life, reality, resembles the slapstick sight gag. Objects flew on the wind.

"Let's get behind the sheds," Clayton shouted.

It sounded like a good idea, to get behind something solid, but I didn't move. I was transfixed at the sight. The sea beyond the mouth of the Crack ran white with streaks of spray snaking in the troughs, while great waves marched rank after rank from as far out as I could see toward the opening of the Crack. The wind had wiped away the clouds and fog, and now the sky was blue and cloudless, a terrible unending clarity.

The waves disintegrated in stark white explosions against the headlands on either side of the Crack—but a part of each wave kept coming right on through the opening. Their speed and size increased as they drove inward and compressed between the rock walls, where they seethed like the great caldera of an ancient volcano when the earth was still new and unformed. As one wave tried to recede, the next slammed up behind it, then the next and the next, and the energy built on itself until the properties of water itself seemed to change from the familiar into something volatile and unstable, like lava. The fifth or sixth wave, having no other way to expend its force, blasted straight up in the air from the apex of the Crack like a white-hot geyser. I stood there slackjawed until a short piece of wood struck me in the chest and knocked me back a stride. Then I followed Clayton and his bouncing gym bag into the lee of the red shed near the side of the cliff.

I pressed my back against the boards. "Nothing could survive in there, right?" I said. Wind whistled through unseen cracks between the weathered boards.

"I don't know," said Clayton. "Your hand looks like hell, Artie."

"Yeah. It does." I held it up, and we watched it for a little while. It was unusual to have parts of myself broken, disjointed, uprooted. I hoped the pain wouldn't get any worse, so I could concentrate, react.

"God, Dick Desmond. I can't believe it," said Clayton. "We have the same agent, did you know that? I'd see the guy at auditions, he seemed normal, happy . . . as normal as anybody in the business, I mean. He had a family, kids. He showed me a picture of his kids once. Two little towheads at the beach. You can't ever tell who's going to turn out to be a psycho these days."

It was possible to walk to the edge of the Crack but

too scary in the face of forces I never imagined I'd actually see, let alone approach.

"Artie, maybe he's just after the publicity, you know? Maybe it's just some kind of twisted stunt."

"It's already gone too far," I said in a cold voice I'd never heard before. "Thanks for showing me the shortcut, Clay."

"Sure, Artie. He's my favorite dog, too."

I crawled to the edge of the Crack, trying not to drag my finger. It was hard to see through my salty glasses and all that spray in the air, and that enhanced the surreal quality. Each wave seemed to reach higher than its predecessor, and soon, I thought, they'd top the cliff and wash me off. After a wave passed, the water level plunged down over the rocks with a scary sucking sound.

Not a single stairway remained on the rock. I could see their broken bones crashing around in the maelstrom. The floating docks like the one the Hampton boat had been tied to was gone. The railroad-tie rack from which the sub had been launched showed no signs of ever having existed. Obliterated. All of it.

There were three vessels in the water. Broken, awash, sunk, they sloshed around like bathtub boats. Each of them, it occurred to me dimly, was from away. There were no islanders' boats broken in pieces down there.

There was the submarine. The sea had stripped it of its tanks, hoses, pipes, and other external fittings; its plexiglass bubble was ripped away. It was nothing more than an orange steel tube full of water, but there must have been some sort of flotation inside, because the pathetic ruined thing hung near the surface, and every wave dashed it against the rocks near the apex

of the Crack. The dark granite was slashed with orange paint.

Near the sub, being driven against the same rocks,
was the black-clad strangers' Cigarette boat that had
circled Dog Cove. How long ago was that? Its red bow
poked the surface every so often. Then I realized that
the bow section was all that remained of the boat. Its
back had been broken in two. The engine half was
probably on the bottom. That's probably where the hip-
sters were, too.

And then there was *Seastar*. My heart sank when I
identified it. There wasn't much left. I put my forehead
down on the rock to cry or moan or something, but
pebbles blew into my eyes. I looked again. The boat
was upside down. Its bright green bottom pointed at
the sky. The propeller was gone, and the thick shaft
was bent like my finger. Splintered pieces of the cabin
and the deck swirled in and out with the waves. Had
my dog been aboard that boat when it went over? If so,
I'd never see him again.

25

I scuttled like a crab away from the Crack, back toward the faded red shed, where Clayton waited. He was pale, his eyes fixed on mine. What had I found? Jellyroll drowned and sloshing around down there? Tears welled up in his eyes. Clayton and Jellyroll loved each other. I told him about the wrecked vessels I'd seen, the submarine, the Cigarette boat, the black sportfisherman, but no people and no dogs. "Maybe we beat Desmond here," I said.

"You want to wait?"

. . . How could I wait? Maybe they were never heading this way. Maybe they only told Crystal that so she'd tell me and I'd take off on a wild goose chase. What to do? Mostly, I like to do nothing; now here I was making these sorts of decisions, potentially life and death decisions, while staring at my hand with a grotesque fascination. So do I wait in ambush while Crystal stands chained to a tree in the storm? I wished I had my gun. That would have made it easier, all that power to destroy, even if destroying didn't make any sense. Psychos beget psychos.

"What's in this shed, Clay?" I demanded.

"Christ, Artie, I don't know, I haven't been here since I was ten. Since the night I killed my father, I guess. They used to store railroad parts and equipment in there. All the stuff was greasy, I remember. Too greasy to play with."

I knelt down to look through a chink in the weathered boards. I moved to hood my eyes with my hands so I could better see into the darkness, but I rammed my finger into the side of the building. I howled in pain. Besides, the goddamn shed was empty inside. "Jellyroll—" I called, nonetheless. Silence, of course. Hearing his name out loud, I started crying.

Clayton put his hand on my shoulder. "Why don't we wait in the depot?" he suggested.

The depot—that would be a good place for us to wait, or for Desmond to hide.

I turned to look at it, across the clearing from us, about a block away. Windblown objects bounced against the boarded-up facade. Nature had leached all the moisture from the wooden structure; the naked boards had contracted, nails had rusted away, and the roof had sagged in the middle. The wind and salt had scoured off the paint, but a red-with-white-trim tint remained deep in the grain of the old boards like a shadow of the past. You could still see KEMPSHALL ISLAND in the stain of once-white letters over the boarded door. The depot was the cliché of rural American whistle-stop stations, yet in miniature, almost half-scale. Maybe that toylike quality had been a whimsical touch by Clayton's old man. Now it just felt grim, depressing, and weird, a death house, the sort of place where serial killers leave messages for each other.

"Was this your toy, Clay?"

"Fuck no, it was his toy. He'd put on his engineer's suit, you know, with the hat, one of those old-fashioned oil cans, and hang out the window, waving like he was just a jovial old eccentric fellow." Clayton's lips were tight as he remembered.

We stepped from our shelter behind the shed, put our backs out into the wind, and it spirited us across the clearing faster than I've covered ground since high school track. We ducked out of the jetstream behind the railroad station barely panting, because the wind had done all the work.

Two of the rear windows weren't boarded up. A few panes of glass were missing. The door was closed, probably locked, but boards were not nailed across it. This would be a fine place to hang if you were a dog stalker with no means of escape, the situation spinning out of your control. I looked in. So did Clayton. The room was starkly empty. The old tongue-and-groove wood floor was mostly covered with dust and bird shit. Shafts of light from holes in the ceiling fell on piles of it. There might have been some small mammal droppings mixed in, rats, voles, porcupines, etc.

"Strange, isn't it?" whispered Clayton.

"What, specifically?"

"These are practical people who live on islands. Yet here are vacant buildings right on the harbor where they'd be most useful, but nobody ever chose to use them, not in thirty years. It's not like an ownership thing. I gave the people everything for the taking."

"Why, then?"

"I'm not sure, unless the old man freaked them out that bad."

Something moved inside— We grabbed each other's arm. Then we heard it again, a thunk. Something was in there, something we hadn't seen—

A woman suddenly began to scream in staccato blasts—"Wah! Wah! Wah!"—like the siren in Nazi occupation movies.

I didn't think, I just acted, always surprising to me. I stood up, circled for momentum, then kicked the door in. It took me two kicks, concussion jolts of pain shooting up my arm, before the ancient door fell at my feet. I charged in. This would have been a good time to have my gun, I thought. I eventually skidded to a stop in the animal shit, straining to stay up as my eyes adjusted to the gloom.

"Wah! Wah! Wah! Wah!" She was in the corner— I peered into the gloom. I saw her. She was clutching her knees to her chest and screaming, "Wah! Wah!" in that staccato way. It hurt my ears.

Her boyfriend cowered beside her. He was on his knees. His black pants were smeared with white slashes of bird shit. He held one hand up as if that might fend off bullets. I looked into the other corners. Jellyroll was not here. No one else was here. Acrid dust hung in the air.

"Wah! Wah! Wah!"

"Look," he pleaded, "there's no point in killing us, we haven't seen shit, we've been in here the whole time, we don't know nothing, we're not worth the fall—but money, we can give you some bread if that'll help you out, cash, we can lay some *cash* on you—" He spilled bills in wet little wads from his tight, shit-stained jeans. "Take it all, man, hell, I'll give you my fucking Gold Card! I'm a Frequent Flier, you can go anywhere!"

"Shut up!"

"Okay, man, okay, you name it."

"Who are you!" I demanded, feeding off his fear of me, even unarmed and caked with black mud from the chest down. "You're the people from the speedboat, aren't you?"

"Right, that's right! You're the guy who lived here all your life, we're just yachtsmen, visiting yachtsmen! We're a cruising couple, got sick of the rat race, you know, followed our bliss, and—!"

"Bullshit. You're not yachtsmen. You're lying. Who are you?"

"All right, all right, you're right, man, I can see you're a bright guy, it was a little dark before. The fact is, we're here to buy some weed off an asshole who calls himself Dickie the Red. Maybe you know him. Maybe you'd like a piece of the action off the top, I don't know, or maybe you want *all* the action. That's cool, too. Is that cool with you, babe?"

"Yeh," she said, her finger in her mouth.

"We never even laid eyes on Dickie's stash, so I can't guarantee its quality, but I talked to the gardener, and the cat knew what he was doing. Take it, it's yours, we've had enough. This is fucking nautical hell out there! Crusty, smirking Yankees knew the storm was coming. They split in time. They stole away. Did they tell anyone? Fuck no!"

"They told us," muttered his girlfriend. Her long, shiny black hair was streaked with bird shit. I felt sorry for her, but I was glad she'd stopped screaming and sucking her finger.

"Well, they might have told us, but who can understand those accents? Look, can you put us up for a little while, just till the storm stops? Hey, we'd really appreciate it. We're nonsmokers."

I had no idea what was going to happen next. I couldn't have these two ginks trailing along as witnesses. "Did you see anybody aboard the other boat when you got here?"

"What other boat? The black boat?"

"Yeah, was anybody aboard? Was a dog aboard?"

"A . . . dog?"

"Yes! A dog! A dog!"

"No, no, I didn't see no dog aboard. Did you see a dog aboard, babe?"

"No. It was whataya call it? Parked. With ropes."

"Docked?" he said.

"Yeah, docked. It was all closed up. There was nobody."

"You'll be safe here," I said.

"Listen, man, we're freezin' our tits off here—"

"I'm sorry, I am too. I can't help you. You can hire a boat when the storm passes." I turned and walked out.

"Hey, nice finger you got there, neighbor," he shouted at my back.

It was a relief to get back into the woods out of the wind. That kind of wind wears you down, makes you old. We moved fast.

"Why'd you do it, Clay?" I asked as if making conversation with a companion on a day hike. "Do you remember?"

"Kill my father, you mean?"

"Yes."

"I've been remembering a snowstorm. While you were crawling to the edge of the Crack, I was remembering the night of a snowstorm. It was because of a panda."

"A panda?"

"It was a big stuffed panda. It was as big as I was. He bought it for me at F.A.O. Schwarz. I remember he made a big show of buying it in the store, the generous, nurturing father routine, but I loved it anyway. I slept with it. We were inseparable. One night—that night, I think—he pulled the panda from my arms. Then he took his penknife from his vest pocket—he always wore vests—and he sliced my panda open from its neck to its crotch. The son of a bitch disemboweled my panda. Then he handed it back to me." Clayton fell silent. I had grown used to that gym bag full of his father swinging in his hand.

It was hard to sustain a quick pace over the rocky, hummocky ground. We tripped and stumbled. My hand hurt constantly, and combined with fear and rage, pain had drained my energy. I imagined some sunny morning in the future—a cup of coffee, Ella and Louis singing "The Nearness of You"—when this would be over, with a happy ending, I imagined, but regardless, over.

We arrived at the outer reaches of the swamp—and immediately began to sink. The wind blew big drops of water from the swaying treetops. Trunks creaked. Mud still blackened the water in billows from our last crossing. Vaguely it occurred to me that there was a sexual quality to the way the swamp wanted to suck us in. We followed the billows into the water.

"Clayton, why'd he do that to your panda?"

"Because he saw how much I loved it, the fucker!" Clayton shouted at the memory. "I tried to sew it back together. I used a shoelace because the wound was so big. But it didn't work!"

I stopped short in the center of the swamp when it dawned on me: that was the panda Crystal had found in the bedroom, only it wasn't a panda, it was a teddy bear. And it wasn't as big as Clayton remembered, but it had been slit open and sewed back together with a shoelace—

"That night, I went into his bedroom. He didn't like that, I knew, but I was frightened of something, and I wanted . . . something. He was lying in bed on his back reading a copy of *Railroad* magazine. I couldn't see his face from the foot of the bed, just the nose of a black locomotive steaming straight at me from out of his chest. 'What do *you* want?' he said. I left. But I came back. I came back."

It's a gift of the human psyche that return trails always seem shorter.

"With my Cub Scout hatchet."

We arrived at Sonny's body. Nothing had changed for him, reposing in the ferns. I circled looking for my shotgun.

"What?" asked Clayton.

I told him, and he began to circle. But we couldn't find it. Why? I knew where I'd fallen and in which direction—

"Here, look," called Clay. Bending, he disappeared into the ferns.

I assumed he'd found the gun, and delighted to be rearmed, I went to get it, but he hadn't found the gun. He'd found the guy's video recorder. We never found the gun. I ran the rest of the way to Crystal's tree—

She was gone.

I began to shiver looking at that empty tree trunk. This is what I feared most when I left her. The chain lay in a pile between two thick roots. It was absurd. Leave your lover chained to a tree— My knees wanted to sag. I picked up the chain. Wait a minute, the heavy padlock was still locked in place. The chain had been cut. It was a stout chain; you'd need a serious set of bolt cutters for that job. That might be good news—I couldn't see Dick Desmond running around with heavy-duty cutters slung over his shoulder.

Clayton was watching me wordlessly. "Let's try the boathouse," I said.

We ran. I tried to keep my finger from flapping.

I stopped near Jellyroll's woodpile to watch the place. Was there life inside? If so, whose? I heard nothing. I walked quickly, quietly to the foot of the stairs and stopped again. Clayton came with me, and I suddenly noticed he was carrying the dead guy's camcorder as well as the gym bag. If Desmond, or some other psycho I didn't even know about, was in there, he'd hear the boards creaking as I came up. But maybe Crystal and Jellyroll were waiting for me and everything was jake. We'd spend the evening peacefully, reading about wildflowers, listening to water lapping. I peeked in the back door—

The stairs creaked. Someone was coming down!

"Artie—!" It was Crystal! She had appeared around the side of the house.

I moaned with joy, but Jellyroll was not with her. We hugged each other. Crystal was crying into my shoulder.

"He's here, Artie. Desmond is inside, and he's got Jellyroll. Hawley's here. He got me off that tree, but Desmond sent him to get the other guy's video camera—"

Jellyroll must have heard us. He began to bark. This was his alarm bark. It is a high-pitched, continuous sound, like a wailing, that penetrates the brain. I felt confused and inadequate. I hunched my shoulders.

"He's okay, he's not hurt," Crystal was saying. "Desmond's got Jellyroll hostage. He's holding him by a rope around the neck, and he says he'll kill him if we don't do what he wants. He's got a machete—"

"What does he want?"

Clayton had gone around the other side of the boat-house, and now he came back— "Hello, you must be Crystal," he said. "I'm glad you're safe."

Clayton and Crystal had never actually met, only spoken on the phone. I introduced them.

"Is that the video camera?" Crystal asked.

I told her about the dead guy, the son, and all this time Jellyroll was barking in fear. It was breaking my heart, but I wasn't tired anymore. The adrenaline began to pump. "What does Desmond want, besides the camera?" I asked.

"Publicity. He says the press is waiting over in Mic-mac until the storm dies. And he wants to have the most media present when he releases Jellyroll."

"Releases?"

"That's what he says."

"You don't believe him?"

"No."

"Jellyroll," I called gently but loudly enough to get through to him on the other side of the wall, "no barking."

He didn't completely stop, but close. I was afraid that the barking would cause Desmond to crack.

"Good boy," I said. Crystal had felt so good in my arms.

"Who killed the son?" Crystal wondered.

Hawley came hustling out of the woods. When he saw Crystal, Clayton, and me standing by Jellyroll's woodpile, he waved the shotgun over his head and ran toward us. "That guy's stone fucking dead out there in the ferns! His head's split—" Something, our body language, told him we already knew about that. "You already got the video machine, the asshole sent me for it— But I found this here. This is a murderous fucking weapon right here."

Hawley was agitated. "Clayton, you don't want to be carryin' him around in that gym bag like that. That's just askin' for trouble."

Clayton had it hung over his forearm by the handles while he fiddled with the camera.

"So what do you want to do?" Hawley asked. "If you want me to, I'll kick the door open and blow the asshole through the wall."

"I don't think so," said Crystal.

" 'Course it'd kill the dog, too."

"That's all we want to do here—" I said. "Get Jellyroll back safe. Understood?"

Hawley promised he wouldn't do anything hasty.

I told him he had been right and I had been wrong about Desmond. I told him he could keep the gun as long as he didn't use it until after we had Jellyroll safe. I asked Crystal if Desmond was coherent. I didn't know what I was going to do, but since he was my dog, I guessed I was in charge.

"Oh yes, he's coherent, but he's real nervous. That's what scared me about him, how tense he is."

"Oh, Jesus—" said Clayton. He was looking at the tiny TV screen at the back of the video recorder.

"What?" everybody asked.

"Wait, let me rewind."

We hunched shoulder to shoulder around the little screen, no bigger than a playing card, while he did so. There was nothing to see but snow. He stopped the rewinding, hit play. The image was so tiny, we had to scrunch even closer together. Crystal and I gasped in unison—

It was Sid aboard the black sportfisherman. He was sitting in the stern. The shot was taken from an elevated angle, as from the flying bridge. Water was rushing by. Sid was grinning slightly at the camera. What the hell was he doing on that boat? Undercover work? Then Sid turned and looked back toward the wake. Then there was a flurry of motion in front of the camera. The image resolved itself into a man's back—the man was stepping into the camera from below and behind, and he was moving sidelong toward Sid. The man had a club in his hand. It looked like a fat, stubby baseball bat, and the man held it cocked like a slugger stepping into the pitch. We all cringed as the bat struck Sid, full swing, in the back of the head. Even on the grainy little screen, we could tell that Sid was dead before he hit the deck.

He dropped in his own footprints. His face came to

a rest staring up at the camera. His eyes were flat. Then the man stuck his own face into the frame. He had to bend over to do that. He was making funny faces, mugging as people often do in front of these cameras at, say, the office picnic on Memorial Day, all good fun. Crystal whimpered. Somebody else was whimpering, but it was unclear who. Maybe me. I put my hand over the screen, but the tape had already ended. Dick Desmond was the man in the home video, the giddy one with the bat.

"Mr. Desmond," I called, and Jellyroll started barking again, "I'm coming in. We've got to talk."

"Just you! You'd better come alone!"

Crystal gave me an encouraging kiss before I went into the house.

26

When Jellyroll saw me come in the back door, he pronked straight up in the air. His tail helicoptered, and, tongue trailing, he surged to the end of his short rope. He went up on his hind legs and waved his forepaws.

"You stop right there!" Dick Desmond shouted at me. He held a machete or some other kind of long, flat-bladed knife cocked above Jellyroll's skull. The blade was rusty.

I froze two steps inside the door. "Good dog," I said with a reassuring smile. Actually, the sight of him there moved me, a lump rose in my throat, but I pinched it back to concentrate on saving his life. I had to look away—

Desmond's eyes were wild. His khaki pants and polo shirt were caked with mud. He had slid the wicker couch against the rear wall so we couldn't sneak up behind him. He crouched on it with his knees drawn up under him in a prissy way. He was barefoot, having abandoned his Topsiders, like two lumps of earth, under the couch. He gave Jellyroll's rope a yank, and I caught myself on the verge of diving for his throat. My broken finger would prevent me from strangling him effectively, and he still might get Jellyroll.

I crouched down on the floor because Jellyroll always likes it when we're at his level and because I wanted Desmond to see how nonthreatening I could be. Who was this guy? What was going on inside his brain, and how did I address it? "I love that dog, Mr. Desmond," I began, feigning calm. "I don't want you to hurt him. I'll do whatever you want so he doesn't get hurt. Okay?"

"Everything's different now. Everything." There was finality in his voice. He pushed it theatrically. You could picture him running his lines in front of the mirror, liking what he saw.

"What do you mean different?"

"My son is dead. Well, he wasn't really my son, but he was *like* my son—I still had to kill him."

I nodded, jaw agape. I had no idea what to say, and I didn't dare look at Jellyroll, the sadness of his pose, head between his paws at the end of the rope.

"I had to!"

"Sure you did. It's a complicated relationship," I babbled.

"I didn't want it to be like this. Killings. I didn't want all these killings. Killings weren't my plan."

"What was your plan?"

"I was desperate. I had a series once, now I have shit. I had esteem once. Esteem, I'm telling you, esteem! Now I have none. The word for that is has-been!"

"Okay, take it easy—"

"You don't know what it's like! You live off your dog! I'd go up for parts, parts I was perfect for. Perfect! Nothing, not a smell. Not even a callback. 'Here comes that old fossil from *Ten Pins,*' which everybody thinks was just a rip-off of *The Waltons* in a bowling alley! I can see it in their eyes when I walk in! And some of these kids today, hell, they never even heard of *The Waltons!* My health insurance expired two years ago, and now I'm losing my hearing. I'm going deaf! Do you know what it's like to go deaf?" he shouted. Then he began to cry. He lowered the knife to rest on his thigh.

I considered rushing him.

But he cocked it again. "I needed something, a shot in the career arm, something a little quirky, a little off-beat to get their attention. But I never meant for anybody to get hurt. And I never meant to hurt the dog. I was going to make a big show out of letting him go. Then say on TV how I was having this drinking problem, break down a little, be real. It'd make every news and entertainment spot from coast to coast. Five weeks at the Betty Ford Center and I'd be working again. But he started killing! Always the killing!"

"Who did he kill?"

"Besides, he tried to make an independent deal with the studios. You can't do that! Hell, it was my concept! . . . Who did he kill? Those people in town, he killed them. Your friend Sid Detweiler, he killed him. For no reason. For kicks! That's not the kind of attention I seek, Mr. Deemer."

"Call me Artie. I know how you feel. It's a tough business. I've seen it, from the outside, of course, but

I can empathize. Look, this dog right here can help you get work. You know Clayton Kempshall?"

"The actor?"

"Yes, he was just in a Jellyroll movie, juicy role, an evil high school principal. I couldn't guarantee anything, but I could set up a serious audition for his next feature."

"Oh, was that the movie young Kevin James directed down on the piers?"

"Yes."

"He rejected me. Young James rejected me, too." Desmond wiped his eyes on his shirtsleeve like a little boy.

Poor Kevin. But I wanted to stay away from that, I didn't want to inject the reality of a murder rap. "What do you want right now?" I asked. "So we can end this."

"I can still kill this dog," he assured me.

"I know it. That's why I'm asking." I could feel Jellyroll's eyes on mine.

"But if I did, then I'd no longer have any protection, would I? You'd probably kill me then, you and your friends."

"Look," I said, "it sounds like we can work this out without any more killing. Let's not get sidetracked with killing. You said yourself there was too much of that."

"That lobsterman type, he'd kill me."

"No, he won't—"

"How do you know what the fuck he'll do? He's obviously insane!"

"He promised me he wouldn't."

"Promised. Right."

"Look, I can guarantee nobody will hurt you. Nobody has a reason to hurt you. He's my dog, and *I* don't want to hurt you."

"People are funny about dogs. . . . When I was on *Ten Pins,* people used to send me bowling sheets as a kind of fan mail. So I used them, give it some identity, some character to the whole thing, for the media. They love that kind of thing. But what happens? It turns into a bloodbath because of my no-good stinking son. He was always that way. Incorrigible. He was incorrigible from birth. The wife and I always— Did that fisherman find my son's camcorder?"

"Oh yeah, do you want it?"

"What do you think?"

"I'll bet you do. And I'll get it for you, but why don't you release my dog first? You let Jellyroll go, and I'll give you a boat. I saw your boat—it's a total wreck. You get in my boat and go as far and as fast as you can. There's nothing to connect you to any of the killings. Somebody'll eventually find the body out in the woods, but nobody will know about you."

"Jellyroll? That's his real name?"

"Yes."

"That's cute. You mean that boat right out there?"

"Sure, take it."

"Let me be sure I have it. I take the boat and vanish. Somebody finds the boy's body— No, it won't work. The cop has seen us together, thanks to that crazy fisherman. As soon as they find the body—"

"Well, suppose they never find the body? It's a big ocean."

"You'd get rid of it?"

"I would."

"I'd have to take the dog as insurance that you wouldn't try—"

"Nope."

"Nope? What do you mean, nope? You do what I tell you to do. You can't reject me!"

"You can't take Jellyroll."

"What can you do about it?"

"Look," I reasoned, "you said yourself that everything's different because of your son's murderous tendencies. If you try to go on with your plan, they'll connect you with the murders. I'm offering you a way out completely. Look, the guy who did the killings is himself dead. But taking Jellyroll from this room is going to fuck up the balance."

"Yes, but how will you stop me?"

"Why, I'd murder you. Eventually." Maybe on some level this is what he wanted to hear, so I laid it on. "But I wouldn't do it quickly. My friends and I would sit down and think up the most hideous possible ways to torture you—"

"Okay."

"Okay?"

"I get the video camera—and the tape. You get Jellyroll."

"Sure. I have some personal effects I want out of the boat. When I come back, I'll give you the camera, then you give me Jellyroll, and I give you the boat. Is it a deal?"

"What about the others?"

"What about them?"

"They've got to go up in the woods. I don't want them around to attack me."

"They won't bother you. They want this to be over, just like me. Okay?"

". . . Okay."

"It's okay," I told Jellyroll. "I'll be back in two minutes," I said to Desmond and dashed out the door.

Trying to hear, Hawley, Clayton, and Crystal had
gathered in a semicircle around the stoop. I skidded to
a stop before running over them.

"He's coming out. He's going to give up Jellyroll, and
then he's leaving in the boat. I told him I'd give him
the camcorder and that you'd move back away from
the house." I wanted to stop and hug Crystal and have
her tell me that I was doing the right thing, but I barely
paused before sprinting down to the boat. The wind
was dying. My pants were stiff with dried mud. It fell
from me in clods as I ran.

The ebbing tide had left the boat up on the flat rock.
Cradling my wrecked hand to my chest, I planted my
feet, leaned against the side of the boat, and shouldered
it off the rock. . . . I looked out across the water as I
strained. Poor Sid was down there somewhere. Maybe
the tide had already swept him into the deep water
beyond, maybe he'd never come up. The hagfish would
have him. Even as a pro, he didn't recognize the level
of psycho he was dealing with when he went aboard
their boat. I went aboard mine. . . .

When I returned to the house, my friends were standing shoulder to shoulder looking at the little screen on
the back of the camera. Their faces were ashen.

Clay handed it to me and shook his head. "Desmond
did it. He killed them all, and his son took the pictures.
Jesus, you should see what they did to Kevin James."

"Desmond did it all?" I whispered.

"It's all in here," said Crystal, tapping the video recorder, her eyes wide.

Then I went back into the house. I remembered Desmond's face, his young face, not his present lined and lifted face. He was handsome then, and he had a quality about him, he had a presence. The good qualities of masculinity. I remembered thinking of that when I saw the program on a black-and-white TV mounted on the wall in the officers' family rec room on an air force base in the California desert, a cinder-block and linoleum room full of orange molded chairs. And remembering, a fog of depression rolled over me, but I snubbed it off. I couldn't give in to it now. Later. I put the camcorder on the floor beside my dog. "I've held up my end of the deal," I said. "Now let him go."

"Believe me, that fisherman is a killer. You better not turn your back on that man," said Desmond.

"He won't hurt you," I said.

And then he released Jellyroll, who sprinted into my arms. He yapped and jumped at my legs as I beat it out the back door. He tangled in my legs and tripped me halfway to the woodpile, and there in the mud we cuddled. I hugged his body to me, while he twisted around to lick my face. His whole being beamed with delight. "Let's go see Crystal," I said, but here she was. He jumped to kiss her until she dropped to her knees, and then they cuddled in a mass. I love dog delight. Then he spotted his old pal Clayton and went to him for further cuddling.

Desmond, having gone out on the porch and down the stairs, peeked from around the house at a scene of joy. Wordlessly, he turned away and hurried down the sloping rock to the boat. We could see the boat from the woodpile through sparse but thick red pine tree trunks. We couldn't see Desmond until he emerged from behind the house. Desmond sat on the gunwale and pivoted his legs aboard.

"Come on," I said to Crystal, taking her arm. "Come, Jellyroll. Come on, everybody," I said, leading the way toward the rear of the house.

Clayton came right along, but Hawley lagged, watching poor insane Dick Desmond start up the boat.

The shock wave hit the house before the sound arrived. Windowpanes rattled in the French doors. One pane near the top collapsed and tinkled to the floor. One instant Hawley was standing up, the next he was sitting down. I guess that's the way of it with gasoline explosions, things happen fast, but luckily no debris made it through the trees to take his head off. I guess you could say things worked out.

When Crystal, Clayton, Jellyroll, and I looked around the corner of the house, the fireball had already formed and risen with an air-sucking whoosh. The rich red flame dissolved into a broiling black mushroom cloud that lingered in the air. Wooden pieces of the poor Hampton boat still pirouetted in the blue sky above the mushroom cloud. They seemed to hang up there as if in slow motion. The big stuff came down first, some of it on the boathouse roof, then the smaller stuff landed, peppering the surface of the water and clattering the porch.

I knelt to reassure Jellyroll. "Want some water?" I asked him. He views cold water as a treat, so I always keep some in the refrigerator. "I'll get it," Crystal said. We went inside. Hawley and Clayton went down to the flat rock to see what was left of Desmond.

"Let me see your hand."

I held it palm up for her, and she examined it without touching. My hand was grotesque. I looked into Crystal's eyes for a measure of just how bad it was. She gasped through barely parted lips. Then she asked me to turn it over.

My finger flopped like a dead eel.

"Let's wash it off and see what we have here." She held her own hand under the water as she regulated the temperature for my comfort. I was getting dizzy now. Jellyroll stopped drinking, watched me. The sink ran black for a while. The mud looked like blood going down the drain.

Crystal held my wrist and looked again, brow furrowed with concentration. When Crystal concentrated, only her right brow furrowed. I loved that. I felt like weeping with the power of my love for her brow—

"Let's go in the bedroom," she suggested. She led me gently by the wrist. She closed the door, then sat on the edge of the bed. I stood before her, and she gently cradled my hand in hers.

"It's very painful now, isn't it?"

"Yes." I was regressing. Mommy would make it stop. I stared at her moist eyes as they examined my injury.

"I don't think it's fractured. I think it's dislocated. It's always best to reduce dislocations right after they happen before everything has time to tighten up in there, get all angry. By the way, how did this happen?"

"I tripped over a dead body."

"It's been a while, so it's going to hurt. But I think I can do it on the first try. Why don't you look away?"

She didn't dally. As soon as my head turned, she clutched my finger in her fist and pulled it straight out.

The pain drove me to my knees. I moaned. When I was a boy, the men in the movies never moaned in pain. Their jaw muscles twitched when it got really bad. I buried my face between Crystal's breasts, hugged them around my face, a fine place to be when the next wave of pain landed. . . . But it didn't.

"It's in," she said.

The pain was gone! I peeked out. Was it going to stay gone? She stroked my hair. "It's in!" I giggled. I could feel my grasp on reality slipping away. I could let it go now, what the hell, my loved ones were safe from the devils in the dark.

"Good, good, there's no pain now, is there?"

"None."

"Artie?"

"Hmm?"

"You knew that was going to happen, didn't you? You knew the boat would explode."

"Yes."

"Did you cause it to explode?"

"It might have exploded anyhow."

"But you intended for it to explode?"

"Yes. How do you feel about that?"

"I feel okay about it. But I want to go now. Okay?"

27

We said our good-byes to Hawley and Clayton. Clayton still had the gym bag in his grip as we cleared the cove and turned for Micmac aboard Sheriff Kelso's boat. This last crossing of Cabot Strait was rough and cold, though the sky was so clear it seemed we could see the curvature of the earth.

Nobody spoke much on the way across. Out of sight of land, Jellyroll hooped in the stern. I wiped it up. I loved that he was still around to hoop, but that was only my perspective. He had just disgorged this nasty puddle of yellow bile in the back of Kelso's boat, and Kelso's gaze at me was as chilly as the sea. He was probably glad we were going. I guess I couldn't blame him. Although on another level, depending on how you wanted to look at it, we had solved his Micmac murders for him. Of course, on the other hand, we had brought the killers to his neighborhood in the first place.

I put my arm around Crystal's shoulder, after I'd

thoroughly wiped my hand, and we let the wind slap our faces. Only the wind kept my head up, I was so tired. Crystal, too.

"Remember those country inns?" said Crystal in my ear.

"Sure."

"Let's stop at one."

Most of the Jesus people had dispersed. Here and there small groups remained on the hillside, packing their belongings. Others, singly or in family units, were walking out of town. They didn't seem particularly dispirited. They seemed like folks heading home at the close of the company picnic, weary and spent but not disappointed. Sleepy boys and girls rode like lemurs on their fathers' shoulders. Mothers and daughters walked hand in hand. Two of their number were dead, and it didn't seem that anyone had been saved, at least not to me. Where would they go now? Did they have other prospects and possibilities?

Dockside, the town went about its business. Fishermen in black rubber boots threw crates of ice from their decks to colleagues up on the dock. A lobster boat backed off the dock, another took its place. Several people from away ate on the porch at the Cod End, gulls circling. The guy from the marine store wheeled a barrowful of heavy gear out to a big rusty commercial fishing boat at the end of the dock. He nodded to us.

"Sheriff, have you seen the face in the lichens?" I asked.

"Yeah, why?"

". . . I just wondered. I was thinking of having a look. What's it like?"

"I'll show you if you want."

"Thanks. Do you want to see it, Crystal?"

"No, I don't. I think I'll stay down here."

I could understand that position, but I still wanted to see. It seemed important, a kind of closure. I helped him tie up the boat. Then we started up the hill.

A few people, volunteers perhaps, had stayed to pick up the litter. They were spearing it into garbage bags tied to their waists. Where the incline was still shallow, we passed a white-haired man of retirement age wearing a multicolored jogging suit trying to spear a soda can. It kept rolling from under his point. We said good afternoon. He stamped it flat, then speared it up.

I looked back over my shoulder as the hill steepened near the top. The setting didn't look real from here, a perfectly round harbor with Round Island right outside, white light shimmering on the surface all the way to the horizon. It was a place out of time, yet there were Crystal and Jellyroll, waiting.

"It was right here," said Kelso, pointing to a vertical crag of the same pink granite that formed Kempshall Island.

About the size of a suburban garage door, the exposed rock was fissured and crinkled. It had been exposed to the elements for thousands of years. Now it was almost covered with a growth of tan, olive, and yellow lichen. The short, coarse plants somehow found sustenance here. Did they draw nourishment from the rocks themselves? If so, they were the smartest creatures around this coast.

"It's gone." Kelso put his hands on the rock as if to summon it up again. He turned to me with a stricken look on his face.

284

"Gone?"

"Yeah, the goddamn thing's gone. It was right here!"

"What did it look like? Did it look like a face?"

"Well, yeah. I saw it when somebody pointed it out to me. Yeah, you could say it was a face in profile. You see a lot of things in the lichens if you look. I know. I sat here and tried it. But the face was right here, I'm certain."

"It's gone." It was the man who'd been spearing trash. He stood below us cradling his weapon in the crook of his arm, his bag hanging from his belt. He shielded his eyes from the sun with his hand.

"Where'd it go?" asked Kelso.

"Stolen."

"What do you mean, stolen?"

"Yep. Last night. Somebody stole it. Just took the face with them when they left. Most people left, you know, because of the murders."

"How'd they take it?"

"Scraped it off with a pocket knife, put it in their pocket, probably. You can see the marks. That ruins it for everybody. I think you should arrest him."

This whole matter seemed to depress Kelso as if it affirmed some darkly held vision. He stared at the place where the face had been.

"Last night it happened. We discovered it at dawn. I think you ought to arrest him," the man insisted.

"Arrest him?" snapped Kelso. "On what charge?"

"Yes. *That's* the problem." The man turned and continued spearing his way down the hill.

"Well, I guess I'll be going," I said. "If you have no objections."

"No, none."

"Would you give this check to Dwight—for the boat?" I asked. I would have asked Hawley to give it to Dwight, but I forgot.

He took my check, folded it into his shirt pocket. "Say, just between us, you didn't set that up, did you, the explosion?"

"He neglected the sniff test. That's what Dwight called it, the sniff test."

"Artie, I'd just as soon you don't come back."

"Okay."

"I mean, I know none of this was your fault, but I think it'd be best for everybody concerned if you didn't come back. No hard feelings?"

"No."

"Take care, Artie."

"You too, Ted."

I looked down the hill at Crystal and Jellyroll. She was leaning against a dock piling, and he was lying at her feet. They seemed small and vulnerable. I wanted to enfold them in my arms, and my chest ached with love as I watched.